# DESTINY'S

# KISS

Printed in the United States of America

First Printing, 2015

ISBN -13: 978-0692416372

ISBN-10: 0692416374

Published by: Charmed Hearts Books


http://juniper479.wix.com/charmed-hearts-books

# This book is dedicated to

### Tina Edgar

*My Teacher, My Mentor, My Guide*

### My Mom

*You always thought my writing was perfect, even when it wasn't*

### Tina Jesse

*My Best Friend and Sister-in-Heart*

### James Jesse

*The hardest person I know, with the softest heart*

*And finally,*

### Jonah Eli

*Mommy did it!*

**\*`Thank you all for believing in me~\***

# *Table of Contents*

# *~ONE~*

There was a mad rush in the old Victorian home, as preparations were made for the matriarch's return from Chicago. Workers were fervently cleaning, putting things away, and making them look perfect; polishing furniture, dusting, mopping floors, vacuuming carpets, and replacing old flowers with fresh ones. The cook was in the kitchen, preparing dinner, and the maids were setting the table. It had been two whole weeks since the mysterious telegram had come, and Margaret Carter Wallingford had rushed away, leaving her two grandchildren, Caspian and Evangeline, with the staff. This was the first time that they had been without their grandmother since their father had died. She was all that they had in the whole world, and they missed her terribly, especially since they were not used to being in the house without her, and the home that they resided in was so big.

The wind picked up, and sent a cluster of maple tree leaves flying passed the window in the foyer, where the young teenagers were waiting to see their grandmother's car drive down the street. Evangeline jumped as a newspaper flew up and smacked the window that her face was practically pressed against. She looked at the headline, "**Troops Return Home, Many to Be Laid to Rest.**" She pointed at it and looked at her brother, with a puzzled look on her face.

"What does that mean, Caspian? The troops are coming home, but some are being laid to rest??" Her innocent question made him sigh with sadness.

"It means that some of the soldiers died while overseas, and they are sending their bodies home to be buried."

"Like father?" Her eyes filled with tears, and she leaned on her brother's shoulder, still staring at the paper, even as it slid down the window, and landed with a slosh on the front stoop.

"Yes, Evangeline… Just like father....But, father fought hard for our country and he died a hero, and he is with mother now." He stroked his sister's reddish-brown hair.

Six years had gone by since they had been taken from their home in Philadelphia, and driven to Boston to live with their paternal grandmother in her home. She had taken them in when their father was shipped out to serve his country. Their mother died while giving birth to Evangeline. They had no other grandparents, as they died before Caspian was born, nor did they have aunts or uncles, as neither of their parents had siblings. They barely knew their Grandmother, Margaret, yet they adjusted quickly to living with her. She was strict, but loving, and she raised them as she knew her son would want them to be. The men in the suits came to their grandmother's door nine months after they had moved there, to tell them that he had died, trying to save some prisoners from their captors. They were freed, but he was caught and killed. Margaret was devastated, as that was her only child, her son, but now she was given the challenging task of raising her two grandchildren.

Caspian and Evangeline were given every advantage, from the best schools, to the nicest clothes. They never wanted for anything, and they were happy, despite the recent loss of their father at such a young age; Caspian had been ten, and Evangeline was only seven. They had their grandmother, and they loved her. For that reason, they waited eagerly for her to return to them. A flash of chrome caught their eyes, and they got excited.

"Is that her?! Caspian, is that her car?" Evangeline pressed of her face to the glass again.

"It sure looks like it. Evangeline, please get your face off the window. She's going to see you, and you will leave smudges!" He pulled his sister away from the window, and used his sleeve to wipe away the smudges that her hands and face made on the clear glass. He took his hands and straightened her hair out, and brushed her dress out to make her look presentable. He smiled at his work, turned around and rushed her to the base of the staircase to welcome their grandmother home. "Crud!! I forgot the flowers!! Stay here." He pointed at his sister, and then steered his wheelchair to the dining table, to grab the bouquet of roses that were bought for the homecoming. He laid them gently on his lap, whipped his chair around and sped back to his sister, just in time to see the large front door open. "She's back, Miss Ruth!!!!" He hollered to their caretaker as he had whizzed by the sitting room. Miss Ruth rushed out and stood about three feet from the young adults, as if she had been eagerly anticipating her friend's return as well, and not just sleeping in the chair in the other room, which she was.

The door swung open, and they locked eyes. As if she anticipated her reception, she had her arms swung wide open already, waiting for hugs.

What she got was a shocked stare from her granddaughter, as she spotted what was behind her from under her right arm. Everyone else just looked curiously, but then looked pleased to see Margaret home.

"Who's That!?!" Evangeline blurted out, a snarl on her face that no one had ever seen before. The question caught Margaret off guard, and she cleared her throat, and stood erect, a stern look on her face.

"Is that any way to welcome me home?! Can't I, at least, get some love from my dumplings before you start asking what I brought home for you?" She spread her arms even farther apart, almost as if trying to hide what, or who, was behind her. Caspian quickly rolled forward, and turned his chair so he could hug his grandmother without running over her toes.

"Welcome home!!! We have missed you so very much." He clutched her tightly. As he released her, he caught a glimpse of a sapphire-eyed, auburn- haired, cherub-faced young woman peering over her shoulder. He gave her a small grin, a wink, and a small wave. She smiled back, and gave him a wave with one finger. He, then, handed the roses to his Grandmother and rolled back so his sister could get to the woman.

"Oh Grandmother, I missed you tremendously. Please never leave us again!" Evangeline approached her and wrapped her arms around her grandmother's waist. She sneered at the girl, and stuck out her tongue.

She, then, stepped back, pointed her finger at the girl, and demanded, "Now, Who is she!?!" She screamed, and stomped her patent leather shoe onto the marble foyer floor.

"Evangeline!!!" Margaret and Caspian said, in unison. "That is not the way a lady should act." Margaret continued, sternly.

"Sorry, grand-mama" the young lady bowed her head, in shame, and backed away.

"All your questions will be answered in a few moments. Go into the sitting room, and I will be there momentarily. Go on...." She motioned for her grandchildren to go into the other room. She then turned to the gentleman standing by her side. "Robert, Take all of her things up to the Periwinkle room, please?" Then she looked at the young girl, clutching a beautiful porcelain doll to her, which was a gift from her new caretaker.

"Amelia, Darling, follow Robert up to your new room and I will be there soon. I must go speak with Caspian and Evangeline." She ran a loving finger down the girl's cheek and pointed up the grand staircase. "Your room is just up those stairs, turn down the left hallway, and it is the third room on the right."

"Your granddaughter doesn't want me here." The girl sighed, quietly.

"She will. Just give me a chance to talk to her." She kissed the girl's forehead, and pointed up the stairs.

"Thank you, ma'am..." She gave Margaret a small smile and then proceeded up the stairs.

After watching her new ward ascend the grand staircase behind her steward, she removed her long coat and scarf, and handed them to a young lady standing at her elbow. "Thank you, Eloise." She walked to the sitting room, and shut the double doors behind her.

*****

Meanwhile, as they waited for their grandmother to join them in the sitting room, Evangeline was pacing and mumbling to herself. Caspian could only make out certain words, but he knew that she had better get her temper under control before their grandmother entered the room.

"Maybe she is a relative, Angie. You don't know anything about her. Why are you throwing such a fit?" Caspian sighed, as though he was used to his little sister's outbursts.

"Maybe she isn't a relative, Caspian. *You* don't know anything about her. And I am mad because I am the only girl in grandmother's life. Is she what grand-mama ran off to Chicago for??" She stopped her pacing as her grandmother entered the room and closed the door. Evangeline immediately sat down on the large armchair next to where Caspian had positioned his wheelchair.

"Evangeline, I am very surprised at your behavior. I thought that you would have behaved a little better than that, seeing as you are oblivious to the circumstances of our guest's arrival. Not another word out of you until I explain." Evangeline nodded, as if it was a binding agreement. "To answer your question, Amelia *is* the reason that I rushed off to Chicago. This is what happened, and I will tell you all of it, as you deserve to know the whole truth."

"Her name is Amelia? That is such a lovely name." Caspian said, ignoring the nasty look that his sister flashed at him from where she was sitting. "Keep making those faces, Evangeline Colette, and you'll stay ugly like that forever." He flashed his sister a serious look, which startled her so much that she looked in the first reflective surface that she could find to make sure she had not turned ugly. "Go on, grandmother. I apologize for interrupting."

"Oh, that is fine, Caspian, dear. It is, in fact, a very lovely name." She cleared her throat, not only to get back to what she was about to tell them, but also to catch Evangeline's attention. "As I was saying, Amelia *was* why I was called away. You see, her father and your father were the best of friends growing up. They went through school together and even joined the service together. I thought of him as a second son. He was a fine young man, and he and your father complimented each other, as they brought the best out of one another. When your grandfather died, he was at the funeral, and acted as a pallbearer. He did the same when your father was killed. He has kept in contact all these years, writing to me and sending me pictures, just as he did with his own mother. His name was Oliver Landon."

She stepped over to her desk, opened a drawer, and pulled out an album, which was bulging with letters and pictures. She opened it, and set it down on the table for the children to look at. On those pages, there were many pictures of their father with another man, whom they assumed was Mr. Landon, their father's best friend. They saw pictures from parties, school, graduations, weddings, the military, and so on. It was as if these pictures were telling the story for them. Caspian picked up one picture in particular, one of the two men standing side-by-side, his father holding a small boy, himself, and his friend holding a beautiful baby girl with scarlet curls, whom he could only assume to be the girl upstairs, Amelia. He flipped the picture over and it said, "Proud daddies, Rick and Ollie." There were more pictures of the girl as she grew, but the pictures stopped somewhere around the age of six or seven.

"You said his name *was* Oliver Landon…" Caspian set the picture back down.

"Yes, that is the next part of the story. You see, like your mother, Oliver's wife died in childbirth with Amelia. So, Oliver was a single father as well. He had people to take care of her while he was away, but they had lives and families of their own, and could not care for her any longer. She was taken to a children's home, and it was there where she was living up until about a week ago. Her father was just killed in action, and they are shipping his body home with the troops. Amelia's extended family couldn't be found, if there is any, and they were going to send her to an orphanage until she turned eighteen, but they found my name and address on a medical form for her, and that is why they contacted me."

"So, what you are saying is that she has nowhere else to go?" His grandmother shook her head to answer his enquiry. "I see. So you brought her here and are going to care for her until they find her family?" Again, without speaking a word, she answered her grandson in the form of a nod. Caspian looked at his grandmother with awe. "You are so kind to do that for her. I promise that I will do the best that I can to make her feel at home. After all, she is our guest. Right, Angie?" He shot his sister a stern look, as if making certain that she heard him and understood.

"So this is just temporary. She is just staying for a little while?" A spark ignited in Evangeline's eyes as she realized that this strange girl was not going to be a permanent fixture in her home.

"She can stay for as long as she chooses to stay, Evangeline. There is always a possibility that her family may not be found, in which, we shall become her family. When did you become so selfish? She is a young girl in need. She just lost her father!" Caspian rounded on his wheels, and looked right at Evangeline. "You were in her place once, too, or don't you remember?!" Caspian looked at his younger sister as if he didn't know her at all, mostly because the behavior she was displaying was not anything he had ever seen before.

"Okay!! I get it. I'm sorry. It's just that Grandmother was gone for two weeks, and I didn't expect for her to bring someone home with her! We've had her to ourselves for all this time. I don't want to share her with anyone else!" She pouted. "I am sorry if I was acting selfish, but she is a stranger to us. I acted like anyone else would act if put in my place." Evangeline crossed her arms, and began to pout.

"You are acting like a spoiled little brat. You stuck your tongue out at her!!" He spun around and rolled toward Grandmother. "If you'll excuse me, I would like to go introduce myself."

"That's my boy! Be the kind of gentleman that your father was." She kissed him on the forehead. She, then, gave a stern look at her granddaughter, who was cowering on the chair. "Evangeline, I taught you better than that. What has happened to your manners? I would strongly suggest you go up and apologize to Amelia for that rude gesture. Then, you are to come back down and write lines!"

*****

Amelia sat on the edge of the bed, staring out the window. To other girls, this would be like a room in a castle, but to her, it was just another well decorated prison. She missed her home, the home she lived in with her father. Her room here was very much like her room back home, except fancier. Here, she had a bay window she could sit in on nice days. Her bedspread here was fluffier and not held together by patches. The room here actually had a magical quality, and the more she looked around, the more she actually began to like it. She set her new doll down gently at the head of the bed and walked over to the window. She was just about to climb up on the cushioned seat when she heard a faint knocking at the door.

"Come in. It's open." She turned quickly and backed herself to the window, as though trying to hide the tattered state of her dress, which sadly was the best one she had. It had a huge stain on the back of it, from falling in a pan of paint at the children's home. She quickly pushed some hair and tears from her face.

The door swung open slowly, and Caspian rolled in. Amelia immediately felt a little more at ease, knowing that it was the sweet boy that came in, and not that horrible girl, who was so rude earlier. Unsure as to what to say to him, she just smiled a little, but kept her eyes lowered, as if she felt that making eye contact would be a sign of disrespect.

"I don't mean to intrude when you are just getting settled in, but I wanted to come up and formally introduce myself." He stopped his wheelchair at the edge of her bed, a clear five feet from her.

"No intrusion, I assure you. I was just looking out the window. I am Amelia Landon, Mia for short." She still stared at the floor, even as she gave a small curtsy.

"It is a pleasure to make your acquaintance, Miss Mia." He bowed in his seat, and then looked up at her, noticing that she blushed a little when he said her name. "I'm Caspian Wallingford, Cass for short." He flashed a toothy grin, but was not sure that she saw it, as her eyes were still fixed on an unspecified spot on the plushy carpet. He decided to make a small game of it, and looked down at the carpet where he figured that she was looking. "What exactly are we looking at? Is the floor dirty? The carpet not the right color?" He joked, quickly glancing up to see her reaction. Shocked that she may be offending him, she looked right at him, and gave him a panicked response.

"No...no. The carpet is perfect, clean and pretty. I love it." She rambled out with a shaky voice, which Caspian noticed sounded as if she were about to cry. He rolled over to her, and took her hand, gently, in his hands, and craned his neck so he could look at her face.

"It's okay, Mia. I was just joking with you. You needn't get upset. I am sorry if you thought I was being serious. It's just that you have looking at the same spot on the floor since I came in the room." He whispered to her, with a calming and apologetic tone. For a fleeting second, it felt as though she was pulling her hand away, but she didn't. Instead, she took a deep breathe, and closed her eyes tightly, like she was trying to prevent tears from streaming out.

"My papa told me that a large majority of the upper class take offense to you looking them right in the eye, because to them, it means you have no respect for them, and you consider them your equals, instead of better than you. You *are* better than I am, because I am in a lower class than you are, so I didn't look you in the eye as a sign of respect."

"She has a point there, Caspian." Evangeline said as she entered the room, obviously proving that she had just been eavesdropping. Caspian shot her a very disgusted look.

"No, she is sadly mistaken. Walking into someone's bedroom without knocking or being invited is disrespectful." He hissed at his sister, and then turned his attention back to Mia. "There is no upper or lower class in our home, and so there is no need to worry about that, despite what my misguided sister or anyone else may say. Now, if you will excuse me for just a moment, I will be right back." He released her hand gently, and in the same motion, snatched the skirt of his sister's dress and dragged her out into the hallway, leaving the door open a crack behind him.

"What is your problem, Caspian? I didn't need to knock on the door because it is *my* room." Angie screeched, straightening her skirt, and putting her hands on her hips.

"It *used* to be your bedroom. It's Mia's room now, and it would be best that you remembered that!

"Oh, it's *Mia's* room, huh? You call her Mia!? I suppose that in the five minutes that you have been up here, you became instant friends, and now you gave her a nickname! She is just temporary, Caspian. She will leave soon, and things will be back to normal, and you will have to deal with your pet, Mia, being gone forever and never giving you a second thought!"

"You are wrong. She is not my pet. Mia is a girl in need of a safe and loving environment, and in need of a friend. I want to be that for her." He grabbed her wrist. "She deserves to be cared for, while she is here. She will come to care for us as well."

"She doesn't care about you! I am your sister, and I care. She is just a lowly trollop that is going to leave you. Who is always on your side and who is always going to be looking out for your best interests....That are ME!! It's best that you remember *that*, before you get your heart crushed." Evangeline yanked her arm out of her brother's grasp and stomped down the hall, into her other room, and slammed the door behind her. Caspian sat there in the hallway, shocked and surprised at his sister's words and accusations. *"She isn't my pet, Angie. Why....How could you be so mean?*

*How could you say such things to me?"* Caspian thought to himself, his heart aching with sadness, as he thought about what she had said, and how he knew exactly what she meant by it. While he sat there in the hallway, hearing Evangeline's hateful and crushing words echo in his head, he was unaware that Amelia had heard every word of it, and was standing in the doorway of her new room, tears streaming down her cheeks. She saw the sad look in Caspian's eyes, and wept for him. Out of compassion for him, she walked slowly out into the hallway, around behind his wheelchair, and quietly pushed him into her room, closing and locking the door behind them. It was only after he heard the click of the lock, which he became suddenly aware of where he was.

"I'm sorry if you had to hear all that. My sister has fits sometimes, and half the time I don't even think she is aware that she says things until after they are said." He said, with a low almost monotone voice.

"Don't apologize to me for her. It wasn't your fault, and she had no right to say those things to you. You have been more than hospitable to me since I came here, unannounced, and intruded on your happy life. You have been kind, and sweet and you made me feel so much better." She was kneeling down in front of him, her hands on his knees. He looked into her eyes, and he felt a warmth in him he hadn't felt since his father was alive.

Without thinking, he put his hands on hers, and gave them a squeeze. The gesture caught her off guard, and she pulled her hands away, but then instantly regretted it. She jumped to her feet, as he immediately put his hands on his wheels, and began to go for the door. He had his hand on the lock, when she leapt forward, and grabbed his hand, and held it between hers, level with her heart. "Please, don't go. I didn't mean to pull my hands away. I just reacted. I have not had physical contact like that since my father was alive. Don't leave. Stay here and talk to me a while." She pleaded with him, but Evangeline's words still echoed in his head, and he could not shut them out to hear what Mia was saying.

"I'm sorry but I have a terrible headache and I need to go lie down for a while. Please excuse me." He removed his hand from her grasp, and rolled out into the hallway, and down the hall. Right before he turned into his room, he looked back, saw her face, and rolled in, closing the door with a soft thud. Mia was just about to retreat into her room, she saw Margaret come down the hallway towards her. *Should she tell her all that had just gone on? Did she hear the commotion from downstairs?* Confused and scared, she retreated to the window seat and stared out the window, sobbing. She jumped slightly when she heard a knock at the door, but did not look, or say anything, but sniffled and sobbed some more.

"Amelia? Sweet girl, what is the matter? What has happened?" She sat down on the seat next to the young girl and lifted her chin with her hand. "Tell me, my dear, why you are crying so hard?" She wrapped her arms around the young girl, and rocked her softly. "Shush shush...calm yourself. Tell me what is troubling you."

"I can't..." She sobbed. "...I can't stay here. I appreciate what you are trying to do for me, but I have done nothing but caused chaos since I arrived. Your grandchildren are at each other's throats, and saying such hateful things to each other...all because of me. I don't belong here. I want my dad..." She began to sob harder.

"Oh darling, I know you do. He was a good man and he loved you so very much. You were the only reason he had for living, and it breaks my heart that he is gone. That is why I came to get you and bring you here. He was like a son to me, and I couldn't let his little angel be alone during this sad time. Besides, he would never have wanted you to be shipped to that awful orphanage. You need to be with people that love you, and will care for you." She spoke in a soothing tone to the young girl. "You are our guest, and if my grandchildren, or rather...if my granddaughter doesn't like it, then she will just going to have to get used to it. You belong here, and that's final, so this is the last I will hear of the subject." She lifted Amelia's head so she was looking at her in the eyes, making sure that she understood.

"Yes, Ma'am…" She answered. She wanted to ask some questions, but was unsure as to how to ask without being rude or disrespectful. Margaret could see that Amelia wanted to say something else, but looked conflicted, so she decided to see if she could help.

"Now, You said that Caspian and Evangeline were fighting about you…can you tell me what they were saying?"

"It wasn't really as much Caspian, as it was Evangeline…but I am not a snitch, so I respectfully cannot tell you. Besides, if I did tell you, Evangeline would hate me even more than she already does." She spoke quietly, still remembering what was said and how hateful her words had been. "But, if you wouldn't mind, may I ask you a question?"

"By all means, ask me anything you wish to know." She smiled at the girl, her arms still wrapped around her.

"Well, I know it isn't any of my business, and it won't change anything by knowing or not knowing, but..." She swallowed hard, looked toward the door, and then asked the hard question she needed to ask. "…if you don't mind me asking, why is Caspian in a wheelchair?" she prepared to be yelled at, like she usually did when asking personal questions at the boarding home she was at.

"My goodness…that is a very good question, Amelia."

"Thanks, ma'am, but, now that I think about it, it really doesn't matter. Forget that I asked, please. I really don't need to know why, because it really doesn't change who he is."

"You are right, Amelia. It doesn't change who he is, but if you are really curious, and you really would like to know…I would be happy to explain."

"Maybe some other time, I may feel the need to know, but I don't need to know right now. But can I ask you something else?" She smiled as she was answered with an enthusiastic nod. "Can you tell me about my father?"

"Oh, well, I thought you would never ask…" She laughed and began to tell her her all about her father and how much he meant to her and her family.

*****

After all was said and done, Mia felt kind of glad that she had talked to this kind woman. It took a weight off of her chest and made her feel a little less out-of-place, hearing about her dad, the kind of person he was, his relationship to Margaret's son as well as to her, and even how he had met her mother. It made her feel closer to him, as well as to the woman next to her.

"So, being as you will be staying here for a bit, I suppose we should discuss what you should call me. I appreciate the propriety and respect you have shown by calling me 'ma'am,' but that makes me feel old, and you are practically part of the family." She smiled at Amelia, and got a smile in return. "So, from now on, I would like you to call me Grandmother."

"No disrespect, but I don't think that I should. Evangeline will protest to that, and she already hates me. I don't want to make any more waves...." She grimaced at the thought of how Evangeline would react if she heard her call her that.

"Good Point..." Margaret set her finger to her temple and tapped it, as though trying to coax an idea out. After a few moments, Amelia's eyes lit up.

"May I call you Gran?"

"Gran...hmm....I suppose that would be fine, and if you call me that, Evangeline doesn't have a reason to complain. Gran, it is. Well, now that we have that settled. I will have Robert prepare the car, so I can take you up to town tomorrow morning to buy you some clothes. You deserve to wear clothes that are not tattered, torn or stained." She stated, noticing the stain on the back of the girl's dress.

"As much as I appreciate that, I would rather you didn't. I saw the clothes that you and the others wear and I couldn't possibly ask you to spend that kind of money on me. Besides, I will be here for a short time, and I doubt that Evangeline would wear the clothes after I have gone."

"Why would she wear them? Wouldn't you want to take them with you?" Margaret looked sad, as if her feelings would be hurt if Amelia didn't take the clothes with her, and would rather keep her old clothes instead.

"Oh, I have already gotten too much from you...you have been so kind to me. I would feel as though I was taking advantage of that kindness." She furrowed her brow, and spoke with her heart.

"It wouldn't be taking advantage, sweet girl, because you didn't ask....I offered. And if you *do* leave us, you are to take the clothes with you. I insist." She got up, set on not taking no for an answer. "I am going to go find Robert and inform him of the plan for the morning. Dinner will be served in a few hours. Why don't you unpack some of your things and then feel free to get acquainted with the house...." She kissed Amelia on the top of her head and then headed to the door. "But before I leave, let me let you in on something. The only way that you will stop Evangeline's behavior....is to fight fire with fire!" She nodded, winked. "However, do not compromise yourself and who you are, to put her in her place." She waved and left the room.

"I have to hand it to you, Gran....you are feisty!" Amelia laughed as she got up and opened one of the trunks that contained her belongings.

Deep down in Amelia's heart, she knew that she needed to say something to Caspian, to reassure him that what his sister said was totally wrong. If she were to leave tomorrow, she could never forget the kindness and sincerity that he showed her. His face was burned into her memory, and she would think of him often. Her heart yearned to heal the emotional wound that Evangeline had caused in him. For someone that claimed to be on his side, and cared the most for him, she was probably one of the few people that could hurt him the deepest.

She realized that she had been staring at her own reflection in the vanity mirror. It was, then, that she decided to take a tour of her new home, and so she walked out into the hallway, and began her new adventure.

# *~TWO~*

The sixth chime from the massive grandfather clock in the hallway echoed, telling Mia that she had better start back toward the main staircase, to head down to the dining room for her first official meal in her new home.

She had been in awe of this massive estate. What she had seen had not even come close to what she had expected. Instead of old war paintings of descendants in massive and ornate frames, she saw pictures of children, family gatherings, and quite often a snapshot of her father with a very handsome man, whom could have been Caspian, but had to have been his father. She loved that her father had such a true and loving friend, and second family. Maybe it was fate that drew her to Caspian. Their fathers had been such good friends and maybe they, too, were destined to be friends as well. And as silly as it sounded, a part of her felt as though they knew one another from before; another time long, long ago.

Mia had also seen many different rooms. She came across a large room filled with books. A couple mahogany tables sat in the center of the room, with Tiffany-style lamps on each end. There were large burgundy armchairs near the windows, stretching from the floor to the ceiling.

There was a darkroom, which she knew was used for developing photographs. There were jugs of different solution lined up on shelves, and a table with several large rectangular pans. A string ran three feet above the table, with small clips. She thought about maybe asking for a camera, so she could take advantage of this room.

There were plenty of rooms, all with different color themes. Obviously, this used to be quite the place to come when Gran was young. She probably had parties, and these were rooms that guests stayed in when they were too inebriated to leave. There were at least twelve that she had counted so far, and every one of them was different, and well-coordinated. Her favorite room was the yellow room, because she felt like she had been standing in a large sunflower, which was one of her favorite flowers.

Mia made her way back to the main upstairs hall, when she stopped dead in her tracks. She stood and watched as Robert, Gran's helpful and kind servant, picked Caspian up out of his chair and carried him down the large arched staircase, followed by Eloise, who was carrying his wheelchair, which she had just folded up. Caspian still had the same look on his face as he had when he had left her room a few hours earlier. She hadn't seen or heard from him since then. *Was he still dwelling on what Evangeline had said to him in the hall? Had she even gone to apologize to him?* She quietly followed a few feet behind the maid, as not to call attention to herself or the fact that she was watching the whole production. She waited until Caspian was back in his chair and around the corner before she proceeded to the dining room.

The dining room was beautiful. There was a large chandelier hanging above the table, which was covered in a silky royal blue table cloth and decorated with dish after dish of deliciously scented entrees. The table was long, and could have seated about twenty people. Gran was sitting on the north end of the table, Evangeline to her right, and Caspian to her left. She hesitated to sit down. Gran spotted her out of the corner of her eye, and motioned for her to come in and take a seat. Evangeline looked up from her lap, where she had just placed her silk napkin. She gave an odd smile and pulled the chair next to her out and patted the cushion, obviously offering the seat to Mia. Very slowly, she walked over to it and sat down. She placed her napkin in her lap, and folded her hands on top of it, as all the others had done. Everyone had bowed their heads, so she did as well. As soon as she had, Gran began to speak.

"Heavenly Father, we thank you for this bountiful feast which you have graciously supplied to us, for the nourishment of our bodies. We also want to thank you for another beautiful day, and for the presence of our new guest, Amelia. Bless her as you bless us and all those here on Earth. In your name, we humbly pray. Amen" With that, everyone raised their heads.

Eloise began to serve them their food, and everyone was very quiet. When she ate dinner with her father, they would talk about everything and anything. Obviously, there were some things that she would have to get used to. She went to pick up her spoon to start eating her soup, when Evangeline set her hand on hers. Mia dropped her spoon with a clink.

"I believe I owe you a very large apology, Amelia. My behavior toward you...well, my behavior in general, has been beyond reproach, and you didn't deserve it. I really do hope that we can move past this and start over. I overheard what you had said to my brother..." Amelia knew in that moment that she had been eavesdropping at the door. "...and I am afraid that I misjudged you and your intentions here. Please say that you will forgive me." Evangeline seemed to be sincere, but something in her eyes told her that she was only apologizing because Gran had reprimanded her. Was she going to find a snake or spider in her bed tonight? Mia simply played along, and smiled and nodded, patting Evangeline's hand in assurance. She immediately flashed Caspian a quick look, as if to ask, "*Are we okay? You and I?*" She breathed a small sigh of relief as he gave her a wink, but his expression was still sad and vacant of the sweet smile he had had on his face earlier in the day. Maybe she should try talking to him after dinner, she decided as she began to eat.

Dinner went by quietly, aside from silverware clinking on plates, napkins being folded and unfolded, the occasional clearing of throats, and so on. Amelia was the first to ask to be excused from the table, as she could barely endure the silence, when there were so many unspoken words to be said. She returned to her room, to find her bed turned down and a plush cotton robe and silky pajamas lying across the foot of the bed. Periwinkle-colored, fuzzy slippers were on the floor by the edge of the bed. So, this is how the upper class lived. She grabbed the robe and went into the bathroom across the hall. This room was almost as big as her bedroom. There was a large, dog-footed porcelain tub off to the right, with gold fixtures. Bath salts of all kinds were sitting on a small table next to the tub. She grabbed one that smelled like springtime, and poured a cupful of it into the tub, as she turned on the water. The scent was intoxicating and she couldn't wait to soak in a nice warm bath. As the tub filled, she walked over to the vanity and searched for something to clip her long crimson brown hair up. After she was sure that her hair was securely fastened up, she began to remove her clothes.

The bath relaxed her, and she was totally refreshed when she got out, and dried off. She had decided, as she mulled over in the bubbles that she was going to lay low for a while. She would avoid Evangeline whenever possible, but she needed to talk to Caspian as soon as she could.

The next week passed quickly. They all attended a memorial service for her father, and there were a lot of people there, making her realize that her father had made an impact on many lives. It meant a lot to her to see so many people coming to pay tribute to him. Her father's body was taken to be buried in the cemetery in Washington D.C.

During her trip into town, she asked for a camera, explaining that she loved photography and would like to take advantage of the darkroom in the east hall, and Gran gladly let her get all the supplies that she would need. It took three trips for Henry, one of the house stewards, to bring in everything that had been bought. She had so many new dresses and outfits, including one for riding horses, and she couldn't wait to wear each and every one of them. She got her first chance to wear her Khaki riding outfit just two days into the week, and she wore her baby blue dress and new black patent leather flats to the hairdresser's, in Gran's attempt to tame her auburn mane. Though she felt like she was really taking advantage of Gran's kindness, she felt just like a princess.

Following the memorial service, the only time that she saw Evangeline was at meals. It wasn't too hard to spend time alone with Caspian, as he was a frequent visitor to her room. They talked quite often about her life in Chicago, and the friends that she had made at the boarding school. She told him all the things that her father and her used to do, and broke down a few times, but Caspian was there to comfort her. They discussed their favorite books, reading being one of the things that they both enjoyed. They were forming a bond, much to Evangeline's dismay. At meals, they would make funny faces across the table when Gran wasn't looking. Evangeline would try to join in, trying to be included, but was usually spotted by Margaret and reprimanded for her table manners.

Amelia was adjusting pretty well to her new life, and tried to abide by the house rules, though sometimes she would slip back into her old ways. On the seventh night since she had come to live there, she started telling Caspian about the pictures she had taken that day, and was quickly put back in line, as there was no talking at the dinner table. She apologized, politely, and she excused herself from the table, first, just like every other night. She had gotten into a ritual of getting her bath right after supper, and then going to her room to read and wait for Caspian to visit and talk again.

She grabbed her robe, as usual, and headed to the bathroom. Using a different scent every night, she ran her bath, and undressed. This time, rather than throwing her clothes in the hamper to be washed or dry cleaned, she absent-mindedly left her dress in a heap on the floor by the tub.

As she stepped into the tub, she was unaware that she was soon going to have company. Over the water running, she couldn't hear the door creak open. She leaned forward as the door had stopped creaking, shut off the faucet, and sunk down in the tub to relax. It was only when she saw the reflection of Caspian and Evangeline in the mirror that she realized what was going on. *"Crap!! I forgot to lock the door!! What am I gonna do now?!"* She panicked and quietly sunk lower in the water until it was up to just below her nose. She pulled bubbles over the top of her to cover her woman parts, and hoped that they would leave without noticing her presence...especially Caspian.

"I really thought I just heard the water running....oh well…" Caspian sighed. "So, what was it that you wanted to talk to me about, Evangeline? And why must we talk in the bathroom?"

"I figured that here would be a safe place to talk, since Amelia is probably still wandering the halls, and I don't want her to eavesdrop. This is a sister-brother conversation, and I don't need her running to grandmother. I had to write lines for two hours because of her."

"I beg to differ. You had to write lines because *you* got caught again, making faces at the table. Not to mention you purposely stabbed Amelia with your fork... She has no one except grandmother, and us for now, and you are starting to ruin that. I wouldn't be surprised if she decided she would rather live in that nasty orphanage back in Chicago. Why can't you just stop being such a brat, and give her a chance?" Caspian asked her, taking his sister by the hand. "You two could be really good friends if you only gave her a chance."

Evangeline looked at him with a confused glare, and then her eyes widened, and her face got really red.

"YOU LIKE HER!!!!!  That dirty nasty disgusting...She is barely in this house for a week and you have a crush on that common street trollop!!"  She squealed.

"STOP CALLING HER THAT!"  He growled back at her.  She got a shocked look on her face, gasped at his outburst, and then went to a stern whisper, afraid that what she was about to say would echo through the house.

"You remember what I said before...about her not giving you a second thought once she is gone...well, I meant it.  Do you think that she sees you the same way as you see her?  When she looks at you, she sees that wheelchair."

"You don't know that!  You don't know her!!  How can you make such accusations?  All I want to do is be her friend...to get to know her...to be there for her as grandmother was for us when we lost *our* father."  Caspian grimaced, like he was being stabbed or cut, which is what his sister's words felt like.

"I love you, Caspian.  You are my big brother, and I know that it is your job to protect me, but since you can't do that, I will be the one to protect you.  You are in a fragile condition and you don't know what you are feeling for her, but it isn't love.  And no matter how hard you try, you could never *make* someone love you. You are a smart guy, and one day you will finally realize that there are just some things that women do not look for in a prospective husband, and one of them happens to be a disability such as yours, a disability that probably cannot be cured. I am your sister, and I only tell you this because I love you and I accept you for you. And despite what you may think, I DO know *Miss Landon*, or girls just like her. When they look at you, they don't feel love, or adoration....they feel pity...So, I would suggest that you leave the compassion or devotion or whatever you think she needs... to grandmother, as far as Amelia is concerned. And heed my warning; don't get your heart invested in her, because I guarantee...it will get broken into a million pieces."

Amelia had to hold her hands over her mouth to keep from interrupting, or even making a peep. Obviously they didn't know she was just a few feet from them, almost near drowning herself. She had known at the dinner table that Evangeline had just said those things, the first night, to please her grandmother, and nothing more. Evangeline was thirteen years old, and yet she had the ice cold heart of an old miserly woman in her later years. For her to speak to her brother like an inferior being was beyond contempt and Amelia was about ready to take Gran's advice and fight fire with fire. She *did* like Caspian. She looked at him and saw the same kind and loving man that her father had once told her he wished for her to find....with those steel Grey eyes that looked like the night sky, and the smile that could melt an iceberg......*Snap out of it, Mia!!! So what if he's gorgeous...it's inappropriate to think such things of the grandson of you guardian.* Amelia could feel her cheeks get hot as she caught Caspian's profile in the mirror.

"A part of me really wishes that Amelia were walking by at this very minute, so I could tell her to her face what I really think of her." Evangeline snickered, looking down at her brother's face, which was beginning to contort into, not a frown, but a half-cocked smile, as he saw a reflection of a face behind him in the mirror. He had figured out that they were not alone in the bathroom about two minutes after they came in, because he saw the same sunflower dress crumpled on the floor as the one that Amelia had just been wearing at the dinner table. He was amazed and impressed that she had kept as quiet as she had, especially considering all the things that Evangeline had said. Somehow, this seemed like poetic justice; however, he had hoped that she hadn't heard what his sister had said about him having a crush on her. His cheeks flushed slightly.

"Um, Angie...I would be very careful what you wish for." He said, trying to keep a straight face. He saw out of the corner of his eye that Amelia reached for a large towel, as well as the pitcher on the bath-side table.

"I'm serious, Caspian. I would love to see her poor little face when I tell her that she is a no one and that I will be long dead and buried before I let her get her charlatan hands on you, my poor defenseless brother."

"Okay, But don't say that I didn't warn you!" He said as he slid down in his chair, smiling, and covered his head.

"What on earth are you doing?!" She blurted out, not a second before she caught sight of the pitcher, and a large splash of warm bath water went right into her face, drenching her from head to toe.

"Gee, Evangeline....Seems like you are all wet. Do you want a towel?" Amelia managed to get herself covered up before Caspian could get a good look. She threw a towel at her, but she was in such shock that she didn't grab it and it just smacked her in the face, before hitting the wet floor in front of her. Amelia went to step out of the tub, slipped, and landed right in Caspian's lap.

For a split second, everything around the two of them went blurry. Caspian's heart began to race like it never had before. His hand, out of instinct, had gripped her thigh just above the knee as she had landed perfectly in his lap. His eyes were locked onto hers. In the fall, her hair pins had come undone, and it was now a tousled mess around her face. He wasn't sure if he was delusional or what, but he had never seen such a beautiful sight in his life. Her skin was the color of pure ivory, and it was silky and smooth, and perfect. Her eyes were the color of sapphires, with just a hint of amber along the edges. Her lips were like rose petals, full and flawless. Caspian began to lean in, his eyes swiftly moved from her eyes to her lips and back again.

Amelia felt strange, almost tingly as she looked up at him. It was like it was supposed to happen, her falling and him being there to catch her. She wasn't sure whether to stay there, or get up and run, but for the moment, she was unable to do anything aside from breath. There she was, sprawled across his lap; his hand on her thigh, and all she could do was breath and look at him, blankly. It took her a few moments to pull herself from his eyes, his fantastic, deep, soulful eyes. His nostrils flared, in an effort to breathe without his mouth, as he had that clenched in an awkward way, half smiling, half trying not to breathe heavy on her. His dark brown hair was wet from being so near to his sister, and it stuck in curls to his forehead. This situation could easily turn into something very weird between them.  Her mouth dropped open, as if wanting to say something, but the words never came.  Together, they glanced up at Evangeline, who looked like a red hot tea kettle ready to explode.

"Hold on!" Caspian whispered in Amelia's ear, and he whizzed around his sister, into the hallway, and straight into her bedroom.  The door slammed shut as the kettle blew.  They covered each other's ears.

"GRANDMOTHER!!!!!!!!!!!!" Evangeline screamed at the top of her lungs, in an octave higher than imaginable.

In that moment, to break the possible tension between the two of them in this sudden awkward and compromising situation, they looked at each other and laughed harder than either of them had laughed before.  She leapt off his lap, while he was still laughing and holding the door shut, as Evangeline was now trying to push it open, screaming and yelling.  Quickly, she ran behind the dressing curtain and got dressed.  She stood there, hidden from his view, and tried to get her bearings.  Her heart was pounding like mad, and her breathing was labored, both from laughing and from her *intimate* moment with Caspian.  Though they were at that age, when feelings such as these were very common, she couldn't help but wonder what Gran would think of what had just happened between them.  Her mind wandered slightly, and she felt all strange as she thought about how he had looked at her. It was only when she heard a knock at the door

that she snapped out of her daydream, and came out from behind the

curtain, and went to answer the door, Caspian still laughing slightly, but

trying to get his bearings. She didn't dare look him in the eye, as she may

freeze in place, and be caught up in his mesmerizing gaze again. She put

her hand on the door knob and opened the door, greeted by gran, and a

still-soaked Evangeline.

"I need to know something. What Happened?"

"Evangeline got wet." Her calm face only set Caspian off again,

and he busted out laughing again.

"Enough, Caspian!" Gran, said sternly, and he stopped

immediately, and cleared his throat. She turned her attention back to

Amelia. "I can see that she got wet, but what I would like to know is how

and why? And also, why is the bathroom floor flooded?"

"Well, I was taking a bath; she came in, without knocking, and

started saying things to Caspian, that were inappropriate. So, I doused her

with a pitcher of bath water. I'm sorry for flooding the bathroom, so I will

go clean up my mess. I however, am not sorry for getting her all wet. In

my opinion, she deserved it."

"I must say that I am disappointed in you, Amelia. That goes for you as well, young man…and you, missy." She looked at Evangeline, who was shocked to hear that she was in trouble as well. "This was something I could see children doing, but not a thirteen, fourteen and sixteen year old. I would expect that you would all work out your issues in a more appropriate manner in the future. Now, all three of you are to clean up the mess in the bathroom, and then, the two of you need to get out of those wet clothes." She rolled her eyes, gave Amelia a wink of approval, and then walked toward her room, mumbling. "What have I gotten myself into…three teenagers in one house…I'm too old for this nonsense." She closed her door behind her. Evangeline shot Caspian and Amelia a look and she turned, headed toward the bathroom. Amelia shot Caspian a smile and waved for him to come and get the cleanup over with.

As the two of them joined Evangeline in the bathroom, she shot up and looked at Caspian. She walked over and began to roll him out, but he put the brakes on the wheels.

"What are you doing? Grandmother told us *all* to clean up the bathroom."

"You can't do it. You're in a wheelchair." She said to him, sounding sympathetic to his situation.

"That is what started this whole thing, Evangeline!" Amelia spoke up, finally speaking her mind. "Gran told all three of us to clean up, so that is what we are going to do. Caspian is more than capable of doing his share. He's in a wheelchair…so what!? I would suggest you get off your soapbox and start cleaning." She handed Caspian a towel, to dry off the sink, and she began to soak up the floor with towels. Evangeline just stood there, staring at her. Caspian's heart began to beat hard as he stared at this angel in front of him, taking a stand for him.

"How dare you speak to me like that! I happen to be his sister and I think I know what he is and isn't capable of. Who do you think you are, standing there; acting like his savior…you are nothing to him! You were the one who spilled the water all over the place…you clean it up…alone. You need to learn your place, anyhow. Come on, Caspian…let's leave her to do her chores." She reached down to unlock his breaks, but he pulled her hand away.

"She is a guest in this house, not a servant. You do whatever you want to do, but I am staying here and helping her clean up. And you better believe that I will let Grandmother know that you refuse to do what you are told. You think you are better than her, but it's the other way around. At least she doesn't treat me like an invalid, unable to take care of myself or protect myself. Well, I am very able. You have changed. You are not acting like my loving little sister. I don't know who you are anymore." Caspian's eyes were beginning to fill with angry tears, as he released his sister's arm, and rolled forward. "If it weren't for your behavior, we wouldn't have to be in here right now." He turned his chair so he was facing her.

"I wasn't the one who threw a pitcher of water…" She pointed at Amelia, hissing. "…She was! She has gotten under your skin, and turned you against me. Mark my words, big brother, she is just using you. She doesn't love you. She doesn't know you, what you have been through. I have been here, every day, watching you struggle with your disability. You say I have changed. Well, if I have, it's because she walked in the door and I *knew* that all she would have to do is bat her eyelashes and give you a pretty little smile, and you would be stuck on her. She targeted you, and you fell right into her trap. I know girls like her, and you will end up with your heart broken, and she will walk away laughing. And I refuse to stand by and watch." She turned on her heels and stormed off, slamming her bedroom door behind her. Moments after she left, the only sound that could be heard was the pipes knocking in the heat register and the ticking of the clock in the hall. Amelia had no words to say, nothing that she could think of that would take the sting from the air. She didn't care how Evangeline felt about her. If she thought that she was out to hurt, Caspian, she was dead wrong. The helpless feeling that Amelia felt, as she looked at Caspian, was more than she could bear. She watched him, as he fought to hold in the sobs that were shaking his body. She wanted to go to him, but she was unsure as to how he would react. So, she said the first thing that came to mind.

"Evangeline is right. I made the mess, so I need to clean it up. You need to go talk to your sister. There is something going on, and you need to work this out." She sighed, trying not to show any emotion other than sincerity. He looked at her, almost as if trying to read her face. When he couldn't see anything ill-minded, he unlocked his wheels and wheeled out of the room, toward his sister's direction. Before he had disappeared from view completely, he looked at her, tears still in his eyes. "Thanks, Amelia." She nodded, and then got back to straightening up the tile floor.

Caspian knocked on his sister's door for a few minutes before she finally clicked the lock open, and cracked the door. He rolled into the room, and closed the door behind him.

"What has gotten into you? Why have you become *this* person, hateful and hurtful?" He moved his wheelchair over to the side of the bed, where Evangeline was sitting, Indian-style, on her comforter, her dark copper hair hanging over her face like curtains. She sniffled, confirming his assumption that she had been crying.

"Nothing has gotten into me, Cass. I just don't trust her, and I honestly can't trust you when you are around her. You know nothing about her, and yet you are caught in her web. I saw the way you look at her, and I am sad for you, because you think that you will have a happy ending, but you won't. You will just end up with a broken heart, and I will be here to pick up the pieces."

"I am not caught in anyone's web. You are wrong, I do know her…we've talked. And you would know her too, if you took the time. You say that you know what she is like because you know girls like her…but the truth is, you haven't even given her a chance. She could be a genuinely nice, sweet girl, but you don't care. You don't want to allow her to prove you wrong." He reached for her hand, and took it in his. "You are my sister. It is my job to protect you, not the other way around. I am a big boy, and am fully capable of safeguarding my own heart. I am not some terminally-ill, fragile invalid, that you feel you need to play bodyguard to. I am a human being, with feelings. I have come to terms with my situation, but obviously, you are still struggling with it."

"I am not struggling with it. I just hate it. I hate that you will never walk again, that you will never be able to live a normal life…not like before. And people will take advantage of the fact that you are in a chair…like…other people, and you will get hurt."

"Well, I hate that I am in this chair too, but it doesn't mean that I am any less than a person because of it. I can lead a normal life, regardless of my ability to walk. As far as me being stuck in this chair forever, it's not definite. I may be able to walk again someday, but for now, I am going to make the most of it."

"At least I know that she hasn't totally got you under her thumb, because you are in here with me, and not cleaning with her. I don't care what you say, Cass, but I don't trust her and I know she is trying to get between us…she almost did tonight." She smiled her devious smile.

"I hate to burst your bubble, but Amelia is actually in there working alone, because she insisted that I come see you, and we work things out. She even said that you were right about the mess being all her." He raised an eyebrow at her, as though to say that her opinion of Amelia was wrong.

"You are making that up!"

"If I'm lying, may God Himself smite me right here on the spot. I am dead serious." He looked at her, and his expression became serious. "I want you to do me a favor and give Amelia a chance. Quit calling her names, and quit being such a brat about her being here. If she had been a he, you would be falling over yourself to make him feel welcome." He sighed, and rolled back, away from the bed. "I think that your problem with Amelia is simple…" He gave her a sideways look, and she couldn't help but wonder what her big brother thought of her. "I think it is as simple as this…she's a girl. And she isn't just any girl; she's a very pretty girl, whom your brother happens to…" He cut himself off, before he openly admitted how he felt about Amelia, but Evangeline finished his sentence.

"You DO like her! I knew it. You look at her with puppy dog eyes, and start to get a goofy look on your face." She leapt off her bed and jumped around, overjoyed that she had been right.

"Stop that!" He made an attempt to grab her arm a couple times, but she jumped out of his reach. "I am being serious, here. You have a problem with the fact that I …"

"Say it! Say it!" She taunted him.

"I like her, okay? There…I admitted it out loud. Now, as I was saying…you are afraid that if any girl were to come into my life, like Amelia for instance, that she will steal me from you. Am I warm?" After hearing what he had just said, she stopped dancing around and looked at him, and a familiar look was in her eyes. She swallowed hard and stared at him, almost looking like a deer caught in headlights. He knew that he had hit the nail right on the head. All of her behavior toward Amelia boiled down to the fact that she felt as though, if there was another female in her brother's life, she was going to be pushed to the foreground and eventually forgotten. "What you need to understand is that she's just a girl…you are my sister. No matter what happens in life, how many girls may come and go in my life…you will always be my sister. Don't you understand that? No girl could ever replace you in my life. However, you have got to understand that I do deserve to be happy, and I am allowed to like girls. I am allowed to have female friends. The things that you have said to me since Amelia got here have been mean, and hurtful, not to mention the things that you have said to and about her."

"You are naïve to think that a girl is just going to fall for you, sincerely. I am not saying that it has anything to do with your wheelchair, either. We have money, or at least we are part of a family that does. There are girls out there who are just looking for wealthy guys to dig their nails into. I have met girls at the academy who only want to marry wealthy men when they grow up, so that they can live in luxury. How do you know that Amelia isn't just like that?" She whispered to him, watching the door.

"I know she isn't like that. She told me she wanted to go back to her home, in Chicago. She had a life there…probably had friends there too. She got ripped from her home and brought here, just as we did. She is not any different from us, just a girl in need of a home and a family to love her. The least you can do is cut her a break. She just lost her father. You know how much that hurts."

"Okay. I'll admit that I haven't been very fair to her…or to you. I just don't want you to get hurt." She hugged him.

"Alright. I am going to go check and see if she needs any help with the bathroom." He turned his chair around and headed out into the hall. The clock in the hall chimed nine times as he headed down the hallway. As he approached the bathroom, he heard an interesting sound. It was almost as if someone had turned on a radio, but there was no music, just singing. He leaned into the doorway and saw Amelia, standing at the vanity, singing. His heart leapt up into his throat.

As she ran the tarnished brass hairbrush through her long wavy auburn tresses, she was switching between singing and humming. Her hips were swaying to the notes she sang, and she looked almost surreal, the lights silhouetting her profile in such a way that she looked as though she were glowing. Her figure was petite, and yet curvy. She filled out the silk pajamas she was wearing in all the right places, even for a fourteen year old girl.

He sat in the doorway, watching her, quietly. He almost felt like he was intruding, but he couldn't take his eyes off of her. The sweet and sad melody she was singing was intoxicating, and he held his breathe, afraid that his labored breathing would call her attention to her unknown audience. Maybe his sister was right. Maybe she did have him under her spell. His whole body would do strange things when he was around her.

He jumped out of his trance when she stopped singing, set her hairbrush down on the vanity, and turned toward the door. He swiftly and quietly backed out of her sight, and into a small cubby in the wall next to the door, as though he was a peeping tom, attempting to keep from getting caught. He saw her shadow approach the doorway, and then it was gone as the light was switched off. He quietly wheeled back a little further, to observe her from the shadows.

He thought that she would head straight to her room, but what she did caught him totally off-guard. She walked toward his door, and knocked, ever so softly, on his door. She stood there, waiting for him to answer the door. He felt horrible as he was not in there to answer it, but in fact, lurking in the shadows, watching her like a creeper or stalker. She waited a moment longer, bent down and slipped something under his door, and then leaned toward the door, and said something to it, as though trying to whisper something through the mahogany barrier. He couldn't hear what she had said, but how he wished he had. She leaned her forehead against the door, ran her hand softly down the wood, and then walked toward her door, a look of disappointment on her face because he had not answered her.

After he was sure that she was in her room, and the door was closed, he glided softly to his room. He was about to open his door, when a sliver of light crept into the dark hallway. He froze, afraid to move. Suddenly, he saw her sneak out of her room, a satchel over her shoulder, and her coat on. *Where is she going?* His first instinct was to call out to her. However, he didn't want to startle her, so he decided to follow her. She headed down the hall, and was standing at the top of the grand staircase. *Is she running away?* He sped up and caught her wrist right before she began to descend the steps to her escape. She squealed in surprise, and stumbled, yanking Caspian out of his chair, as he was still holding tight to her wrist. They hit the landing with a thump, and his wheelchair clamored as it got knocked back, right into a wall. He had landed on his side, pulling her down on top of him.

"Caspian! My God! Are you alright?!" She propped herself on one elbow, and looked at him.

"Please tell me you were not just about to run away..." He gasped, as the wind got knocked out of him, not only because he hit the floor, but also because her body was pressing hard onto his. When she couldn't answer him, truthfully, she looked at him, sorrow in her eyes. "Why would you run away? Mia, please, explain to me why you would leave." His body was in agony, but he didn't care. He was closer to her, physically, than before and it was driving him crazy. The urge to grab her face and finish what he had started in the bathroom before, surged through his veins and he tuned his face from hers. The scent of honeysuckle wafted from her hair into his nostrils.

"I can't tell you. I just have to go." She got to her feet, and stepped over him, retrieving his wheelchair. She locked the wheels and reached down, for him to let her help him back into his chair. As much as this situation hurt his pride, having her help him, he took her help, without complaint. He wrapped his arms around her neck, and used what strength he had, to assist her in lifting him. After several attempts, they managed to accomplish their task, and sat, winded. "Are… you… okay?" She asked him again, between the gasping for air.

"I'm not sure. I seem to be all in one piece." He sighed, trying to let on that he was in a lot of pain. To prevent her from taking off until he had answered his questions, he snatched her satchel off the floor. The sudden movement sent a sharp pain up his side, and he winced, and hissed.

"You are not okay! You're hurt!" She leapt forward and gently lifted his arm, and pulled his shirt up. In such a short time, a large purple and black bruised had formed over his ribs. "My God! I have to get Gran." She moved to go around him and get help, but he grabbed her with his other hand.

"Please, don't…not yet. I need to know why you want to leave. Please don't go…" The pain was getting worse now, with every breath he took; it felt like knives stabbing him. He became very light headed, and his olive skin became very pale.

"I promise I will tell you, but not right now. I have to get Gran!"

When she finally got Gran, and had told her what had happened, they raced to his side. He was slumped over in his chair, out cold, most likely from the pain.   An ambulance was called immediately, and Amelia knelt next to him, trying to wake him.  She patted his cheek, begging him to squeeze her hand, and sobbed about being sorry.  After what seemed like an eternity, the ambulance finally arrived.  They came with a stretcher. After strapping him down to the back board, and putting the neck brace on him, the men carried him down, and headed out the door, Margaret at one side, and Evangeline at the other.  Right before they put him in the ambulance, he came to, and pulled his grandmother close, and whispered in her ear.  In the midst of all the chaos, no one saw Amelia slip out the front door and head down the street, still sobbing.

Evangeline raced into the house, hell bound on finding out what Amelia had done to him. She took the steps two at a time, and blew though Amelia's door. The room was dark, and void of life. She flipped the light on, and looked everywhere she thought that Amelia could be hiding. When she had exhausted every option of a hiding place, she noticed that there was an envelope on the bed, with her name on it.  She opened it, still furious at seeing her brother take off in an ambulance.  Her eyes read the words, and her heart began to slow, her breathing less raspy.

Evangeline,

By the time you read this, I will be gone. I have caused your family pain, and it is obvious that I am tearing you and your brother apart. I will always be grateful to Gran, for taking me in, even if it was just for this one week.

Contrary to what you may believe, my intentions were never to hurt anyone, especially him. He has a kind and loving heart, which is very rare in my experience. Though I may not be what you would want for him, I would never have used him, and then broken his heart.

Take care of him. Take care of Gran. Take care of yourself.

Amelia Landon


She dropped the note on the floor, and ran back down the stairs. She couldn't understand why Amelia was wearing her coat earlier, but now she was sure she knew. She hadn't done anything to Caspian. He caught her trying to run away and tried to stop her, and something must have happened. She needed to tell her Grandmother. It hadn't been very long, so she couldn't have gone very far.

When she got to the bottom of the stairs, she realized that the ambulance has already taken Caspian to the hospital, but that her grandmother had stayed behind to wait for Evangeline and Amelia, so they could head to the hospital together. When Margaret saw Angie alone, she thought that her granddaughter had done or said something to prevent Amelia from joining her.

"Where's Amelia? We must go. The ambulance has already left, and I don't want him there alone."

"Grandmother, Amelia's gone."

"What do you mean, gone? What have you done?"

"Everything! This is all my fault, and I am ready to take responsibility for my actions. She ran away, grandmother."

"Poor child…she must have snuck out while we were tending to Caspian. You and I need to have a serious talk when I get home." She moved quickly to her study, where she phoned the police, and reported Amelia missing. When she hung up, she rushed back to the door, where Henry was waiting with her coat. "The minute you hear something, let me know. I have to go be with Caspian." She gave an awful look to Evangeline, and then went to the car, leaving her behind in her guilt.

# *~Three~*

The police were combing the streets in less than twenty minutes after Margaret had made the call. She told Evangeline to stay home, just in case Amelia returned home. She told the police to contact her at the hospital, as she needed to get there to be with her grandson.

The house was dead silent, except for the fall of Evangeline's footsteps on the marble floor, as she paced back and forth. She realized that what Caspian had said was true. She had misjudged Amelia, and it took her note, and her running away to make her realize that. The streets of Boston were unfamiliar to her and she could easily get lost, or hurt. She never wanted anything bad to happen to Amelia, but her behavior had pushed her to this drastic measure. The funny thing that stopped her in her tracks was what Caspian had said to her, about her not accepting his situation. It wasn't until Amelia came, that she even began to make such a fuss about him being in that damned wheelchair. It was as if, unintentionally and subconsciously, she was trying to belittle her big brother, so that he would not leave her, by telling him that no one would love him because of his disability. Obviously, the wheelchair hadn't mattered to Amelia. She hadn't heard her say anything about it, except to defend his capabilities despite it.

She took a seat on the bottom step and watched the front door, almost willing Amelia to walk through it. Caspian was in the hospital, Amelia was wandering the streets of Boston, and there she sat, feeling utterly helpless to help anyone, then an idea struck her.

"Eloise!" she bellowed to the maid, snatching her coat and boots from the closet by the door. Eloise came running.

"Have we heard anything about Master Caspian…or Miss Amelia yet, miss?"

"No, but I have an idea. I am going out, and I need Henry to drive me…I think I know where Amelia might be." She waved Eloise to go get one of the stewards, as she laced her boots and got her coat on. In no time flat, the Rolls Royce pulled out front and Evangeline was out the door.

"Where to, miss?" Henry beckoned back to her.

"The bus station, Henry…and step on it." No sooner had she gotten the destination out of her mouth, the car sped down the road. It took close to ten minutes to get to the station, and she was unbuckling her safety belt. Henry parked the car, and they raced towards the buses that were being loaded, headed to Chicago.

They looked on four of the five buses headed to Chicago, and were about to check the last one, but it started rolling away before they had a chance to look for Amelia on board. Evangeline was about to give up hope of getting to her in time, but then the bus rolled away, and there, on one of the benches, was a reddish-brown head of wavy hair, and an old tattered coat.

"Henry! There, look!" She took off at a run, and stopped with a skid in front of Amelia.

Amelia looked up, her eyes red and puffy, and her hair a complete mess from the wind. Evangeline sat down next to her, and looked at her. "Missed your bus, huh?" Amelia answered with a shake of her head.

"I couldn't get on it. I have no home in Chicago anymore. My house is gone, my father is gone, and I am too old and too poor for the boarding home for Girls that I was staying at. All I would have is the orphanage, and it is pointless, cuz no one would adopt a fourteen year old.

Everyone wants babies. But it is my only choice. I have nowhere else." She wiped her runny nose with her sleeve, and sniffled.

"You could always come home. Grandmother's worried sick."

"I'm sure she is worried, but it is for Caspian, not me. I am the reason he got hurt. I ended up hurting him after all. You were right about me. I'm sure you are happy to hear that, especially by me."

"Actually, I was wrong about you. I misjudged you completely. I'm thirteen. I act stupid sometimes. I am so sorry. I really am."

Amelia turned her head and looked at the face of the girl sitting next to her, trying to catch that glimpse of maliciousness in her eyes. But, to her amazement, there was nothing malicious there.

"I appreciate you apologizing, but you were still right…I hurt Caspian. I can never take that back." She began to sob again. She sat there and sobbed, but suddenly jumped when she felt Evangeline put her arm around her shoulder, almost expecting her to trick her in some way, but nothing happened.

"Let me see if I can guess what happened…Caspian caught you sneaking out, tried to stop you, and got hurt somehow." Amelia nodded, and then Evangeline continued. "Would you have even attempted to run away, had I treated you as a welcomed guest, like he had? You ran away because you felt like you were just causing problems and tearing our family apart, but the truth is…I made you feel that way, so I was the reason that my brother got injured. It wasn't your fault. It was mine. Now stop being stupid, and come home." She got up and offered Amelia her hand. Hesitantly, she took her hand and they walked back to the car, followed closely by the giant black man in a suit and nightcap. He gave a big, bear yawn, and then started the car, after securing the two girls in the back seat.

Rather than going straight home, Henry took them to the hospital. He escorted them in, got directions to Caspian's room, and walked with them. When the girls went in, He stood outside the door, like a security guard.

They walked in, and turned around the curtain to see Caspian, a bandage around his midsection. His eyes lit up as he saw Amelia's face. Amelia was greeted by a giant hug from Gran, and then a splotch on the behind.

"Don't you ever run away from home again! You were close to giving this old lady a heart attack." She looked at Amelia, kissed her forehead, and then looked to her granddaughter. "Where did you find her?" Evangeline and Caspian traded looks and then answered her question in unison.

"The Bus Station."

"The bus station? Where were you going, my dear?" Margaret stepped forward, embracing Amelia. "I wish that there was something or someone in Chicago waiting for your return, but there is nothing there. Your life is here now." She held her at arm's length, and then motioned for Evangeline to come get some hugs too.

Caspian looked at Amelia, searching her face, but, as before, she wouldn't look him in the eye. He knew that what needed to be said between them, it needed to be said in private. He waited until his grandmother and sister had released each other from the warm embrace, and then asked to have a few minutes with Amelia, alone. They left, without argument. When the door had closed, and it was just them, he reached for her hand, but winced and quickly put his arm back down, and clutched his side.

"Do I need to call a nurse?" She started to step toward the door, but he shook his head, and softly waved for her to come over to him. Slowly, she edged her way over to his side. He patted the bed, urging her to sit down. She hesitated, looking worried that she was going to hurt him more.

"It's fine, Mia. Please, sit down." She did as she was asked, and he took her hand in his free hand, his other still clutching his side. "I'm fine. I have a couple cracked ribs, but they will heal. I will be able to come home in a day or so. I just have to take it easy for a while, which shouldn't be difficult, seeing as my life is nothing but taking it easy since I am wheelchair bound." He tried to joke with her, but the pained look on her face told him that it wasn't as funny as it sounded in his head. "I'm sorry. I was just trying to ease your mind. I will be fine, I promise you."

"It's my fault you got hurt, Cass. I shouldn't be allowed anywhere near you, now."

"Now, Mia, that is ridiculous. You shouldn't be so hard on yourself. If I hadn't grabbed your arm, and startled you, you wouldn't have almost fallen down the steps, and therefore, I wouldn't have lunged out of my chair to keep you from getting hurt. If my injury is anyone's fault, it's my own. No worries. You are safe, and sound, and here. That is all I care about." He said, softly, looking deep into her sapphire eyes.

She began to get all warm inside, and her heart began to beat a little harder. She couldn't understand why he had this effect on her. It was as if she had no control of herself when she was around him. She felt drawn to him, like a magnet, and somehow felt at peace yet energized at the same time. She must have gotten lost in his stare, because she didn't feel herself move closer to him, nor did she feel his hand find its way to her cheek. She felt the warmth of his touch, and she leaned into it, instinctively, putting her hand on his, to prevent him from pulling away. Her eyes closed, and she felt the treacherous storm in her mind come to a halt, and, instantly, she was calm and felt safe. But it came to an abrupt end, when she heard him suck a quick break through his teeth. Her eyes flew open, and she was startled at the fact that her face was nothing more than two inches from his. She could feel his warm breathe on her face, and it mingled with her own breathe. They had been in this same awkward position just a few hours before, in the bathroom, her dressed in nothing but a bath towel. Her heart was leaping in her chest, and she swallowed hard.

"Are you in pain? Am I hurting you?" She whispered, unable to speak any louder. She realized that she was leaning into him, and pushing down on his chest. She tried to pull away, but his other hand, which had been clutching his side, was now settled at the nape of her neck, his fingers entangled in her hair. She had nowhere to go, but forward, and that fact terrified her, and excited her all at once. She had never kissed a boy, nor has a boy ever attempted to kiss her. She swallowed again, and looked at him. Part of her knew that she wanted it to happen, needed it to happen, and it was that part that was urging her to go for it. However, the other part of her was telling her that she wasn't ready, and that if it went badly, they would never be able to look at each other the same way again. Her eyes filled with tears, and she swallowed hard. Her body began to shudder, and he could feel it. She shut her eyes tight, trying to shoo the tears away, but it didn't work. With a hard sigh, she opened her eyes, and looked at him, and pulled his hands from her face and neck, and leaned back, still clutching his hands in hers. "I can't…I'm not ready…not for this…it has to be just right, or …"

"…or it ruins everything." He gave her an understanding look, and gave her hands a soft squeeze. "I know what you mean." He pulled her hands to his lips and brushed his lips against her knuckles, so soft, that she wouldn't have known he had done it if she had not seen him. "When the time comes…when you are ready, can you make me a promise?" He looked at her, holding her hands in his, and pressing them to his chest. She blinked and nodded. "A kiss is very special, but a first kiss is a treasure to be earned, not just given away to the first guy you meet. Promise me that you will save the honor of being your first kiss for someone extraordinary. You will feel it in your heart when you have found the right guy…the one worthy of receiving such a special gift. After all, you only get one 'first kiss,' so keep it to yourself for as long as you can. Whoever earns the honor....I will envy them for all eternity, which is all I have to say. They are going to be very lucky, and they better treasure it." She could hear the strain in his voice, telling her that he was on the verge of becoming emotional. "Promise me, Amelia... "

"I promise, Caspian. With all my heart, I swear." She wanted to tell him that she could have easily have given him the honor just moments before, if he had truly wanted it, but she felt that he knew he could have had it, but had sacrificed his golden opportunity, out of respect for her.

In those moments, as they sat there, holding onto each other's hands, in silence, they both knew that this night would change them both, forever.

# *~Four~*

Life went on after that night in the hospital. Amelia was enrolled into Blakemore Academy, the school that Evangeline attended. As promised, she got the best education that her Gran could offer, as well as all the advantages that being a member of that family could give. Amelia and Evangeline took the time to get to know one another and found that they had a lot in common after all.

All the chaos that came with the first week after Amelia had arrived seemed like a distant memory. No one spoke of it, except to joke about how absolutely ridiculous the whole ordeal was. And, the "near-kiss" in the hospital was kept as a secret between them; however, their intense feelings for each other became less apparent over time. And the note that Amelia had slipped under his door, prior to her attempted escape, was tucked away, unopened, in his favorite book in the library. Many times, He found himself in the room, holding the envelope in his hand, debating whether to open it or not, but, again, he would slip it in between the pages, still sealed, and put the book in its slot, exiting the room.

Because Holbrook College didn't have accommodations quite yet for wheelchairs, Caspian was homeschooled for his college courses. His day started when the girls left for school, and ended when they walked in the door. He looked forward to seeing them walk passed the window in the study, and often found his heart jump when he saw Mia approach the front stoop, but he hid his feelings and emotions from her. Although the physical attraction had come to a halt for her, or so it seemed, his feelings for her hadn't changed. He regretted not taking his chance, but knew that if he had kissed her, he would have stolen that golden moment from her for his own selfish reasons. And though he denied it, Evangeline knew that he still harbored those same feelings for her ex-nemesis, now best friend. And though it made her uncomfortable to think about it, she knew in her heart that they would never feel the same for another person, as they did for each other, despite both of them going through blatant denial.

The wind was blowing hard outside, and it sent a flurry of snow up against the windows, making the elegant design of frost more visible. Cars were moving at snail speed down the street, and the people brave enough to be outside in the chilly weather were bundled so much so that no one could recognize the person beneath the layers. Caspian was in the middle of a Shakespearian sonnet, when he heard the heavy front door swing open and heard the girls laughing. He looked to his instructor, gave a big gin and a wink. The older gentleman did same as he did every day, which was, roll his eyes, close the big book that they were reading out of, and wave him off.

"Class dismissed." The instructor sighed, exasperated.

Caspian raced himself in the foyer to greet them, and met with a face full of snow. As soon as he had cleared the cold, wetness from his face to welcome them home, he got two more snowballs, one more to the face, and the other to the stomach. There was an uproar of echoing laughter. He couldn't help but laugh along with them. But, as quickly as they had bombarded him with snow, they were there to help clean him off.

"I think I got some up my nose this time." He chuckled, as he shook his ivory sweater free of snow. "Good aim, Angie." He laughed as he took a chunk off his lap and, stealthily shoved it down his sister's blouse. Mia was picking up the scarves, hats, gloves and coats up from the floor and shaking them off, before hanging them up to dry on the coat rack, and shot him a coy smile. She shook her head, causing the snow in her hair to spray all around her.

"We better change out of our uniforms, Angie. Gran will be peeved if they are all a shambles for school tomorrow." She laughed, stepping over the remnants of snowballs on the marble flooring. She used her hand to shake some snow from Caspian's hair, before hopping up the stairs, trailed closely by Angie, still laughing. He watched the two girls ascend to the upper floor, and sighed. Both of them had grown and matured quite a bit in the years that had passed, but there was still a trace of the thirteen and fourteen year old versions in them that could be seen, for instance, when they attack him with snowballs for the pure joy of it.

His sister, Evangeline, was once a small statured, gangly little thing, her legs and arms slightly too long for her body. However, now, the rest of her body had caught up, and filled out. Her nose, which used to come to an upward point below green eyes that looked a little close together, now was more like a button beneath those same emerald eyes, which also separated slightly, making her face more symmetrical. Her mousey red hair, which she used to keep in tiny pin curls, framing her face, was now long and straight, with streaks of blonde, thanks to her hairdresser, Carlos. He didn't invest too much thought into her body, as it made him feel creepy, because it was his sister.

Amelia's appearance however was a whole different subject. There was not a day that went by that he had to pull his eyes from her direction. She was beautiful when he first met her, but the years had been so very kind to her. Her reddish-brown tresses, which used to be out of control most of the time, were now tamed down quite a bit, often pulled back in a semi thick ponytail, or up in a sloppy bun. Her skin was no longer ivory, as she spent an enormous amount of time outside during the sunny days, and had a soft tan. Her beautiful sapphire eyes were brighter now, and the amber tint was less visible. She filled out even more than anyone had expected, yet she still stayed petite. Caspian got chills whenever she was near, because he thought that there could be no woman who could come close to her when it came to raw sexual appeal. Every move she made was graceful, and flawless, and she had a smile that could melt an iceberg.

As much as the girls had changed over the years, Caspian had changed more so. His hair, which used to be cut short, was now hanging loosely around his shoulders. Margaret had allowed him to grow his hair after graduation, because with his hair short, he looked almost identical to his father, and she often got weak in the knees when seeing him out of the corner of her eye, as she could swear that her Richard was back from the dead.

Another thing that had changed was his physique. He had spent a large amount of time using weights, trying to strengthen his arms and upper body, to eliminate the need of assistance transporting in and out of his chair. He was now strong enough that he could hoist himself to the second floor on his own, by climbing the stairs with his arms, going backward. He even got a second wheelchair, and left it at the top of the steps, eliminating the need to drag his chair up and down all the time. After all the strength training, he was buff from the waist up. And though Amelia still acted as though she wasn't attracted to him like before, he had caught her looking at him a few times, biting her lower lip and, that same look in her eyes. He would laugh inside when he caught her, and she'd blush and look away. It was moments like that that kept hope alive for him, that he would not have to steal her first kiss, but that she would give it to him willingly, as he felt was always meant to happen.

He rolled to the stairs, slid off onto a step, pushed his chair to the side, and began to make his way up the stairs. When he was about three steps from the top, the hair on the back of his neck stood up, and he stopped and turned his head, slightly. With a smile on his face, he leaned back and propped his elbows on the step behind him.

"Hey Gorgeous…" He crooned, not even looking to make sure it was her and not his grandmother or Eloise.

"How do you do that? Do you have eyes on the back of your head?" She giggled, sitting down on the step next to him, tucking her skirt under her, and propping her feet on the step down, so her knees were nearly to her chest.

"I told you before…I have super senses." He laughed, mocking her slightly. "So, how were your classes today…Any new gossip to share from the old Academy?" He gave her a sideways look, as he couldn't look her straight in the eyes, as that would set him off.

"Well, classes were good. Mrs. Sheffield announced her retirement for the end of the school year. I got an A on my trigonometry test, my Spanish exam, and on my report of the Roman Empire. I got the solo spot in choir, like you said I would. And, I have an exam in Applied Science on Friday, so I could use your help studying for that." She rattled out the info, all the while, staring at the tips of her tennis shoes peeking out from under her skirt. "So, can you find time to help me with my studying, Cass?"

"It depends. What do I get out of the deal?" He shot her a crooked smile.

"You get the satisfaction of knowing that I am not going to fail my test because you helped me study…" She smiled her cheesiest smile, as she tossed the statement at him in the form of a question.

"Good enough for me." He softly smacked her knee, and held his hand out to make the deal official, and she gave him a genuine smile and a quick shake. He could feel a shock of electricity in the instant that her skin made contact with his, and his heart skipped a beat. "Now, what's the gossip? I wanna hear all the juicy details." He rubbed his hands together in anticipation.

"Hmm, let me think. Let's see…Oh! Billy Cassidy got a three-day suspension for setting a lizard, from science lab, loose in Dean Cumming's office. Meghan Brenner was caught in the janitor's closet with…wait for it…Matt Harper!"

"Ewwww" they both said together, their faces both scrunched up. They started to laugh.

"I tell you, that girl will make out with anything with lips." He chuckled and sighed. "Anything else…"

"Well, there is the dance coming up…and…I still have not been asked." She got a sad look on her face.

"I am surprised that you weren't the first to be snatched up….I thought you would have a line of guys asking you…" He craned his neck to look at her.

"Nope. Not even Matt Harper asked, and he is the last guy I would want to go with, but at least it would have been someone. I don't think I am going to go. It isn't really that important anyway." She started playing with a stray thread on her skirt hem.

"It is important to you… I know it is. Even if you and Angie just go to have fun together, at least you can say you went."

"I can't go with Angie." The words exited her mouth, slowly, as though she didn't mean to say them.

"And why not, may I ask?" He sat straight up. She had his full attention, now. She turned and faced him, her hands out in front of her, as though she needed to protect herself for what she was about to say.

"I can't go with her….because she has a date…Please don't get mad!" She winced and flinched, looking at him from squinted eyes. He instantly closed his eyes, and began to rub the bridge of his nose.

"How long has she had this date? When did the cretin ask her to the dance?"

"She hasn't had a date for that long…maybe a week…and a half." She grimaced, after telling him.

"A week and a half! Are you serious? And this is the first I am hearing of it?" His shoulders and hands began to shake, and his face got red, as he held his mouth clenched, trying not to scream. Mia jumped up, moved in front of him, and grabbed his hands tight in hers.

"We were afraid to tell you for this reason. We all knew that you would get upset, but she is growing up. Please don't ruin this for her. It means so much to her. It's her first dance. Come on, Cass. Calm down." She grabbed his face between her hands, and made him look at her. "You will be able to meet him prior to the dance, and talk to him. Okay?" At her last few words, he exhaled slowly, and placed his hands over hers, and nodded. At that moment, he was concentrating more on trying to calm his temper, and not on the physical contact between Mia and himself, which would have sent him into overdrive. When his color went back to normal, and he had calmed quite a bit, he opened his eyes again, and he was face to face with the reason his heart continued to beat harder than normal.

"Are you calmed down now?" She said softly, and he nodded, still looking at her, his hands still over hers. "You can let go of my hands now." She suggested, with a smile. He shook his head, no, a glint in his chocolate eyes. "Let go, Caspian." She giggled slightly. He shook his head again, and intertwined his fingers in hers to get a better hold. Her giggling stopped, and she looked at him, almost sternly. He slid her hands off his face and held them together in front of him, leaning his forehead against them.

"Why can't you just give me five minutes of this…actual physical contact, instead of the cold shoulder?" He looked up at her, with a pleading look in his eyes. She swore she could even hear a waver in his voice.

"Why are you doing this, Caspian? Just let go of my hands, and talk to me." She tried to sympathize with him, but he closed his eyes, so the eye contact was broken.

"No, I will not let go, but we SHOULD talk. Why do you look at me as if I am a stranger? Why do you treat me like one?" He pursed his lips to minimize the quivering in his lips.

"I don't treat you like a stranger. I mean, at least I don't think I do. If I do, it is not intentional." She whispered to him, trying to figure out why he was acting so strangely.

"You do. So many things have changed between us, and it kills me. You barely ever come near me, and when you do, you avoid physical contact as much as humanly possible. What harm is there in a hug once in a while? My sister hugs me, Grandmother hugs me… but you…you wave, or nod your head at me…"

"I don't know, Caspian. I didn't realize…" She started, but he cut her off.

"Don't tell me that you didn't realize that you have been treating me like some kind of disease, afraid to touch me, for fear of catching something. I am not a contagious virus. I am a human being, for goodness sake." He didn't notice that as he spoke his words, he was squeezing her hands, and she whimpered. He opened his eyes, looking petrified at the realization that he had caused her pain, and loosened his grip slowly. Staring at his hands, and then at her, he tried to apologize, but the words weren't coming out. "I…I…Oh God…I'm so…I didn't mean…" Without a word more, he got to his chair, and rolled down the hall to his room.

She stood on the step, at a loss for words at what had just happened. Tears welled in her eyes, as she rubbed her fingers. She ran up the stairs, down to Angie's room and ran in, slamming the door behind her.

After telling her best friend all that had just happened, she looked to Angie for a response.

"I don't know what to say, Mia. I would tell you that my brother was wrong about what he said, but, to be totally honest, he wasn't." She sat down on her bed, and looked at Mia, sympathetically.

"He wasn't... what? Wrong?" She got a pained look on her face, not wanting to believe what Angie was saying.

"He wasn't wrong. You may not realize it, but you have gotten very cold toward him. It has gotten progressively more noticeable as time passes. When you put your hands on his face...it was the first time that you, willingly and intentionally, made any meaningful contact with him. And after a long span of nothing, I am not really surprised that he reacted that way. Now, I can't make excuses for him hurting you, but I know that he would never hurt you on purpose. He was upset. He's hurting..."

"My fingers..."

"I'm not talking about physical pain, Mia!" She got a stern tone in her voice. "He's hurting here." She pounded her clenched fist on her chest, over her heart.

"I hurt too, Angie. And I am not talking about my fingers, either. It broke my heart to see him like that. He hasn't gotten that emotional for a long time. I hate seeing him like that. What should I do?"

"Well, for one, stop feeling sorry for him. He doesn't like people feeling sorry for him. He doesn't need your pity." Angie crossed her arms over her chest. "What he needs is…you." Amelia's eyes shot open wide and stared at her friend. "What I meant to say is that you have turned away from him, away from what used to be a really solid and loving friendship, and now you treat him as nothing more than a useful object that you pull out only when you are in need of it, and then shove it back into a drawer when you are done with it."

"I do not!"

"Oh, but you do, Mia. Your sole purpose for going to talk to him was to ask him to help you study for your science exam. You didn't go to him to spend quality time with him, or to just be around him. Sure, you guys talked a little, but that was just the price you needed to pay for his help…five minutes of your time."

"Now we are back to this, Angie. I am only using him. I don't care about him. I am going to break his heart. I have heard this all before, and I thought we were past it...four years ago." She stood up, and took a defensive stance against the accusations.

"Me too, Mia. I thought we were long past it, but you know what they say...history has a way of repeating itself. The only difference is that, back then, my accusations only brought the two of you closer. Here's hoping that it has the same effect the second time around. Maybe, I will actually see my brother's smile reach all the way to his eyes again...like they used to, before you became a frigid bitch!" As soon as the words escaped, she clapped her hands over her mouth, in shock that she had actually said them before she could sensor herself. Mia's eyes filled with tears, and she turned her back on Angie, and began to sob, her arms wrapped around herself. "Oh my God, Mia, I am so sorry! I didn't mean to say that." She reached for Mia, but Mia pulled from her hand.

"Yes, you did. You meant every word of it. The sad thing is..." She sniffled, and turned around to finish her sentence. "...the sad thing is that you are absolutely right. I am a frigid bitch. Caspian hasn't smiled like that for years. The light has gone out in his eyes and it is I who extinguished it. It wasn't until I saw the look of utter desperation in his eyes, pleading for just five minutes of physical contact from me…I don't want to be responsible for making him stoop so low as to beg for a simple touch, but I am. I'm scared…scared of what might happen if I give him what he so desperately needs from me…scared of what I might do if I let down my walls."

"Wait…what? You're scared of letting down your walls? What walls, Mia?" She walked over and put her hands on her friend's arms, as if trying to steady her. "What are you talking about?"

"I spent a long time, wondering…if I distanced myself from him, slowly, if the feelings that we felt for one another would just fade away eventually. So, I slowly built walls, and pulled away from him. I thought it was starting to work…but, after how I saw him just then, I think that I only made things worse." She began to sob again.

"What are you saying, Mia?"

"I can't do this to either of us any longer…I can't…" She broke from Angie's grip, ran out the bedroom and down the hall, and threw open Caspian's door, with a loud bang.

Caspian, caught off guard by the sudden intrusion, nearly jumped off his bed. He had been sitting in the dark, his hands over his face, and his head leaned back against his headboard. Now, his arms were bracing him on the bed, and he was sitting straight up. He squinted his eyes to make out the face of the figure in his doorway, as the only light in there was coming from the hallway behind them. He heard heavy breathing and sobs, and slight whimpering.

"Cass, I...I'm..."

"Mia, is that you? What's wrong? Are you okay? I swear, I didn't mean to hurt you earlier...I would never..." His words were cut off, as she flung herself at him on the bed, and wrapped her arms around his chest, and clung to him as if her life depended on it. Her face was buried in his chest, and he could feel her body shaking erratically as she sobbed harder than he had ever seen. He didn't know what to do with his hands. "What's wrong? Did something happen? Mia, talk to me." Her arms were wrapped up under his, and her fingertips were clutching his shoulders from behind. He could feel the wetness of her tears soak through his sweater, and make contact with his skin underneath. His heart was thumping hard under his ribcage, and he let his instincts take over. His arms wrapped tightly around her, and he bowed his head, so his cheek was now resting on the thick cushion of silky hair. He was so overwhelmed by the moment that his body started to shake, as his emotions got the best of him. They sat there, clutching each other, and were oblivious to the girl, standing in the doorway, her hand over her mouth, masking the sobs that escaped her as well. She leaned forward, and grabbed the knob, slowly closing the door, allowing them to have some privacy before dinner.

*****

Two hours passed by, and there was no sound coming from Caspian's room anymore. Angie couldn't hear either of them, and wondered if they had maybe left the room, and gone down to supper without her. She descended the steps, and noticed that Caspian's wheelchair was still at the bottom of the steps. She looked toward the top landing, and there was no chair there. She crept back up the stairs, and knocked quietly on the door, calling for either of them in a whispered voice. When no one answered she decided to go looking for them in any of the other rooms.

However, they were not in any of the other rooms, but rather, still in Caspian's bedroom. After an unknown length of time had passed of their mutual emotional release, they had unintentionally drifted off to sleep, still holding to each other. Something that sounded like light knocking at his door, roused Caspian, and he slowly opened his eyes. As his eyes adjusted to the dark room, he noticed that the silhouette of his body was unusually fuller, he had a weight across his upper body, and the familiar scent of honeysuckle tickled at his nostrils. It was, at once that he remembered what had happened, and he, looking down at his chest, moved a strand of auburn hair from the face of the girl nestled, comfortably, against his chest. He had never actually seen her when she was sleeping before, and as beautiful as he thought she was normally, she looked amazingly more so as she slumbered against him. Her hand had found its way to his chest, and was laying, softly on it, her fingers clutching his sweater material. He tried to look at his watch, to see what time it was, but he couldn't make out the hands on the watch face. He did not want this moment of absolute serenity to end, and so he just leaned back again, and rested his hand over hers, and closed his eyes. He could hear the sound of her breathing, and it was as if that sound would forever be etched in his memory as one of his favorites.

After a short time, of just lying there, he heard the chime of the clock in the hall, beckoning Caspian back to reality. It was only after he heard the seventh chime ring out, did he realize that they had both slept for supper. But, why, if they had missed their evening meal, had no one come looking for them? Though he hated to bring this magical moment to an end, he needed to find his grandmother and explain why neither of them were present at the table.

"Mia…Mia…" He tried to rouse her from her peaceful rest, but her response to it was going to send him into a sort of frenzy. She, sleepily, slid her hand up, and wrapped her fingers in his hair at the base of his skull, which sent tingles down his spine and made bumps pop up all over his body. He untangled her fingers from his hair and brought her hand to his face. He laid several feather soft kisses across her palm. "Hey, sleeping beauty….Mia, wake up." When she only sighed, and nuzzled her face more into his chest, he resorted to gently tickling her cheek. She jostled a little and then, stretched slightly. Her eyes began to flutter open, and a smile swept across her lips and she looked up at Caspian.

"Hey you…I must have dozed off. Why didn't you wake me?" She sighed.

"You were sleeping so soundly, and obviously, you needed it, so I just let you snooze away."

"You fell asleep too, didn't you?" She giggled, catching him trying to act all noble.

"Um, yeah…yeah, I did. We both must have needed it, because we slept straight through supper."

"Are you kidding me?" She shot up, startled that they had slept that long. "Why didn't someone come and get us? Where's Angie?" She got up and straightened out her clothes, or attempted to in the dark. Caspian reached over and clicked on the bedside lamp, and they both winced at the sudden light.

Like she had heard her cue, Angie knocked and then peeked her head into the room, and sly grin on her face.

"Did you guys have a nice nap? I hope so, because I had to cover for you at supper. If Grandmother asks, you guys were up here, studying for that science exam." She could tell, instantly, that they had been sleeping by the state of their clothes and hair.

"My God, thank you, Angie! We owe you one!" Mia sighed, relieved that they wouldn't have to explain their absence to Gran.

"Oh, you most definitely do! Both of you." She giggled and then left, closing the door behind her.

Mia slunk back down onto the bed, and looked over at Caspian, who was looking at her very strangely.

"What's wrong? Do I have bed head? Did I drool?" She checked her hair and wiped her cheeks and chin for any wetness. He laughed, and grabbed her hands.

"No, you are as beautiful as always, I swear. But there is something on my mind…As much as I truly enjoyed…this…" he tried to use his hands to explain what had just happened. "…as happy as it may have made me to hold you again…what happened? What were you so distraught over, that you would come to me like that? I mean, we haven't exactly been very touchy-feely for a long time…and after what happened out on the steps earlier, that was the last thing that I ever expected to happen…"

"You were upset. I know that you never intended to hurt me. You needed to tell me how you felt, because I really had no idea that I was making you feel like that." She leaned back, propping herself against him. "By the way, you are really comfortable to sleep on." She snuggled up close to him, and laid her head against his shoulder. "And, also, you are like a big heating blanket."

"Thanks, but you are just complimenting me to avoid answering my questions." He looked at her, a stern look deep in his eyes.

"Am I? I was just making some observations, that's all." She stated, sweetly, playing with his fingers. He pulled his hand away, and sat up, forcing her to fall backward. He scooted to the edge of the bed, and pulled himself into his chair to put some distance between them. "Hey, what is wrong? I thought you wanted…this." She used her hands to mimic his actions from a few moments ago.

"Do you think this is a game? Am I a joke to you?"

"No, of course not! Why would you think that?" She sat back up and looked at him, offended.

"Answer my questions, then. Why the sudden turnaround? I need to know what has changed. You couldn't get far enough from me, but now you are all clingy and needy…if you are just messing with me, I swear, Mia…" She reached for him as she saw him get very agitated. He wheeled further away. "Please, Amelia, don't touch me right now. I need answers."

"What do you want me to tell you? Do you want me to say that I was just satisfying your need for affection? Huh? Do you want me to say that I did it so that I could gossip about it to my friends? It is obvious that you want me to be the bad guy, to tell you something that would make it easy for you to hate me, so you can brush aside your feelings, cuz you are tired of loving someone who could never love you back. Well, guess what…If I said all those things, I would be lying to you and to myself, like I have been lying to myself for four damn years! Why do you think I have kept my distance from you?" She was now standing, words spilling from her lips, and tears from her eyes. Caspian was caught off-guard, unable to process everything she was saying, before more came at him. When she stopped, momentarily, he looked at her, confused. She repeated the last question so he could understand her. "Why do you think I have been so cold and distant toward you? Would you venture to take a guess?"

"That is what I have been wondering. I don't know what is going on in your head, or your heart. You never talk to me anymore. You're either very distant or you just avoid me altogether. But, as far as what you said about me wanting you to give me a reason to hate you….that is not true. Even if I wanted to, which I don't, I couldn't hate you. I just want to understand what I did to you to make you hate me!"

He was yelling now, and it was so loud and intense that it could be heard outside of the room they were in, and a small crowd of people had gathered outside the room, curious as to what the shouting was all about. Margaret had come up from her study, and was the last to join the small congregation surrounding the bedroom door. Angie was crouched on the floor, with her ear to the door, trying to make out what was being said, since it sounded like a garbled mess to everyone else. After a moment's hesitation, Amelia responded, weeping.

"Hate you?! You think I hate you?! That is the furthest thing from the truth."

"Why have you been acting so cold toward me, if not for blind hatred? No one could treat someone they cared for the way you have treated me!"

"Well, unlike you, I don't express my feelings for people as easily and as publicly as you do. My feelings for you scare me. They terrify me! I can't tell you how many times I have wanted to...how many times I have tried..."

"Wait a second...what?" He leaned forward, trying to figure out what it was she was saying, but his head was swimming. "Back that up a little bit! You are trying to tell me, because you are scared of your feelings, you have stood by and watched me suffer with mine 'publicly' and done nothing. It has torn me to pieces, seeing you, day after damn day, treating me like I am nothing."

"You have no idea what the distance between us has done to me! I have lost sleep because of it."

"Oh, you've lost sleep! You were the one that put the wall between us in the first place! If it was half as hard on you as it has been on me, you still couldn't have stood the pain. And yes, it kills me to know that I fell in love with someone who could not love me in return. I fell in love with someone who would rather hide behind an invisible wall, and protect herself from the pain that comes with loving someone, then to allow me to go through the pain at her side!  And when I say her, I really mean YOU!" He had, inadvertently, just admitted to her how he felt, and the look in her eyes made him believe that he had made a big mistake by letting the cat out of the bag.

"If you love me…truly love me…with all your heart… Kiss me." She looked him straight in the face.  This was the ultimate test for him.  If he kissed her now, in the heat of an argument, then that magical moment would be lost forever.  On the other hand, He did love her with every fiber of his being and kissing her would prove that to her.  He rolled over to her, reached and pulled her onto his lap.  He slid one hand to the small of her back, and the other went to the nape of her neck.  Her body began to tremble as he drew her face closer to his.  As he closed the distance between their lips, she closed her eyes, and swallowed.  Her hands found their way to his face and the waterfall of silky hair at the back of his head. Just when he was about to close the last inch remaining between them, he felt his heart ache.  He lowered her face and pressed his lips firmly to her forehead. He closed his eyes hard, and choked on the lump that rose in his throat. He felt her let out a shaky breath.  He lifted his lips, and raised her face so she was eye-to-eye with him.

"I refuse to rob you of your first kiss. If that means that I don't love you, then so be it." He laid a kiss on the tip of her nose, and moved his arms so she could leave if she chose to. She didn't release her grip on him, hoping that he would change his mind. After a few moments, she gently tugged his hair, pressed her forehead to his, and sighed. She leaned to the side and whispered in his ear, and the words she spoke sent an electrical current through his whole body, and he closed his eyes, fighting tears.

"You're wrong…You *do* love me. You just proved it. Just know that when you are ready…my first kiss is yours, and yours alone….it always has been and it always will be. I'll be waiting, till the day I die." She kissed the side of his face, and then got up and walked toward the door.

When she had reached the threshold, she laid her hand on the doorknob, and looked down at the floor. Before she left his room, she needed to set the record straight, because she felt that she had finally built up enough courage to tell him what she felt he deserved to know.

"Just, so you know, to answer your questions…I pulled away because I have always felt that you deserved so much better than me. I thought the distance would cause all those feelings to fade, so you could move on with your life. I thought that it was working for a while…but I guess I was just in denial, because it was painfully apparent your feelings were as strong as ever. I saw today that, instead of helping you move on, I was hurting you. I never wanted to see that look of desperation in your eyes, and it was a wakeup call. That's why I came to you. I just wish that it could have lasted a little while longer. And despite what you may believe, I do love you. I did when I came to the hospital that night, and I still do. If you don't believe me, ask your sister. Better even, go to the library, open your favorite book, and read the sealed letter that I wrote you." She turned the doorknob and exited the room, not seeing the smile that crept across Caspian's face.

Upon hearing footsteps approaching the door from the other side, Angie leapt back and signaled for everyone to scatter. Henry, Robert, and Eloise took off down the stairs immediately. Angie urged her grandmother down and around the corner, so they wouldn't be seen. As Amelia left Caspian's room, she looked in the direction of the corner where Evangeline and Gran were hiding.

"Show's over. You can come out now. I know you are there." She walked over in their direction, as they came out from their hiding place.

"May I ask what all that was about? Obviously, the two of you didn't miss dinner because you were studying." Margaret gave a sideways glance at Angie.

"No, we weren't studying. If you don't mind, I really don't want to talk about it right now. I'm going to my room." She turned and headed back down the hall.

"You are going to bed without anything to eat?" Gran inquired.

"I'm not hungry, but thank you." She sighed as she got to her door, and entered, closing the door quietly behind her.

Angie shrugged at her grandmother, kissed her on the cheek, and went back to her room, and Gran returned to her office downstairs.

Caspian sat in his chair and pondered what had just happened between him and Amelia. His emotions were raw, and he felt exposed and yet, he felt a huge weight had been lifted from his heart. He had been harboring these feelings for so long, not knowing that she had felt the same way. To know the truth, and her reasoning behind why she had been acting as she did, broke his heart. She felt as if he could do better than her, that she wasn't good enough for him, while at the same time, he had felt the same thing about her...he always had, and a part of him still did.

Amelia sat on her bed, unclear as to why their discussion of their relationship had escalated so quickly into an argument, and then ended the way it had. A part of her wanted him to kiss her, but she was grateful that he hadn't. He had respected her enough to know where to draw the line. Arguing and kissing didn't seem to draw the picture of romance.

She laid back on her pillows and starred at the ceiling. Her heart was still racing, but not because of the argument. It beat hard because Caspian had told her how he felt...he loved her. With a sigh, she rolled over and drifted off to sleep.

# *~Five~*

Ever since their fight, things seemed to be better. The two of them made a point to greet each other, and Amelia tried to spend more time with him, just to talk. She thought that laying all their cards out on the table would have made things less tense, but there were always words to be said that neither of them dared to utter aloud.

Caspian had not found time to retrieve a certain envelope from his hiding place in the library, though he was curious as to how Amelia had even known about it, as no one ever went in there that he was aware of. He did, however, get to meet the boy who had asked his sister to the dance, and after a thorough interrogation, he approved of him. He gave them all thumbs up, and his sister let out a sigh of relief.

Amelia escorted Angie and Gran to the dress shop to get her dress for the dance, and walked out with a strapless silver silk gown, with sequined pattern on the bodice, and a slit that went up the side and stopped at her knee, with matching silver pumps. As Amelia had yet to be asked to the dance, she didn't pick anything out, though she was very fond of a very flattering azure princess gown, with matching satin open-toe stilettos, which she tried on and it gave her an extra three inches and made her calves look fabulous.

They had just walked in the front door from their shopping trip, when Gran nearly stumbled and fell. Robert caught her elbow. Everyone was scrambling to get her to a chair.

"Oh…there's no need to fuss over me. I just got a little light headed. Eloise, please take Angie's dress and hang it up…oh, shoes too." She let Robert and Henry assist her with removing her coat, and then put her hand to her head.

"Something's wrong, Gran. It's time for us to call Dr. Wendell." Amelia handed her coat to Robert and then went to her grandmother's desk and looked up the family physician. This had not been the first time that Gran had nearly collapsed. There had been three other incidents in the last week. She got on the phone and spoke to him, filling him in on Gran's ailments. When she hung up the phone, she rushed up to Caspian's room, to let him know that they were going to take his grandmother to the hospital. Caspian got downstairs as quickly as possible, by flinging himself onto the bannister and sliding down, stopping right near the bottom, and swiveling to land his chair. He had mastered that trick after many failed attempts, some of which sent him flying and sliding on the marble floor on his derrière.

"Grandmother...what happened?" His voice was soft, but she could hear the panic.

"Oh, it's nothing, my dear boy. I'm old. I got a bit light headed, that's all."

"She nearly collapsed again, Cass. That's the fourth time this week. I called the doctor and he said that he would meet us there. We need to get her there right now. Do you want to stay here...wait, what am I saying? You go with her and Angie. I will stay here."

"No, if something happens, I won't be any use to anyone in this thing." He pointed to his chair. "You go. I will stay here. Just call me and let me know what they find out." Caspian shoved Amelia toward the door. He leaned over and kissed his grandmother on the cheek, hugged her, and then moved aside so Henry could assist her out the door to the car, where Robert was waiting with the Town car. He hugged his sister, who was already in tears. Before Amelia had a chance to get too far, he grabbed her hand, and she turned to him. "Watch out for Evangeline, just in case something does happen. She's going to need your support in case this is serious."

"She wouldn't need me...she'd need you. You are her big brother. Please go with them."

"No, I insist that you go. You can talk to the doctor. I would be too worried to talk, that I wouldn't be able to remember what the doctor says. You are more level-headed than I am. You can worry and stay focused at the same time. Go...go go go!" He gave her hand a squeeze and shooed her out the door.

*****

Four hours had passed since they had rushed his grandmother out the door, and sped off to the hospital. Caspian's nerves were raw, not hearing anything of her diagnosis. He had tied to pass the time by keeping busy. He practiced doing wheelies in his chair, had gone through every photo album in the study, read every letter that Amelia's father had sent to his grandmother. After reading those letters, it reminded him of the letter from Amelia. He hurriedly retrieved it, and brought it back to the study, to be close the phone in case the phone rang with news. He used the letter opener on the desk, and slid it under the flap. As he unfolded the paper, he closed his eyes to steady himself for what he was about to read. Taking a deep breath, he opened his eyes, and began to read.

My Dearest Caspian

There are no words to express how I feel, writing this letter, knowing that I will never look upon your sweet face again. You have been very kind to me, and I can never tell you how grateful I am to have met you. My heart aches to know that I will be gone before you even read this. I need to tell you something, that I know I would never be able to say to your face, as I find myself at a loss for words when you are around. I think I may be falling for you. My heart beats a million miles a minute when you are near, and I can barely catch my breath. Why am I telling you this, knowing that I am leaving? That is very simple. I want you to be happy. I want you to find your soul mate. I want you to find love with someone that deserves your love in return. And you will find love, regardless of what your sister may think, though I really believe that she is just scared of losing her big brother. Just remember something. If ever you feel alone or unwanted, just know that I am out there, somewhere, thinking of you and loving you. You have my heart, now and forever.

Mia


The words were slightly blurred as he read them through the tears that had welled in his eyes. He attempted to read the letter a second time, but the desk phone began to ring. Still clutching the letter in his right hand, he picked up the receiver.

"Hello?"

"Caspian, it's Mia. Sorry that it took so long to call you, but they ran all sorts of tests, and the doctor finally came back with the results."

"Well…what did the tests say? Is Grandmother going to be alright?" She could hear a strain in his voice, but was unsure as to whether it was his grandmother's condition that was causing it or something else. "Well, What did the doctor say…MIA!"

"Oh! I'm sorry. The good news is that your grandmother will be coming home soon. Unfortunately, there are going to be a lot of people coming to the house in the meantime."

"What does that mean? What happened?"

"I don't want you to freak out, but the reason that she has been collapsing is because the muscles in Gran's legs are beginning to deteriorate due, in part, to her suffering a mild stroke. The people coming to the house are workers. They are coming to do some revisions on the house, to make it handicapped accessible. Gran will be in a wheelchair, because her legs can no longer hold her weight. Also, she will have a nurse and physical therapist visiting the house several times a week."

"She's going to be in a wheelchair? She had a stroke?"

"Caspian, she's still the same otherwise. Being in a chair doesn't change who a person is…you of all people should know that. The stroke was mild, and there was nothing any of us could have done. The doctor seems to think it happened in her sleep. Gran said that she woke up one morning, feeling strange, but she just thought she was coming down with something."

"Poor Grandmother. Is there anything that I can do?"

"Henry is going to bring Angie and I home. Robert will stay with her, and they agreed to take shifts until she returns home. I will bring home all the papers that the doctor gave to me. We will read them together."

The next day, a slew of carpenters, contractors, and a truck full of materials had arrived at the large home, parking on both sides of the sleepy avenue. Much of the house was taped off within an hour of their arrival. Walls were torn down and dust was flying everywhere, driving Eloise and the rest of the staff absolutely crazy, as they kept the home pristine at all times. Quite a few times, Amelia had to remove a weeping Eloise from a room that was covered in plaster dust and scraps of wood and debris.

A new addition to the house was a motorized lift to carry Margaret to the second floor, moving along a track on the wall of the grand staircase. Caspian didn't need it, as he was fully capable of going up and down the stairs on his own, but for "safety purposes," he took it for a test drive. Though it was much easier than his method, he felt that it took entirely too long to get from point A to point B.

It took longer than anticipated for Margaret to return home to her grandchildren and the home she had loved so dearly. Complications arose, and she suffered another mini-stroke while in the hospital. Fortunately, she was able to return home after almost four weeks. Everyone scrambled to make certain that everything was in place and ready for her homecoming.

The birds were chirping and carrying on as the town car rolled up in front of the house. The house was all a flutter, as she was rolled up the ramp and in through the front door. Immediately, everyone noticed the change in the Matriarch, as she no longer looked young and spry. Her illness had taken its toll on her, and she seemed to have aged years. But despite her health, she wasn't too weak to greet the three young adults with a smile and outstretched arms.

Evangeline, out of instinct, looked around at the people coming in the door, as if she were looking for someone. Amelia and Caspian both leaned toward her, trying to see what she was looking at.

"Who are you looking for, Angie?" Caspian whispered, curiously.

"Last time that grandmother was gone for a long time, she brought home a stray…" Angie remarked, giving a crooked grin to Amelia, who caught the joke and slapped her friend. Caspian laughed; amused that Angie had actually made a joke at Amelia's expense, which was actually funny. Amelia rolled her eyes, and started laughing as well. Hearing the laughter seemed to brighten the older lady's mood, and she greeted them with a wide smile, receiving a group hug in return.

*****

The dressing room was all a flutter as the spring formal had finally arrived. Margaret had Jean Claude, the Hairdresser, come to the house to do Evangeline's hair. Because Amelia hadn't landed herself a date, she was foregoing the dance. Gran had insisted that she get her hair done as well, as she felt that she deserved to be pampered, regardless. Now, they were in the room, getting Evangeline dressed and ready. Her dress was form fitting, and it glistened in the sunlight creeping through the curtains. After she was completely ready, the butterflies in her stomach were flying frantically, looking at herself in the mirror, Grandmother and Amelia in the background.

"You look absolutely beautiful, Angie. Kevin is going to flip out when he sees you. He should be arriving any moment. Are you ready for this?"

"I think so. I really wish you were coming too. You know this is the last dance you are going to be able to attend before you graduate."

"You know that no one asked me, and I wouldn't want to be a third wheel. This is *your* night, Angie. I want you to go and have a good time. I will be fine, right here, with Gran and Cass. And I will stay up so that you can tell me all about your night when you get home." She set her hands on her friend's shoulders and gave them a squeeze. Suddenly, the doorbell rang, alerting them to the date's arrival.

"Don't forget, my sweet child, that you need to be home no later than eleven. If not, I have no control over what your brother will do to that poor boy out there." Margaret said, weakly, to her youngest grandchild. "Your father, God rest his soul, would be so proud of the beautiful young woman that you have turned out to be. So would your mother." She patted her on the hand, and led the way to the door.

In the foyer, a timid blonde boy in black slacks, a blue button up shirt, and black waist coat waited, his eyes looking down at the boxed corsage in his hands. He was surrounded by Eloise, Henry, and Robert, amongst other members of the staff, but one familiar face was not among those waiting to see Evangeline off.

"Where's Caspian? He should be here to see you before you go." Amelia whispered to Angie as they stepped around the corner and joined the others by the door. She wound the film in her camera, and urged Angie to go stand by her date.

"This is for you, Evangeline. My mother helped me pick them out." The boy murmured, as he took the daffodil corsage out of its plastic box, and slid it on her wrist.

"Thank you, Kevin. They are lovely." She lifted her wrist to smell the flowers.

"Alright, you two, look here and smile." Amelia lifted the camera, and clicked a few pictures. "You better get going, or you'll be late." She set her camera down on the side table and went to say goodbye to Angie, but Angie pulled her aside instead. "What are you doing? You have to go."

"I know but I just wanted to say…I hope you have a wonderful night, Mia." She gave a tearful smile, and then hugged the girl she considered like a sister.

"Shouldn't I be saying that to you?" She giggled, awkwardly, as she hugged back.

"Well, yes, but I just wanted to tell you that I hope you do too."

"Oh, yes…a wonderful night is in store for me…I will be in the darkroom, probably developing the pictures I just took." She laughed.

"You never know what tonight might have in store. Those pictures may have to wait." She grinned and turned to leave, grabbing her lace shawl from her grandmother.

"Wait a minute…what are you talking about? What have you been up to, and for God's sake…where is Caspian?!" She tried to get answers from Evangeline, but she was smiling and waving, as she headed out the door, leaving the questions unanswered.

The staff waved goodbye, even after the door was closed, and Eloise started crying again. Henry escorted her to the kitchen as the other staff disbursed to get back to their duties, leaving Amelia and Gran alone in the foyer. She walked over to her, and bent down to look at Gran in the face, her hands on the armrests.

"Do you know what is going on? Caspian is missing, and your granddaughter just told me she hopes that I have a wonderful night. What in the world is going on? By the look on your face, Gran, I can tell that you know something." She smiled as she interrogated the lady sitting in front of her, a weak but sly smile on her face.

"Take me to my dressing room, please, dear, and we can sit and talk in there." She pointed in the direction of where they had just come from, where they got Evangeline ready. Amelia did as she was told and took her back to the room. Positioning Gran's chair across from the chaise, she locked the wheels and sat down.

"Alright, Gran, we are back in here, but why? Are you going to tell me what is going on?"

"You remind me so much of your father…always asking questions, always needing to know all the answers to everything. And, as I told your father years ago, some questions are better left unanswered. It takes the mystery and wonder out of life."

"What can you tell me, then?"

"Well, my sweet, I could tell you that the reason that we came to this room was not just for the purpose of talking."

"Alright. I figured as much, but go on."

"It was very distressing to me that you didn't go to the dance with Evangeline. As she said, this is the last dance before graduation, and you should have gone."

"Gran, as I explained it to you, and Angie, and Cass…I didn't have a date. No one asked me."

"Now, young lady, I don't believe that for a second. A beautiful young woman like yourself had to have been asked by at least one young man, if not more. You know how I feel about dishonesty in this house, so, come out with it. How many times were you asked to the dance?" Gran gave her a stern look, knowing that her surrogate grandchild was keeping something a secret.

"Alright…three…three boys asked me to the dance." She felt ashamed for lying to everyone.

"So, you could have had a date to the dance, but you told everyone that you didn't. Tsk Tsk. Shame on you, young lady. Why did you tell us that no one asked you?" She gave a disappointed look to Amelia, and folded her hands in her lap.

"I didn't want to go with any of them. The one guy that I wanted to go with…"

"…doesn't go to Blakemore Academy anymore." Gran finished her sentence for her, knowing who she was referring to. "You are a strong, independent young woman. Why didn't you ask him, instead of skipping it altogether? I have it on good authority that he would have been elated for you to ask him. Also, a little birdie told me that he was going to ask you himself, but was afraid that you would turn him down." She winked at the young lady in front of her.

"No I wouldn't have. It would have made me so happy…wait, Gran, are we talking about the same guy?" She went from smiling to a confused look.

"I am an old woman, true, but I'm not blind yet. I can see how you look at my grandson, and that he looks at you the same way." Gran's words made Amelia blush and hide her face in her hands. "It is obvious that you care very much for one another."

"But, Gran, it's also very inappropriate. I'm ashamed that I've acted un-ladylike in such a way. He's your grandson, and I'm...I'm...I don't even know what I am, but I know that the way I feel for Caspian is inappropriate." She began to cry.

"Calm yourself, child. There is nothing to be ashamed of. You've done nothing wrong. Caspian is a very handsome young man, and you are a radiantly beautiful young woman. It is only natural that you would care for one another as you do. I have watched the two of you over the years, and have seen how your affection for each other has blossomed and grown. To be honest, this has been a long time coming. Even your fathers predicted this." With her last statement, she handed Amelia a photograph that she had tucked in her pocket.

In the photo, there was a strapping young boy about the age of five by an oak tree, gently clutching the hand of a cherub-face girl of three years. The girl was chestnut-haired, that stuck out in different directions in its beautiful thickness. They were looking at one another, and smiling. Amelia flipped the photo over and on the back was written "Cass + Mia =

Love?." She turned it back over, and ran her thumb over the image of Cass, standing on his own two feet, and tears welled in her eyes.

"Would you mind if I kept this photograph, Gran?" She smiled and looked at the lady in front of her.

"I wouldn't mind at all. As you can see, everyone, including your fathers, knew that it was bound to happen. They used to say that it was destiny."

"How old was Caspian…when he…"

"He was eleven. It happened shortly after the two of them came to live with me, and after their father passed on. He had been outside playing, and saw a puppy in the middle of the road. He went out to get it out of the road, but he didn't see the car coming around the corner. God spared his life, but he has been in the chair since. It took me a long time to forgive myself for the accident, but it was your father who helped me deal with my guilt. The doctors told us that there were procedures to help him to walk again, but that there were no guarantees that they would be successful. Ultimately, it was Caspian's decision, as he would be the one going through the operations." For a moment, it was as if Margaret had gone back to the past in her mind, as she stared at the window. She cleared her throat, and looked back to Amelia, smiling. "But, enough of sad stories…let's get back to you.  Could you please go in that closet?  There is a garment bag hanging in there.  Get it for me, please."

Amelia did as she was asked, and nearly burst into tears when she saw what Gran had asked her to retrieve.  In a clear garment bag, there hung a beautiful Azure princess dress with matching open-toed stilettos, the dress that she had fallen in love with at the boutique.  She pulled it from the rod, and hugged it to her as she turned to face the sweet woman behind her.

"Gran!  It's the dress I…but how…You only bought Angie's dress that day.  How did you get this?  You were in the hospital for a month, and you haven't left the house since you got home…"  She was stammering, tears in her eyes.

"I asked Bernice, the clerk, to put it on hold for me, and I paid for it when I paid the bill on Evangeline's, so I just had to find a way to pick it up without you knowing.  Sweetums, your face lit up when you tried it on, and that dress was practically made for you, so I knew you had to have it, just in case you changed your mind about the dance.  Alas, you didn't change your mind, but Robert had already gone to get it for you, so…"

"So what?  What are you up to, Gran?"  She gave a twisted smile and a suspicious look to Margaret.

"Put it on, my dear." She rang the little crystal bell on the table next to her, and Eloise and Claudette, another maid, came in and began to help Amelia into her dress. Claudette retrieved a beautiful sapphire pendant and matching dangle earrings from the jewelry chest, and put them on her. As Amelia turned to look at herself in the mirror, she had to do a double-take, as she could hardly recognize herself. She looked like royalty. "And, isn't it fortunate that you got your hair done today, as well?" Gran clapped her hands together in delight, looking amazed at the vision standing in front of her. "And now, my beauty, it is time for you to be on your way. You have someplace to be." She rang the bell again, and Henry entered the room, dressed to the nines in a tuxedo. He looked like a bald-headed gorilla in a suit, and Amelia smiled sheepishly, trying not to laugh.

"Miss Amelia, I have come to escort you to the Ballroom." He spoke in a deep voice, as he offered his arm to her. She took it, blew Gran a kiss and went with Henry. She had only been in the ballroom once before, when she was younger, and she had told Caspian that being in there made her feel like she was Cinderella, and she had danced around, with her arms up like she had a partner. But when she saw the sad look in Caspian's eyes, she never went back in there, nor mentioned it to him again.

The doors to the ballroom were open and it looked like diamonds hanging from the ceiling, not at all like the dusty abandoned room she had remembered. There was a light shining in the middle of the floor, and bits of light spinning around it from the mirror ball above. Henry took her to the spotlight, and told her to wait there. From that spot, the rest of the room looked dark. She stood there for a few moments, trying to see if there was any movement from the shadows.

All of a sudden, soft music began to play, and she saw a flash of something in front of her. She watched as Caspian rolled into the light, dressed in a tuxedo, and his hair slicked back. She giggled in delight, her eyes filling with tears. He rolled up to her, handed her a white rose, and put his hand up.

"Milady, may I have the pleasure of a dance with you?"

"You most certainly may, good sir!" She squealed, as she set her hand in his.

He pulled her over to him, patting his lap for her to take a seat. She tucked her dress under her, out of the way of the wheels and wrapped her arms around his neck. He wheeled around the dance floor to the music. They rolled slowly, and turned softly during the slow songs, and sped around wildly during the fast ones, which made Amelia laugh and squeal.

They went on like this for hours, and during one of the last songs, she got off his lap and danced, holding his hand. She even got behind him and wheeled him around. It was going rather well until he tried to spin her out from him and he lost his grip, and she slid across the floor. She just laid there, laughing, spread eagle on the floor. But Caspian, seeing what had happened, was not so amused.

"I'm sorry that happened. Are you okay?" He reached for her hand, and pulled her from the floor.

"Don't be sorry. That was fun!" She gasped through the laughter. She crouched down in front of him, so she could look at his face, and she suddenly stopped laughing. "I'm fine. The question is, are you?"

"No...I mean...yes, I am fine." He grumbled, shooting her a half smile.

"No you aren't. Don't lie to me. What's wrong?" She put her hands on his knees, and he placed his hands over hers.

"I wanted to give you this magical night, since you weren't going to the spring formal. I was going to ask you if you mind taking me as a date, since no one asked you, but...." He hesitated.

"But, what, Cass?"

"…But, if this had happened at the dance, in front of everyone, I would have embarrassed you. Just going with me would have been embarrassing enough, but if that had happened…Dammit!" He jerked his wheelchair back and rolled off to the side of the floor. She stood back up, and watched him. He turned around, and looked at her.

"Stop this right now, Caspian Greyson Wallingford! Stop acting like this…like you are anything less than human. That was an accident, and could have happened to anyone…ANYONE! If you had asked me to be your date to the spring formal, I would have been ecstatic to go with you, not embarrassed. However, you didn't ask me, which is okay, cuz I love this better. Now, get back over here and dance with me." She stomped her stiletto on the floor, and pointed at the floor in front of her, expecting him to put himself right there.

"You love this better…better than a real dance, with actual people…having to sit on my lap rather than standing on your own two feet, showing off that stunning dress in all its magnificence. You cannot honestly tell me that, were you given a choice of me or someone else with working legs…there's not even a doubt in my mind…you would choose them." He had rolled back to her, and she was crouching back down in front of him. "Look at yourself, Mia. You are absolutely breathtaking, a princess right out of a fairy tale, a modern day Cinderella. But, unlike the prince, I can't dance you around the floor like we are on air. I can't even hold you when we are dancing" He threw his arms up in the air, out of frustration.

"Do you think that I care about those things? Do you think that I am that shallow? This night has been everything I could ever have wanted…and you know why? Do you?" He shook his head. "It's because of you...YOU. How many times do I have to tell you that before you believe it?" She looked at him, nothing but adoration and love in her eyes. "If you were able to walk, and dance on your own two feet, I would not look at you any differently than I do now."

"You can't know that… not for certain." He lowered his eyes, looking down at her hand in his. He stroked her fingers with his thumbs.

"I do, and I can prove it." She got to her feet and ran out of the ballroom, leaving him there, bewildered. Moments later, she returned, a piece of paper in her hand, and Henry trailing behind her, her camera in his hand. She knelt back down in front of him, and put the photograph, which she had gone to retrieve, in his hands. "Look at that picture…look at that little girl's eyes." She pointed at the picture. The little girl was looking at the older boy like he was the only thing in the world. "That little girl is looking at that little boy the same way that I am looking at you right now. Do you know who those children are?" Again, he shook his head, and looked at her gaze and then looked at the picture again.

"Is that…not possible…is that you and I? Where in the world did you get this?" He was in awe of the image in front of his eyes. There they were, side by side, hand in hand; young versions of themselves, and he was standing.

"Gran gave me this picture before I came in here tonight. That is the same look I give you every day. I am looking at you the same way then, before the wheelchair, as I am now." She took the picture from him and stuck it in the front pocket of Henry's jacket. "But it is obvious that you need just a little more proof." She looked at Henry, who knew what was about to happen. He walked behind Caspian's chair, reached down, and grabbed him under his arms.

"What the…Henry, what are you doing?"

"Up you go, mister…on your feet. I have myself a point to prove to you, and you are going to cooperate, or I will have Henry drop you on your behind!" With Caspian clear of the wheelchair, she lifted her foot and kicked it out from under him. Henry held Caspian around the chest, as Amelia bent over and locked his knees. When she stood back up, she took his arms, and flung them over her shoulders. "Hug me." When he got a hold on her shoulders, she wrapped her arms around the base of his back. With a nod to Henry, the big man slowly removed his arms from around Caspian, so now his full weight was on Amelia's shoulders. She gripped him hard. With his knees locked, and her bear hugging him, he was actually standing with her. She looked up at him. Tears were in his eyes. She never realized how tall he really was, because she had never seen him fully erect.

"Why are you doing this? What is this supposed to prove? I'm going to hurt you. Henry, get my chair back please." He panicked.

"What are you so afraid of? I have you, you are fine. Just look at me." There was absolutely no strain in her voice, and he calmed slightly. He lowered his head, and looked deep into her eyes, which had caught the reflection of the mirror ball above them, so they sparkled like jewels. It was only when he looked away from her eyes, to see her whole face; he realized that his lips were just an inch or two from hers, as he could feel her breath on his face.

"I…I don't know what this is supposed to accomplish, other than to give you a hernia." He smiled slightly, and saw that she was smiling as well. He looked over, catching something out of his eye. It was when he saw their shadows on the floor, standing in a tight embrace that his heart swelled. He never imagined he would ever see a sight like that again.

"Smile for the camera." A deep voice beckoned him to look in the other direction. He smiled at Henry, and then leaned his head forward, resting his cheek on Amelia's head. A flash went off, and they heard the shutter click.

"One more, Henry." She looked at him and then turned her head so she was looking up at Caspian again. He turned his head, and looked down at her, which was new for him. Another flash went off and the shutter clicked again. "Thank you, Henry. Stand by, just in case." The behemoth man nodded, and walked back into the shadows.

"You are full of surprises."

"Just wait…you are about to be blown away. You said that I didn't know for certain that I would look at you the same way, standing, as I look at you in that chair. This is my proof. Look into my eyes…has anything changed?"

"Other than the fact that …God, you have one of the most angelic faces…your skin is like…it's absolutely flawless and perfect. I feel like I'm seeing it for the very first time. And your eyes…they are the color of the perfect sky at sunset, the deepest blue with flecks of amber and gold…I could get lost in them. It's like looking into eternity, so deep…" His eyes lowered to her lips, a smile tugging at its corners. He couldn't resist those lips, and he closed the gap slightly between her lips and his. It felt as though the ground was dropping from under them. Her breath was intoxicating, so much so that he closed his eyes. He slowly rubbed the side of his nose against hers, the edge of his mouth connected for a split second with hers, and something erupted within his body. He was so close…so much closer than he had ever been before. One small move of his head was all it would take to do what he has waited years to do, and yet, he felt that this was not the moment, not the right time. He moved his face ever so slightly, his lips just a sliver from hers. "I love you." He breathed this, knowing that even a whisper would cause them connect, and all would be lost. That would be the point of no return. She let out a moan, and she gripped him tighter to herself, and he pressed his forehead to hers, widening the space. He opened his eyes, and looked at her. He had finally said the words that he had avoided saying directly to her, and he didn't expect her to say them back to him until she was as sure of them as he had just been.

"Damn you, Cass. Why don't you just get it over with and stop putting us through this torture?" She opened her eyes, and looked at him.

Responding to her, he leaned his face down, and laid a feather soft kiss right at the corner of her mouth, so close, but not close enough to count as a real kiss.

"I get it, Mia. I understand everything you were trying to tell me. I will not doubt you ever again, my love. And, so with that, I have to confess something." They looked deep into each other's eyes. "I think, seeing you this way... it is quite possible that I have fallen even deeper in love with you than I was before. I didn't think it was possible, but it happened. And, I cannot think of anything better than this moment right here."

They stood there through the rest of the song that was playing, holding tight to one another. And like anything good in life, it couldn't last forever. Caspian flagged down Henry as soon as the song was over, and with Mia's help, they lowered him back into his chair. They both thanked Henry, and he left the room, and she climbed back into Caspian's lap. Laying her head on his shoulder, they sat there for what could have been minutes or hours. Neither of them cared how long, because they had had their moment. He had fulfilled a dream of hers; to be Cinderella at her own ball with a handsome prince. And, in turn, she had done the same for him.

Though they hadn't danced their way across the floor, they stood together, and he was able to hold her in his arms...

The grandfather clock called out to Caspian and Amelia, telling them that it was midnight. He had held her in his lap and they spun and glided their way across the dance floor for every delicious second after he had returned to his chair.

"Hey Cinderella, it's pumpkin time...Amelia... Mia" He whispered to her, rubbing her arm. She sighed and nuzzled her face into his neck. She had fallen fast asleep, and he dared not wake her. He rolled himself, and his lovely passenger to the grand staircase. He signaled to Henry, and the large man gently scooped the slumbering young lady into his arms and carried her up to her room, Caspian trailing behind, his own way. Henry waited for Caspian to join him, and they both took Amelia to bed. After Henry had placed her on the large plush comforter, he excused himself.

Caspian hoisted himself up onto the bed next to her, and gently removed the jewelry, setting it all on the bedside table. He swiveled himself around and removed her shoes, carefully lowering them off the edge of the bed, and they hit the floor with a soft thud. He brushed his fingers across her rosy lips, and along her chin. Before leaving her room for the night, he kissed her hand. He slid off the edge of the bed, and back into his chair.

"Sweet dreams." He whispered as he backed out of her room, and closed the door with a soft click. He looked toward his sister's room, and she was standing there, still in her dress, smiling.

"How did your night go?" She whispered, a glint in her eye.

"You have absolutely NO idea." The smile on his lips was enough to tell her that it had went well, however, she had no inkling as to how well. He looked at his sister, and his smile widened. He grabbed her hand and pulled her down to him, giving her a kiss on the cheek. As he was rolling away, he turned his head, and winked at her. "By the way, you look beautiful...a vision of loveliness. Just thought I'd tell you. Goodnight." And he proceeded to his room. She blushed and then adjourned to her room for the night.

# *~Six~*

Last night felt like a wonderful dream, and Amelia would have thought it was just a dream, but she woke up in her dress. She rolled over onto her side, and stared out the window. The sun was shining in golden beams through the tree outside, directly onto her wrinkled dress. She noticed that someone had removed her shoes and jewelry, and she was grateful for whoever had put her to bed. She sat up, stretching, and tried to recollect all the events of the night before. It did feel like a dream, and it was fading. She ran her fingers along the edge of her lips, and stopped, lingering on the spot that Cass had kissed her. It couldn't have counted as her first kiss, but now she knew that she was not going to leave it up to him to make it happen, and it was going to happen soon. He was just teasing her now, and that sad part was he was enjoying it.

She got up, showered, and changed her clothes. She gave her beautiful dress to Robert to have dry-cleaned and pressed, put her shoes in the closet, and returned Gran's jewelry to the chest downstairs. Breakfast was spread out on the table, and she sat down across from Caspian without a word.

"Good Morning, Sunshine. How'd you sleep?" He asked, not looking up from his plate of pancakes and eggs.

"I slept well, thank you...and yourself?" There was a cold, stand-offish tone to her voice.

"Other than mild cramping in my legs, I slept like a log. Thank you for asking." He replied in the same tone. All the while, Evangeline and Margaret sat at the table, confused as to what they were hearing from the two of them. To break the tension that was building, Evangeline decided to speak, though, speaking at the table was not permitted.

"I think that someone should ask me how my night was last night." She spoke up, waiting to hear her grandmother reprimand her, yet again.

"Alright, Evangeline...How was the dance? Did you have fun?" Margaret inquired a smile on her face. Everyone else at the table was shocked that she was actually trying to carry on the conversation, and not bringing it to a halt.

"It was amazing. The Deejay was really good, and my feet are sore from all the dancing. I think Kevin had fun, too. He didn't say much."

"That's nice." Caspian garbled.

"Glad you had fun." Amelia sighed.

Evangeline looked at her grandmother, kind of put out that they weren't really interested, so she decided to mess with them. She winked at Margaret and stated to speak again.

"Yes, I did. By the way, I apologize for getting in so late. After the dance, Kevin and I went to his house and went up to his room…for privacy. Let me tell you, they don't call him the 'Silent Wonder' for nothing. He was amazing…I have never screamed so much in my life…" Margaret's mouth dropped open at the story that she had just heard, and gave Angie a disapproving look.

"He was a very nice boy, Angie." Amelia grumbled, picking at her food with her fork.

"He better've used protection, that's all I have to say…" Caspian spoke up.

"Wait…What!?! You did what?!" Angie's words finally registered in Mia's mind, and she leapt from her chair. "Caspian! Did you just condone your sister having….Caspian!?"

"What can I say? My sister is a big girl. If she wants to be a hussy, she should, at least, do it safely…" He winked at his sister, out of view of Mia, and it dawned on Angie that he had heard her after all.

"I cannot believe what I am hearing right now!" She threw her napkin down on the table. "This house and everyone in it have gone berserk. Now, we are condoning premarital relations…What's next? Are we gonna raise her baby when she winds up pregnant, too?" She was boiling mad, and almost walked out, but Caspian grabbed her wrist.

"Calm down, Mia…" He chuckled, fighting her as she tried to break free.

"Calm down!? You sit there…okay with your sister's promiscuity, but you won't even…Ooooh! I give up!" She turned to the elderly woman at the end of the table. "May I please be excused? I've lost my appetite."

With an approving gesture, she stormed off, mumbling. They all waited until they heard a door slam, when the three of them started laughing. What they didn't know was that it was the front door, not her bedroom door, which had slammed shut. It wasn't until Angie had gone up to Mia's room to explain the joke, twenty minutes later; they realized that she was gone.

Angie snatched her coat out of the closet, flinging it on, and headed out the front door. Caspian followed close behind, hoping to widen the search. After an hour of looking, they both returned to the house, disheartened.

"I didn't think she would get so upset. I was just trying to see if you guys were listening, and then you started…What has gotten into her?"

"I think that I have an idea." Caspian zipped his coat back up. "She thinks that you…ya know…and well….she hasn't even gotten to first base yet, and she thinks you hit a home run."

"What? I hate when you use sports analogies…speak human, not jock, please."

"She thinks that you…had sex…and she hasn't even gotten a kiss yet."

"You haven't kissed her?! What in Hades is wrong with you?" She rounded on her heels and looked at him, her hands on her hips.

"No, but the thing is…I can't do it. I want to…Oh God, do I ever want to…but I get so close and then something clicks in my head and I just can't."

"I understand that you have this nobility thing, but even she has told me that you are just dragging this out. I honestly believe that she thinks that you don't really want to kiss her, but that you just don't have the heart to tell her that."

"Maybe I should have taken my chance last night. I was right there." He made a gesture. "But, I guess I am coward. My thing is….once it's done…that's it! It's all over. It will change the whole game…uh…it will change everything between us. We will know, in that moment, how we truly feel. My biggest fear is that it doesn't go well…we kiss and there's nothing…"

"Do you love her? Like truly, indisputably, undeniably, head-over-heels…that kind of love?"

"I would die for her." He looked up at his sister, and she could see it in his eyes.

"Let's hope that Henry has better luck in finding her." Evangeline looked down at the ground, knocking the remnants of a ball of snow onto the ground.

"Well, I don't know about you, but I am going to keep looking." He rolled back down the street and headed in a different direction. Evangeline followed suit, and headed out as well.

The town car rolled up to the parking area for the Harborwalk, and Henry threw it into park. In the distance, he could see wild auburn hair blowing in the cool breeze. He grabbed a wool blanket from the trunk and started walking toward the girl standing near the water.

Though most of the snow had melted, the grass still crunched because of the frost. She heard him coming, so she was less startled when he came up behind her, and put the blanket around her shoulders.

"How'd you find me, Henry?' She asked, as he sat on the bench next to her.

"I come out here on my days off to think, sometimes. It's a good spot."

"Yeah, it is. I didn't peg you as a 'water' kind of guy. What do you come out here to think about, if you don't mind me asking?" She looked up at him, sweeping hair out of her eyes to see him.

"My wife...my boys..." He stared out at the water, no emotion on his face.

"You have a family? I didn't know that. Where are they?"

"Yes'um, I have a family. I don't talk about them much. They died in a house fire about twelve years back. They buried back home in Al'bama. That's where I'm from, originally." He pulled down the collar of his coat, to reveal scars on the back of his neck and on his shoulder.

"Oh. I'm so sorry. You must miss them very much."

"I do. What are you out here thinking about, Miss Amelia?"

"Caspian...Evangeline...Gran...you know, my family..."

"…Anything that I can help with?"

"Maybe…I know it is personal, but how long did you and your wife date…before you, um…before you kissed her for the first time?"

"Kissed her? As in 'on the lips'? Oh, we didn't miss, not while we were dating. I kissed my Maggie for the first time on our wedding day."

"Seriously?"

"Yes, I am very serious about my first kiss with my Maggie."

"You must not have dated for very long before you got married, then…" She looked back out at the water.

"We dated for six years before I even asked her to marry me. We were engaged for three more years after that. Now, mind you, it was very hard to resist. But, looking back, I am glad we waited. It made the day and our first kiss that much more special."

"That's amazing, Henry."

"You know, Miss Amelia, I heard what you all were talking about at breakfast. Miss Evangeline may be a spitfire, but that girl was raised right. Ma'am would never have allowed the kind of behavior that miss was speaking of. And Master Caspian would not have sat by, calmly, if he thought that someone had taken advantage of his sister's virtue. They were joshing you, and if you ask me, you overreacted a bit."

"I kind of figured that was the case right after I left, but I was just so frustrated, and embarrassed. I needed to go for a walk and think."

"There's nothing wrong with that, Miss. Emotions get the best of all of us at some time or another." He turned his head and looked down at her. "I'm going to give you a bit of advice. Don't rush things. You are young. Don't try to grow up too fast." He paused, brushing hair from her face, which she found very endearing. "I saw you and Master Caspian…the way you two were together…You reminded me of Maggie and me. I suggest that you cut him some slack on that kissing thing. He's like his father, honorable and noble to the core. To him, a kiss is more intimate than anything."

"It's just so frustrating, Henry. It would be my first kiss, and I want it be with him and no one else."

"If that is what you want, for Master Caspian to be your first, no one can stop that from happening but you. You must have will power, and you must, above all, have patience. There's obviously a reason why it hasn't happened yet."

"You know what, Henry...you are a very wise and kind man. You kind of remind me of my father."

"Well, Miss Amelia, I am honored that you would say that about me. Shall we head back now? I'm certain that everyone is worried sick about you." He stood up, and offered her his hand. She put her hand in his, and got up off the bench. It didn't take any time at all for them to get back to the car and drive home.

Amelia had barely walked through the door, and she was bombarded by a familiar swoosh of red hair.

"Where have you been? It's been hours! We were all worried sick about you." Angie held Mia at arm's length, and spoke as though she was scolding her.

"I'm fine. I just got a little upset, and needed to get some air to clear my head. Henry found me at the Harborwalk, and we sat and talked for a while." She removed her coat and handed it to Henry, who had his hand out to take it from her. "I really didn't mean to worry anyone, honest."

"It doesn't matter anymore. You're home, safe, and that is all that counts."

"By the way, you were joking earlier, right? You and Kevin didn't really...you know..."

"Oh! Heck no!" She laughed at the assumption.

"Okay, good." She wiped her brow, as though she were relieved. She turned her head, and Robert was rolling Margaret over to where they were standing.

"What do you have to say for yourself, young lady?"

"I am so sorry, Gran. I know that my behavior was wrong, and that the way I handled the situation was wrong. I swear to you, I will never do it again. I just let my emotions get the best of me."

"Alright, then...Go find Caspian. He was really upset because he couldn't find you."

"He was out there, looking for me?" Her eyes widened at hearing the news.

"Yes, he was. He's in the Solarium. Go." She pointed, urging Amelia to leave immediately.

*****

The hours had ticked away, and he worried more and more, the longer that Amelia was missing. He sat in the doorway leading out to the botanical garden, and jumped at every moving plant. He heard footsteps approaching, and yelled over his shoulder.

"Have we gotten any word on Amelia? I swear, if something happened to her, I will hold everyone responsible, especially myself..."

"You really shouldn't be so hard on everyone, especially yourself...And give Henry a raise." He heard her voice, and spun around.

"I'll give him anything he wants..." He sped forward, and yanked her down into his lap. "Don't you ever do that to me again. I couldn't find you. I wanted to find you, but I had no idea where you could have gone. I was frantic!" He pinched her arm.

"OWW!" She yanked her arm from him, and rubbed it. "It's your fault, talking that bull at breakfast! I didn't know you were joking. Jerk!" She punched him in the shoulder.

"Hey!! That hurt!" He rubbed his shoulder.

"Good! That was payback for pinching me." She poked him in the chest. "By the way, thank you for looking for me. It means a lot." She ran her hand through his thick, dark hair. His eyes rolled back in delight, and Goosebumps popped up on his arms. He let out a shaky breath and a moan. "Are you going to start purring like a kitty cat now?" She giggled.

"I will get down on the floor and meow if you asked me to?"

"That won't be necessary. Besides, I'm a dog person."

"Well, woof woof!" He growled and snapped his teeth at her chin, and she flicked his nose.

"Bad dog!" She laughed, shaking her finger in his face. His response was to pout his bottom lip, give her puppy-dog eyes, and whine. "Awe, I'm sorry." She rustled his hair. "You are so funny."

He reached up, slicked his disheveled hair back into place and looked up at her. He had intended on talking to her about the events of last night when they had finished breakfast, but things always seemed to go wrong. And there was no way that he would be able to have a serious talk, when she was being playful. She could see the conflict in his face, so she took his face in her hands, and looked him straight in the face.

"Something on your mind…You wanna talk about something?"

"Yeah, but it can wait. We were having fun."

"If you have something to talk about, we can play around later. Talk to me." She shifted on his lap, and folded her hands in her lap, obviously showing him that he had her full attention.

"Well, I know that we had that discussion last night, and you told me that the wheelchair didn't hinder your feelings for me, right?"

"I still stand by what I said. I thought you said that you believed me."

"Oh, I do, baby, I do! It's just…When I was up on my feet, I have never felt so free. I feel so limited in this chair."

"I can understand that. You looked really happy, after you stopped being so scared. But, why are you telling me this? Do you want me to get Henry? We can do it again, right now, if that is what you are suggesting."

"Before you did that for me, which I know was strictly to prove your point and set me straight…I felt like this chair was all I would ever know for the rest of my life. Now, I don't know…I feel like I can change that. I don't know if Grandmother told you about how I ended up...like this..."

"She did. I have been meaning to ask you, personally, but it just kind of came up...after she showed me that picture of us as children."

"Oh, no...that's fine. I just wanted to know if she had told you what the doctors told me."

"Yes, but tell me anyway." She gave him a smile, allowing him to share some of his history with her, personally.

"The doctors told Grandmother and I that this might not be permanent. There are doctors out there that specialize in spinal cord injuries. I could walk again."

"Is that something that you are considering?" She was curious as to what he was getting at.

"I have always considered it as an option, but I have never really had a reason to...until now...until you. Last night opened my eyes to everything."

"Caspian, this is a big decision. There is no guarantee that any procedure they do will work. I want you to do this, if you choose to, knowing that you would be doing it for yourself. If you are considering this because of me...don't. You are perfect just the way you are, at least in my eyes." She had his hands in hers, and she wanted to make sure that, if he made the decision to see one of the specialists, that he was doing it for the right reasons.

"If I do this, it will be for both of us. I would do it...to give *US* a brighter future."

"Okay, I get what you are saying. However, what happens if you go through all the procedures, the therapy...and it doesn't work?"

"Then, I will try a different doctor...try a different procedure." He was getting frustrated, and she could feel his pulse quickening.

"And, let's say, you exhaust all your options, and still nothing works...what then? Will our future be ruined? No, it won't. The way I see it is...no matter what you decide to do, I will be here with you every step of the way. And *if* nothing changes, I will still be here with you to deal with whatever future we may have."

He looked at her expression, the sincerity in her words and her eyes, and it warmed his heart.

"I have to, at least, try." He almost pleaded with her.

"You know what...Let's do this. If this is something that you are sure of, I am with you."

"Really? You are okay about it?" She responded by smiling and nodding. "Okay!"

"Make me a promise, though." She placed her hands on his face, and looked him dead in the eye, yet her gaze was still soft.

"Anything! Just tell me." The pure excitement shining in his eyes made her feel bubbly inside.

"We will do this, but you have to promise that, no matter the outcome, you will remember this moment right here... No matter what the outcome, I want you to remember who you are...here!" She put her hand on his heart. "The chair doesn't make the man...this does."

"Are you worried that these procedures will change me...that I will not be the same person that I am right now?"

"Yes, I do. I think that if it doesn't go like you hope, you will lose yourself. Not to mention...you don't know how your body will react to the procedures. Something could go wrong. I won't stop worrying about that." The thought of something happening to him cause her to start to shake.

"You're shaking. This really scares you, doesn't it?"

"Of course it does. It terrifies me. But it seems like you have your heart set on doing this, so I will just have to pray really hard that nothing bad happens, and hope for the best." Her pulse slowed as she took a deep breath and grasped his hand.

"I know this is scaring you, so we will wait until after you graduate. We don't want anything to distract you during your finals. Are you okay with that?"

"Yes, I think that will put my mind at ease for a bit. Besides, having a procedure, after the school year has ended, means that I can concentrate my summer on helping you recover from surgery." She stood up, and got behind his chair, and began to push him back into the main house.

"Where are we going?" Caspian tipped his head back, and looked at her from below, a perspective in which he hoped he would not have for too much longer.

"We are going, my dear, to tell your family the big news." She smiled and looked down at him, and he reached up and caressed her chin.

*****

After gathering everyone together, Caspian expressed his feelings and told his family what he and Amelia had just discussed. Though it went rather well, there was also negative feedback, which was largely coming from Evangeline.

"If this is something that you feel that you are ready to try, you have my full support, my sweet boy." Margaret had a knot in her stomach about it, but didn't want to discourage him, or make him believe that she didn't support him, fully.

"No offense, Mia…you are my best friend, and I love you like a sister…" She looked from Mia to her brother. "…But, I have the feeling that this would not have even been an option if you two were not involved. You had the option to do all this when you recovered from the accident, and you chose not to do it, because there were no guarantees. What makes you think that anything has changed, as far as your odds of a successful surgery?"

Mia looked at Angie, her eyes narrowing, and her lips pursed, trying not to say something hateful. She squeezed Cass's hand, and he squeezed back.

"Actually, Angie…I am very offended that you would think that I had any part in this decision. He made the decision all by himself. I am just supporting whatever decision he makes. I am not going anywhere, whether the surgeries are successful or a failure. I have always been accepting of Caspian and who he is. The wheelchair is part of who he is, who he always has been since I came here. If he wants to take a chance, and possibly walk again, I am not going to hold him back, and neither should you."

"And what happens when he goes through the procedures, and he is still in that wheelchair..."

"Then I will be no different than the person sitting in front of you right now." Caspian piped in. "Yes, part of me is doing this for Mia, but not because she asked me to. Though everyone has told me that being in a wheelchair doesn't make me less of a man...You aren't me. You are not restricted to a wheelchair. You can't understand what I go through, day after day. You don't feel what I feel. I feel like less than a man if I don't try to better my situation. I want to be able to dance with her, take a walk with her, pick her up and carry her to bed, myself, when she falls asleep on my lap..." He glanced up at Henry, who nodded in understanding.

"If she loved you...she wouldn't let you do this. There are risks involved, and you could be paralyzed...you could die! Is that a risk you are willing to take?" She was standing up now, her hands balled into fists. She turned to Amelia. "Are you willing to take the risk of something going bad, and you losing him...because, if you are...you are no friend of mine!"

"I cannot believe that you just said that to me. I only want what is best for Caspian. I want him to be happy. Do you think that he could possibly be happy for the rest of his life, in that chair, knowing that there was even the slightest possibility that he wouldn't have to be? I don't think you want that life for him. Could you do it? Could you live in that chair for even one day? He has lived in it for nine years. He's paid his dues. He deserves a chance. That's all he wants….a chance to walk again."

"He could die!" Angie screamed.

"You could walk out that door right now and get hit by a car…and die. Does that mean that, to avoid that risk, you would never go outside again? NO! You'd take the chance, just so you could walk in the sun. That is all he is asking for…a chance to *walk* in the sun." Amelia's last statement hit a chord and Angie sat back down. Amelia leaned toward Angie, and took her hand. "Angie, there is nothing that I want more than to see your brother happy. I am scared to death that something could go wrong on the operating table. I don't want to lose him. I do not want to see anything bad happen to him. But, I cannot let him make this decision unless he knows that he has my support and the support of his family. That is what is going to pull him through,"

"I get what you are saying, and I am sorry that I said that stuff to you. I am just scared and I feel like he is doing this for all the wrong reasons."

"I am doing this because it is something that I need to do, for myself. I have not complained once to anyone about the fact that I am in this chair, but that doesn't mean that I want to spend the rest of my life in it...especially if there is a possibility that I wouldn't have to. I remember my life before the accident, and I remember how much fun we had, running through these halls. I remember running and sliding across the marble foyer floor...because I could, and it was fun. I remember dancing with you in the ballroom, lifting you up and spinning round and round until we were dizzy."

"Ultimately, this is his decision, Evangeline, and we have to respect it. We don't have to like it, but we do have to have to accept it. He's going to do it, with or without our support." Margaret spoke up, and signaled for Robert to roll her out of the study. "Now, if you'll excuse me, I need to go lie down." She leaned over, as they passed Caspian, and she pulled him close and kissed his forehead. "At the end of the day, my boy, you must make the choice."

"Thank you, Grandmother. Now go and rest." He smiled at the sweet woman, and then turned to his sister. "Angie, I know that you are scared. I am terrified. However, I choose to put my faith and trust in God, and leave it up to him to guide the doctors in what they have to do to fix me. If it is meant to be, then it will be. If I am not meant to walk again, God will see me through. I am strong, and healthy, and I am very ready for this. Please put your faith and trust in him too."

"If this is something that you feel that you have to do, what kind of sister would I be to try to stand in the way of your happiness? God saw you through it, when you were in the accident, so I am sure that he can see you through this." She gave Cass a hug, and then reached over and hugged Mia.

"I make you this promise…no matter what happens with these surgeries, I am not going anywhere." Mia stated, looking at Angie.

"That is really good to know, because if you left him…I would have to hunt you down and hurt you."

"I'll keep that in mind." Mia gave her a serious look, and then all three of them started laughing.

# *~Seven~*

The last few months between Caspian's decision to go through with the procedures, and Amelia's graduation flew by. He had seen three different specialists and all of them were confident that they could do something to help him. He did research on the different procedures that the doctors had described to him, and had to decide which one would be the most successful with the least amount of risk. On the weekends, Amelia and Evangeline helped as much as they could, that is, when they weren't studying for their finals.

Amelia finished third in her class, and proudly walked across the stage on graduation day, and received her diploma. She was overjoyed that she had finished that chapter in her life, but was dreading the events to come. As much as she tried to enjoy the party that Margaret had thrown for her, she knew that everyone in the house was dealing with the tension and nervousness that came with Caspian's procedure.

The morning of the first surgery in a series of five, the staff gathered around Caspian and laid their hands on him, sending him off with prayers and blessings from different beliefs; Christianity, Judaism, Buddhism, and Catholic, all of which made Caspian more hopeful of a good outcome.

They all rode to the hospital together, and they checked him in. Waiting for the surgeon to get there and prep him for surgery was nerve-racking. Amelia held tight to Caspian's hand, and he could feel her shake. Evangeline kept coming over to him and hugging him, before returning to her pacing. Margaret sat in silent meditation, asking her late husband and her dearly departed son, Caspian's father, to be there with him and protect him. She asked God to do his will, whatever it may be, and be merciful upon all of them. The nurse came out, after they had waited for nearly an hour, and called him back to get him settled and prepped for his surgery. Henry and Robert walked over and shook his hand, and Margaret and Evangeline hugged and kissed him several times. Right before the nurse wheeled him back, Amelia took his hands in hers, kissed them both and leaned in to give him a hug. They held each other for a moment, and then, she whispered in his ear.

"No matter what the outcome…I love you." She backed away slowly, his hands sliding from hers, and she blew him a kiss, which he pretended to catch and place on his heart. He disappeared through the double doors, and the waiting game started.

During the four hours that they had been waiting, Amelia had joined Evangeline in pacing the room. The nurse had come to check on them several times, asking if she could get them anything while they were waiting for the doctor to come out to talk to them. None of them could eat anything, but Robert had insisted that they eat to keep their strength up for Caspian. They each had something small to eat and they drank their bottled water, little sips at a time.

When the doors opened, everyone nearly jumped out of their skin. The doctor came out, with no expression, so no one knew what he was going to tell them, but there was only one thing that they wanted to hear. Amelia and Evangeline clung to one another, and waited for the doctor to say something.

"Are you the family of Caspian Wallingford?" They all nodded quickly. "My name is Dr. Clancy. I am the head surgeon here at Boston

Memorial Hospital. My team and I worked on Caspian today." He paused. "Well, I have good news and bad news." Again, he paused, before continuing. "The bad news is that he has four more surgeries that he must go through in the next eight months to a year, depending on how he handles them…" He hesitated, and then a smile crept across his face. "The good news is that this one went very well, and he is in recovery right now."

The room erupted in squeals, laughter, and sighs of relief. Evangeline and Amelia flung their arms around each other and wept, happy that the surgery had gone well. Margaret was mouthing, "Thank you, Lord. Thank you, Cecil. Thank you, Richard."

"Now, he still has a long road ahead of him. However, if the other surgeries go as well as this one did, I don't see why we couldn't see him walking within the next year to eighteen months. Now, you will be able to go back and see him, one at a time, as soon as he comes out of the anesthesia. Congratulations." The doctor's words only caused more eruption of emotion, and he smiled as he walked away.

After two more hours, the nurse came out to escort each of them back to see Caspian, and Amelia, once again, chose to go last. She sat in her chair, twirling a strand of her hair between her fingers, getting updates from each of them as they came back out, to allow the next to go in to see him. Henry was the last one to go in to see him, before it was her turn, and he came out, a smile on his face, and his body still shaking from chuckling. He walked over to Amelia, squeezed her hand, and pointed to the nurse.

"You've waited long enough…go see the knucklehead. He's been chomping at the bit to see you." He was still chuckling as he sat down, taking up a whole couch with the sheer size of him. The last thing she saw was him shaking his head, still amused by something.

The walk was so long, or at least it seemed like it. She turned the corner, led by the nurse, and she was pointed to a curtained room straight ahead. She felt like she was moving in slow motion. Her heart was pounding like a jackhammer and her chest felt heavy. She moved the curtain, and the first thing she saw was his behind facing upward.

"Ooooh, nice butt!" She joked, walking toward the other end of the bed, where he was lying, face down, his head turned towards her.

"Yours, too. I have seen it a million times but I never get tired of it." He said, slowly, still doped up from the medication. He, weakly, reached his hand out to her, and she put her hand in his, and sat down.

"The doctor said that it went well. That's a good sign. We were all out there; going crazy, so good news was just what we needed. How are you feeling?" She leaned down so she could speak quietly and he could hear her.

"Well, right now, I feel absolutely nothing…except for the drool running down my chin…can you get that for me, please." She grabbed a tissue and wiped the drool from his chin. "How do I look?" He asked, smiling as big as he could.

"You look handsome, as ever. Is this how you have to lay until it heals?" She inquired, trying to peek and see if she could see the incision they made, but it was covered with a bandage. "By the way, what did you say to Henry? He came out to the waiting room, laughing. He was still laughing when I came back here."

"I said, 'Hey henry, you know all those times you wished that I wasn't in my chair, so you could stick your foot up my backside…well, here's your chance…it's right there, waiting for your size eighteen shoe. Have at it, because I can't feel a thing.' He found that funny, apparently, cuz he started to laugh and scared a nurse. She thought someone was tickling a bear!" He tried to laugh, but it was hard to do so while lying on his stomach. "Get it…tickling a bear…cuz he has such a deep laugh…ha ha ha."

"You know what…you're right…" she began to laugh, herself.

"Now, what was the question you asked me…if I have to lay like this until it heals…I would hope not.  It would kind of be hard to get me home if I had to stay like this for six weeks. Not to mention, how I would do my business….that would be awful messy."  He winked at her, because he knew that someone would have to wipe his behind.  "No, I think the doctor told me that I just have to lay like this until they take out the stitches, and put a dressing on it." Like she had predicted what he was going to say next, she chimed in.

"What kind of dressing? French…Italian…"

"Ooooh…you're a quick one!  You just stole my joke."

"Alright…That'll be quite enough of that.  This is a hospital, not a comedy club."  The nurse said, coming from behind the curtain, laughing as well.  "He needs to get some rest. You can come back tomorrow to visit your brother…"

"She's not my sister…She's my reason for being, the love of my life…the sugar in my coffee…the…the honey in my tea…She's my everything…"  He drawled on, his eyes slowly closing, his voice getting quieter.  She blushed at his words, and watched him as he slowly drifted off. The grip on her hand loosened and was now laying limp in hers.

"Looks like the medication finally kicked in. Sorry, sweetie…I didn't know…I just assumed…"

"Oh, that's alright. It was an honest mistake. I guess I will be going now." She looked down at his face and slowly put his arm back on the bed. She kissed his cheek, and ran her fingers through his hair before standing up and walking around the bed.

"Don't worry, we'll take really good care of him. He's in excellent hands." She escorted Amelia out of the room, shut the light off and pulled the curtain closed.

\*\*\*\*\*

With the assistance of physical therapists, and advice from Dr. Clancy, Caspian's recovery from the first surgery went quickly. Because of the procedure, they were able to reconnect nerves in his spine, so that they could regenerate and he would regain feeling in his lower extremities. The first time that he felt something in his legs, he screamed, and startled everyone in the house. The second surgery, also, was a complete success. Little by little, more feeling came back, and physical therapy improved his muscle tone. Over the last nine years, Henry had assisted in making certain that the muscles in Caspian's legs didn't atrophy by exercising them several times a week. The doctor admitted that that may help him respond to the surgeries quicker. Amelia took great joy in watching him as he passed milestones, and quickly found out that he was ticklish behind his knees and around his anklebone.

By the time the third surgery was over, he had new hardware in his back. The shattered vertebrae were replaced by prosthetic discs, and they were protected by a temporary titanium cage. Amelia couldn't help as much with his recovery as she was now enrolled in college, full-time, per Caspian's request that she continue her education immediately, and not take the year off to help him. His reasoning was that he had the doctors and physical therapists to help him. Though he loved that she had taken an active role in his progress, his success was also based on eliminating unneeded stress. When Amelia spoke of taking the year off, it upset him, as education was very important to him.

When she agreed to attend college, his mind rested easier and he was able to concentrate on his recovery and progress. However, something else had found him distracted right after his fourth surgery, which was to replace the cage on his spine, with a smaller, permanent one.

Margaret's health was failing rapidly. Her heart was getting weaker, her breathing more labored, and she was often very confused and frustrated by things that never used to confuse and upset her. She started losing memories, and would call Caspian by his father's name, and tell him to stop fooling around with the chair, and go get his father, her husband, Cecil. As her condition worsened, they feared the worst. Caspian wanted to push himself, wanting to finish his recovery, and get to his goal of walking before she was gone. Unfortunately, the harder he pushed, the longer his recovery. He was doing more damage than good by not following the doctor's explicit orders to take it slow, and follow the therapist's specialized exercises.

In the spring, right after he had scheduled his last surgery, against the doctor's recommendation, the day had come to say their goodbyes. They all gathered around Margaret's large four-post bed, and took turns holding her hand and talking to her.

Evangeline had taken her place on one side of her grandmother, and Caspian sat on the other. Amelia stood at Caspian's shoulder, trying to soothe him.

"Grandmother, I just scheduled the last surgery. The end is in sight, and soon I will be walking. Don't you want to stay long enough to see me walk again?" He pleaded, trying to swallow the lump in his throat.

"And, Grandmother, I graduate from the academy in about two months. I want you to be there to watch me walk across the stage. I am tied with another classmate for Valedictorian. Please stay with us until after I graduate." Angie sniffled, holding tight to the lady's frail hand.

Amelia had no incentive, no considerably big event, to ask her guardian to stay with her for. This woman had taken her in, given her everything she could ever have wanted, and she had fought a lot longer than her doctors thought she would. To her, Gran had earned the right to have peace, but she didn't say it aloud.

"My beautiful…babies…You have grown…into such…fine adults" she paused, coughing. "I am so…proud of…you all. I wish…I could…promise…to stay…here with…you…forever." Margaret struggled to speak, and her voice was weak, as she gasped for breath between words.

"We know, Gran." Amelia sighed.

"I may not…be here…to see all…that you become." She looked at Caspian, and tears were welling up in his eyes. "You will…walk again…soon. Don't…give…up." She smiled a weaker version of her smile, and gently squeezed his hand. She slowly turned her head to her granddaughter. "And you…will…be…Vale…dic…torian…because…you hate…to lose…at anything…" She closed her eyes for a moment, then turned her head back in the direction of Amelia, and looked at her. "You…make…me…a promise…"

"What, Gran? Anything…" Amelia leaned over and put her hand on top of Caspian's.

"Take care…of…Caspian. Love…him. Stand…by him. He needs…you. They…both…do."

"Of course I will, Gran. I promise you, I will." She began to sob.

"I am …Blessed! I…I am…going…to…miss…you all. I…love…you, my angels."

The three of them all looked at each other, and no one could hold back tears. Caspian leaned forward, laying his head on her hand, and crying like he hadn't since his father had died. Margaret looked over to the behemoth of a man, standing next to Evangeline. Though he was hardly ever caught showing any emotion, his bottom lip trembled as he looked down at his boss and friend.

"Henry…you and …the…others…have served…me…faithfully…for many…years. I…thank…you. Please…carry on…with my…darlings…when I…have…gone."

"No, Ma'am. We thank you for all you have done for us. I can't speak for everyone, but I will stay and care for them as long as they need me. It has been a pleasure serving you all these years. Rest your soul, sweet lady." He bowed to her, and laid a kiss on her frail hand.

With one last look at her family, she smiled, and closed her eyes. It was a sad moment as they watched her breathe her last breath. Caspian clutched to his grandmother's hand, and wrapped his arm around Amelia, his face buried in her soft hair. Evangeline let go of her hand and ran into Henry's arms.

The funeral was very bittersweet, and there were so many people there, that many had to stand along the back of the church, as all the pews were filled to capacity. Amelia sat in the front row, between Caspian and Evangeline, and they clung to one another. The minister spoke of the many contributions, monetary and otherwise, that Margaret Wallingford had made to the community, and to the lives of all who knew her. The eulogy was beautifully done, and it was a testament to who she was a person.

The cemetery was filled with people, lined up, who came to pay their last respects to her and to give their condolences to the three of them. After they had lowered her casket into the ground, a line of people walked by and each dropped a white rose down into the grave.

Amelia and Evangeline cried almost the whole entire time, but Caspian was stone cold, and emotionless. It scared Amelia to see him like this, and she tried to get through to him, but he just looked away.  It was

almost as if a part of him was in that grave with her.

# *~Eight~*

Caspian, disheartened at the loss of his grandmother, cancelled his last surgery indefinitely. He spent a lot of time locked away in his room, not talking to or seeing anyone. He couldn't see a valid reason for continuing his physical therapy, despite what the doctors, therapists, and Amelia had to say about it.

Amelia, to distract herself from troubles at home, buried herself into her studies. It wasn't long before the professors noticed that she was excelling far above what they had expected of her. Her term papers and essays were above and beyond thorough and well thought out. It was only when the Dean, himself, came to her front door that she even realized that her work had caught the attention of the whole University. A knock came to the large front door. Henry opened it, catching Dean Moore off guard.

"Can I help you?" Henry bellowed

"Is Miss Landon at home? I am Dean Moore, from the University."

"Yes, please come in." He led the man to the study. "Wait here. I will go get her." And he closed the doors. He found Amelia in Evangeline's room, assisting her with her college essay. He cleared his throat, and the girls turned their heads to him.

"What is it, Henry?"

"I don't mean to disturb the two of you. But, Miss Amelia, you have a guest. He is waiting down in the study."

"He? Who would come see me at home?"

"Maybe you have an admirer, Mia." Angie teased. They got up and both followed Henry downstairs. They were chattering loudly enough that it caught Caspian's attention, and he stuck his head out the door.

"What's going on out here? What's all the commotion?" He asked, grumpily.

"Amelia has a guest waiting for her in the study…most likely an admirer from school. Why should you care? It's really none of your concern, as you have pretty much locked her out of your life since Grandmother passed away."

"I do care. And, I haven't locked her out of my life." He huffed, and went to close his door, but she blocked him and pushed her way in, fully intending on giving him a piece of her mind, while she had the chance. Usually, he kept his room locked, and ignored any knock at his door. Henry and Amelia proceeded downstairs and his door slammed shut with an echoing boom.

"Get out of my room, Evangeline!"

"Not until you talk to me, Cass. You have locked yourself in here for the last ten months. You have missed so much. I graduated, top of my class, but my brother wasn't there. I got accepted at Boston University, started dating someone…where were you? In here! And Mia, poor Mia…she stood by you, supported you, tried to help you get through Grandmother's death…you pushed her away. When was the last time that you talked to her?"

"I'm sorry I missed your graduation. I am glad that you got into college. I'm not too happy with the fact that you are seeing someone, but whatever. As far as Mia, it's none of your concern what is going on between Mia and I."

"She's my best friend and you are my brother…so yes, Cass, it is very much my concern. What has happened to you? You just…gave up."

"Get out, Angie!" He turned his back to her.

"What would grandmother think of your behavior?"

"Grandmother is gone, Angie. She can't dictate on how I live my life anymore." His words hit her like a punch in the gut.

"She never *dictated* how you lived your life. She wanted what was best for you. We all did. You were so gung-ho about walking again, and look at you now. You just gave up. Last time that Mia tried to talk to you, you screamed at her, and told her to stay out of your life. I was there...I heard you say that!"

The funk that Caspian had gotten into since the funeral had caused him to push away everyone he loved, and he was especially hard on Amelia. Most of his days were a hazy mess, and he couldn't recall telling Amelia to stay out of his life, but apparently he had.

"I never meant to...I just...she was hovering. She wanted me to go through the final surgery. She used to tell me that the wheelchair didn't matter to her, but she was pushing me to finish the surgeries."

"Oh, get over yourself! She didn't care about anything but you finishing what you had started. She wanted you to do it for you! Grandmother wanted you to walk again, but she was gone before she got a chance to see it happen. You were so close, Cass. Amelia loved you enough to push you…but you pushed her back, and in doing so…you pushed her right out of your life. What happens in her life now, is none of your concern anymore. You lost the right to be involved. I honestly hope that her guest is an admirer. Maybe she can get her happily ever after."

"I was supposed to be her first kiss. I was supposed to be her happily ever after." He murmured to himself, but his sister heard him. She walked over to him, and glanced over his shoulder and saw what he was fidgeting with. In a beautiful brass frame, one of the pictures from their dance in the ballroom was beautifully displayed.

"You could have had that…for the rest of your life. You could have been her happily ever after…but now, that picture is just a daily reminder of what you could have had, and what you gave up. You have no one to blame but yourself. Mia tried, for a longtime. Do you honestly believe that she could look at you the same way again?"

"She doesn't love me anymore. How could she? I thought the day grandmother died was the worst day of my life…but, when I saw the light in Mia's eyes extinguish, and she walked out that door…that day was the worst day of my life. You always were afraid that she would break my heart, but you had it backwards."

"I guess so." She put her hand on his shoulder, and then walked out the door.

Evangeline sat in her room, typing away at her computer when she heard a rapid knocking at her door. She turned and walked to the door, where a wide eyed Mia stood, her mouth gaping open.

"What's wrong? Mia…what's going on?" She shook her friend's shoulders.

"I cannot believe this is happening…"

"What's happening?! Talk to me!"

"The dean was just here…He sent one of my papers to that fashion magazine in Chicago… Fashionista…The Editor-in-chief read it…I have an internship."

"What? Back that up! What are you talking about?" She pulled Mia over and sat her on the bed.

"Dean Moore came to see me. That's who was downstairs. He told me that all my professors were impressed at my work, especially my journalism professor. They took the paper I wrote about the impact of bullying on school morale…they sent it to like ten different newspapers and magazines…Ms. Larson from the Fashionista…the editor-in-chief…offered me an internship. I would be working for the magazine, and they are putting me up in an apartment, as part of my internship."

"Oh My God!!! Mia!! That is amazing!!! I cannot believe it."

"What should I do?"

"You are going to do it, stupid! There's no decision to be made. When do you start?"

"The first of March…one week away…" She looked at Angie, and her eyes began to fill with tears. "I'd be moving out of here…leaving you…and Cass…"

"Don't you dare! I am not going to let you use me as an excuse to pass up this opportunity. And as far as Caspian…forget him! You have your future to worry about."

"He is…was my future…but he doesn't love me anymore. Everything that happened…Gran passing…it was like the Caspian I knew died with her."

"Stop worrying about Cass…"

"I can't. I will never stop worrying about him…I still love him. I know that I shouldn't especially after how he treated me…But I do…I always will. Don't tell him though. I would just look pitiful to him."

"You are a damn fool, you know that?" Angie shook her head and laughed slightly.

"I know…but he is who my heart wants. It belongs to him." She sat, trying to decide what to do. Suddenly a thought occurred to her. She leapt up and tore out of the room, and Angie heard her banging at Caspian's door soon afterward.

"Caspian…Caspian, answer the door. Please, answer the door. I need to speak with you, immediately." After a few moments, the door opened, and she saw his face for the first time in months. The whiskers on his face were now a full-grown beard. It took her a full five minutes before she could finally speak.

"Well, what was so urgent?" He asked, coldly. Not being able to hold it in any longer, she told him everything that had just transpired downstairs in the study. "What are you telling me for? You haven't spoken to me for months…why would you talk to me now?" He looked at her, not giving her the slightest idea that he was both overjoyed to see her face again, but saddened that she was talking to him, just to tell him that she was leaving for Chicago in less than a week.

"I know that we haven't talked…not after you told me to leave, and stay out of your life…" Tears welled in her eyes, and she tried to fight them off as she remembered his words. "…But, the thing is…I won't know anyone there. You need to get out of this house. It's killing you, literally. You are wasting away to nothing. I would ask Angie, but she is still in her first week of college, and she has a boyfriend now…"

"What are you talking about? Get to the point." He grumbled.

"Come with me….to Chicago." Her words echoed in his head. He searched her face, thinking that she was just trying to hurt him as he had hurt her, by teasing him with something as monumental as moving with her. He looked into her eyes, and a glimmer of what looked like hope shined in the deep sapphire pools.

"Come with you? Move to Chicago with you? Just the two of us?"

"Yes. It would be a fresh start. There are so many memories, sad memories here in this house. They have sucked the life from you…come with me. We can start over…at least become friends again."

Hearing her words made his heart leap. She wanted to start over…with him. All this time, he thought that she hated him, wanted nothing at all to do with him ever again. Yet, there she was, standing at his door, wanting him to be a part of this once-in-a-lifetime opportunity for her.

"I appreciate the offer, Amelia, but my place is here. I would just be a distraction to you. This is your chance to do something wonderful with your life. Taking me with you…that would be a reminder of things long gone…" what *was he saying that for?* He wondered, after the words had come out. "Grandmother is gone, but I know that she would want you to do this for yourself…alone." Again, he wanted to punch himself for what was coming out of his mouth. "I mean, this is a golden opportunity. I would just get in the way."

"You don't want to come with me." Her eyes dulled, and her smile faded away. "I just thought…you and I…we could, maybe…" she let out a rattled sigh, and turned away. "Sorry, I bothered you." She turned back to him, tears streaming down her face. "I guess this is goodbye, then." She leaned over and hugged him. Before she backed away, she kissed him on the cheek, and he felt her lips quiver. She stood back up, and turned to walk away. *Don't let her walk away! Grab her!* The voices in Caspian's head screamed and pleaded with him, and he reached for her hand just a moment too late. He heard her, wailing, as she ran too her room, and slammed the door. He sat there, shocked and angry. When he looked up again, his face met with the palm of his sister's hand. The sting lingered, even after her put his hand to the hot skin of his cheek.

"You don't deserve what she was offering. She wanted you to be with her, wanted you to share this with her. How dare you even speak of Grandmother to validate your bad decisions! Grandmother would never have wanted her to do this alone, and would have encouraged you to do this with her. Amelia was giving you a second chance, even after you hurt her. She may not want me to tell you this, but I need to, because I know that this will cause you pain, and rightfully so, you deserve to be in pain..." She looked down the hall, and then back at her brother. "She still loves you. She never stopped. She said that you had her heart. And what you just did...you took her heart and crushed it to dust. After everything she has done for you, how much crap she has taken from you...she thought that she never deserved your love, but I think that it is quite the opposite!" She looked down, and saw that he was still holding the picture. She snatched it, and opened the frame.

"What are you doing?!" He tried to reach for the picture, but she held it out of his reach. "Give that back, Evangeline! NOW!!"

"Why would I do that?" She snapped.

"It's mine...It's all I have left of Mia and I. Give it back! Please, Angie!" The salty tears flooded his eyes and trailed down his cheeks. "Please, don't do it..." He stretched for it, and lost his balance, landing face first on the floor just a few feet from where she had backed up to. He sat up, and reached for his sister.

"The man in this picture deserved her, loved her, and was her future. He's dead now." She dropped the frame onto the floor, and the glass shattered at her feet, the frame broke in half. Caspian shielded his face from flying glass. She took the picture and ripped it in half, and then in half again. With a disgusted look on her face, she threw the pieces of the picture in his face. "Go to Hell, Caspian!" She stormed off, and left him on the floor amongst broken shards of glass and his shredded dreams.

He picked up the picture, piece by piece, and tried to put them back together right there on his lap. Henry came racing up the stairs, followed by Eloise and Robert, as they had heard a heavy thud from down below. Henry lifted Caspian back into his chair, the pieces falling to the floor like falling leaves. Eloise began to pick up the broken glass, and Robert began to pick up the picture pieces as if they were just scraps of garbage.

"Robert, no, give me those!" He tried to snatch them from the man's hand.

"Sir, they are just pieces of paper…trash. I will throw them out for you." He said, holding them away from him.

"Evangeline ripped up a very important picture…the one in your hands, the pieces…please give them to me." He asked nicely, holding his hand out to him.

"The picture is ruined, Master Caspian. Why do you want it back?"

"Please…I can tape it back together…give them here." He reached out, and Robert, reluctantly, put the pieces in his hand.

"Master Caspian, I am sorry, but even if you were to tape it back together, it will never be the same again. Those tears will always be there; no matter how well you piece it back together." Henry rolled him back into his room, and Robert assisted Eloise in cleaning up the hall.

"I know, Henry…No amount of tape will ever fix the damage that has been done."

# *~Nine~*

Amelia had moved to Chicago without seeing or speaking to Caspian again. Her apartment, though small to some, was much too large for just her. She found herself imagining what it would have been like if he had come with her. She stepped out on the balcony, staring out at the Navy Pier a block or so away. Taking a sip of her tea, she hugged her sweater to her, and stared out at the water. She had just tried to call him, but he didn't answer his phone. When she couldn't get through, she called Evangeline, who picked up before the second ring. Three months had passed since she said goodbye to him, and she cried to Evangeline, begging her to give him message after message, though she was unsure as to whether she actually gave them to him.

"Why are you doing this to yourself, Mia? It's over. He isn't worth all the heartache. Get on with your life. Concentrate on your job." Evangeline pleaded with her friend over the phone.

"Part of me truly believes that he wanted to come with me…I could see it in his eyes. Sure, I was hurt…but looking back on it, I understand. And I know you were angry, but what you did…it was cruel."

"I know that I overreacted, and I can never take it back, but I saw your face when you went to your room. I heard your crying and I guess I just felt like I needed to step in and teach him a lesson. You are my best friend."

"He is your brother. He needs you. He's hurting, and he needs you."

"You're hurting. You need me too. Besides, he hasn't said anything to me since that day." She paused and changed the subject. "I have a break coming up. What do you think about me coming to visit? You can show me around Chicago. We can have a girls' night, with tubs of ice cream and watch old movies."

"We'll see." She wanted to say something else, but then her phone beeped in her ear, alerting her that someone was calling in on the other line. "Can I call you back? Someone else is beeping in. I think it might be Katrina, my boss."

"Sure. Call me back. Talk to you later."

Amelia said bye, then clicked over, expecting to hear a squeaky woman's voice on the other end.

"Hello?" The voice made her jump as it was deep and very familiar. "Mia, Are you there?"

"Yeah...I'm here."

"Did I catch you at a bad time? I can call back..."

"No, that's alright."

"I got your message...messages off the machine. I thought it was about time I called you back."

"Well, thanks. How are you?" She walked back into her apartment, and closed the French doors behind her.

"I'm alright, considering."

"Considering, what?" She sat down on the loveseat, and curled her feet under her.

"I know that there is nothing that I could say to you to make up for all the hurt I caused. I was a real jerk, and I have been trying to find a way to apologize to you."

"You were mourning Gran…You were going through stuff. I just wanted to help, but you shut me out."

"It's more than that. I mean, that was part of it, but Grandmother passing…it was just an excuse…"

"You don't have to explain. You don't owe me anything. And you don't have to apologize. I could have fought harder, stayed and toughed it out. I didn't. I just left."

"I do have to explain, and I do have to apologize. And as far as you running off…not fighting hard enough…I pushed you out, I broke your heart... I am stupid, and stubborn, and I destroyed us. You say I don't owe you anything, but I owe you everything. You brought light into our house. You shook up the whole household. Everyone here loves you dearly, and they miss you. Henry told me to tell you that he is grateful for the letters and pictures. Eloise talks to Evangeline about your phone calls and letters, and sometimes I overhear."

"Please stop." She swallowed hard. "You called to apologize. I accept your apology. Okay? It's done. I have to go, now. Thank you for calling…."

"Please don't hang up. Please. I miss you."

"I can't do this right now, Caspian."

"Can I call you again?"

"If you want to…I can't promise that I will answer, though." Her voice was shaking, knowing that if the phone rang, and she thought it was him, she would definitely pick up.

"I don't blame you. I wouldn't answer my phone calls if I were you…but, I want to at least set things right. What I went through was not your fault, in any way. I want you to understand that"

"Cass, Please…"

"Amelia, I know that I don't deserve your forgiveness, but please, give me a chance to earn it…"

"Fine…I get off work around five tomorrow. Call me around seven o'clock. We'll talk." She didn't give a chance to say anything else. She hung up the phone, and clutched it to her chest, trying to steady her breath and compose herself. Even after everything, her heart still raced when she talked to him. The love she once had for him still lingered in her heart, but she had learned that loving him just led to more pain, so she ignored the aching that she felt for him. She took a deep breath, and dialed Evangeline's number. She spoke not a word of her conversation with Caspian, and told her that it had been a wrong number.

At the office the next day, she was very distracted. The planning meeting for the following week's issue was like a fog, and she could tell that Katrina was concerned. Before leaving the conference room, her boss called for her to stay a few moments. She closed the door, and looked at Amelia, her arms crossed.

"What's going on with you today? You barely spoke two words in the meeting, and you are always the first one to speak up with ideas and suggestions. You seemed like you weren't really here."

"I'm sorry, Katrina. I just have a lot on my mind."

"Do you want to talk about it? You know that you can always come to me. You have been a valuable asset to this magazine, so much so that our sales have gone up twenty percent since you started here."

"I love it here, and I love working with you. I just have a lot of stuff going on...from back in Boston...I am sorry if it was affecting my work." She gave her an apologetic look.

"Everyone is allowed to have bad days, Mia. I just wish that you would have come to me sooner. We could have worked this out before the meeting. Everyone thought you were bored, and had no interest in anything that they had to say."

"It won't happen again."

"It better not. Though you are valuable to this magazine, you need to understand that there are hundreds of people wishing to be where you are, who would give anything to have your job." She took a deep breath, and continued with a less stern tone. "Are you homesick? I know that my offer came as quite a shock to you and I didn't give you a chance to say proper goodbyes to everyone back home."

"No, it isn't that...I miss them, yes... but, when I left...I left stuff unsettled with one person in particular. He called me last night...he's calling again tonight, and I am not sure if I am ready for that conversation."

"A guy, huh?" She rolled her eyes, and smiled. "All this drama is over a guy...why am I not surprised? Let me guess...you broke the guy's heart and he wants you to be miserable, so he's calling to tell you how he can never trust anyone again, and you put your career over your relationship..."

"Not exactly...." She looked at her boss, and friend and her eyes narrowed. "Why do I get the feeling that you weren't just talking about me?"

"Honestly, I wasn't. I went through the same thing. But, this is the thing...You don't need him. You are a smart, beautiful young woman.

You could have any guy you set your eyes on. You need a man that will support you and your career, not try to drag you down."

"He doesn't drag me down, and he doesn't want me to be miserable. I have been in love with him since I was fourteen years old. His grandmother passed away and he became severely depressed and pushed me away. Then, I got the internship here…things were left unsaid. We haven't talked to each other until last night, and dust got stirred up, I guess you could say."

"Oh…well, then…" Katrina cleared her throat. "…I guess you will just need to buck up and talk to him. The sooner that that dust settles, the sooner we can get 'our Mia' back." She opened the door, allowing Mia to leave.

Mia tried hard to concentrate and the rest of the day ticked slowly by. She walked into her apartment at five thirty, and noticed her answering machine was blinking. She pressed the button, and sat down on the big arm chair, and listened.

The first message was from Caspian.

"I know that you are at work right now. I just wanted to say that I understand you hanging up on me last night. I look forward to talking tonight." She closed her eyes, and just took some deep breaths.

The second message that came on was Henry. He just wanted to call and say hello, and to ask her if she was going to come and visit soon. His voice made her smile. The third message was from a very agitated Evangeline.

"I'm mad at you, Mia. You lied to me and told me it was a wrong number. Why didn't you just tell me that Caspian called you? You shouldn't have answered his call. He says that he is supposed to call you tonight too. Do yourself a favor…don't answer it."

She got up, hit delete, and went into the kitchen to fix something to eat. After looking through the cupboards, and the refrigerator, she decided to order out. The delivery guy arrived with her food a good half hour later. She paid him, and went to the kitchen. Deciding not to dirty a dish, she took her Chinese food into the living room and ate it right out of the carton. Her quart of sweet and sour pork was almost gone when the phone rang. Evangeline's words popped into her head. *Do yourself a favor…don't answer it.* She put her hand on the phone receiver, and hesitated. By the time she had decided what to do, the ringing stopped. She breathed a sigh of both relief and dread. She took her leftovers to the fridge, and put the teapot on the stove. She stood, watching it begin to steam. After the water boiled, she poured the hot liquid into a mug, dropped a couple teabags into it, and took it to her room. She sat on the bed; her knees pulled to her chest, and looked over at her nightstand. The green numbers on the clock looked brighter than normal, telling her that it had been an hour since the phone had rung. She laid her head back against the headboard, and closed her eyes, mentally debating as to whether she should call him back. As she reached for the phone, it began to ring again. She picked up the receiver and put it to her ear, almost knocking her cup of tea over.

"Hello?"

"Hey." The deep voice answered back.

"Did you call earlier?"

"You told me to call at seven. Did I hear you wrong?"

"No, I told you seven."

"You didn't answer the phone."

"I know. I'm sorry."

"Don't apologize. You've called me lots of times, and I didn't answer the phone." There was a moment of silence and then he started talking again. "I don't know what to say. I have been trying to think of where to start. I have been running through my head what I wanted to say to you, but now…having you on the phone…I am at a loss for words."

"Me, too." She took in a lung-full of air, and started to say something, but he began talking before she could.

"What do you say to someone you hurt? I'm sorry doesn't even begin to cover it."

"But, if you are sincere, it's a good place to start."

"Can you do me a favor, and stop being so nice to me?"

"How am I being nice to you? I almost lost my job today, because of you."

"Good…"

"GOOD?! You think it is good that you almost cost me my job?"

"Oh, no…you didn't let me finish…I meant good, you are yelling at me. Yell, scream, and call me names. I don't care what you do, but don't let me off easy."

"What are you talking about, Cass? I am not going to yell at you or call you names. That's ridiculous. Why on earth would you want me to yell at you or call you names? What would that accomplish?" She wondered what he was up to.

"I don't know, Mia. But, I figured that that is the least you could do, after all the hurt I caused you."

"In all honesty, I was hurt at first. Now, I am sadder than anything. I'm sad that you felt you needed to push everyone away, especially me. I am sad that Gran passed away so suddenly, and that you never finished what you set out to do. I am sad that your fear of leaving that house kept you from moving here with me. I am just sad that I gave you everything I had, and you took it for granted."

"I never meant to take you for granted, Mia. As far as not finishing what I started…I assume you're referring to the surgeries, and I can't give you an explanation. I just felt as though the stress of it all was what caused grandmother to deteriorate as quickly as she did."

"You blame yourself for Gran dying? Do you know how much she was looking forward to you succeeding? She would have given anything to see you walk again."

"I do blame myself. And you're right, she would have given anything…she gave her life for it."

"And you repay her by stopping when you were so close? You got feeling and partial movement back, so something was happening…but, she passed away, and you gave up. The thing you need to understand is that your surgeries were not what killed her. Her health had been fading for years. I talked to her doctor. She was sick for a long time, Cass...even before I came into your lives. She was just really good at hiding it."

"Are you serious? You are telling me this now? How long have you known?"

"When she started collapsing...I didn't want to tell you. *She* didn't want me to tell you."

"Did Evangeline know?" He began to get upset.

"No, Henry took her out of the room. The doctor and Gran both thought it would be better if she didn't hear what was really going on."

"No offense, but we are her grandchildren. We had a right to know. You kept this from us."

"I kept it from you because I swore to Gran, no matter what happened, I would not tell you. She was trying to protect you. Why do you think that she made me promise her that I would take care of you and your sister when she was near the very end?" She sighed, and tried not to cry. "And, just to set the record straight, after Gran died, I told Evangeline right away, and we had agreed to wait until after your surgery to tell you. When you didn't have your surgery, I tried to tell you several times, but you refused to listen. You wanted to be left alone, and you called me a liar when I finally got it out."

"What do you mean?  You never told me that grandmother was sick.  I would have remembered that."

"Do you remember the day that you threw your wheelchair across the room at me?  When you told me that I had no idea what you were going through...I said that you had no idea what I was going through either and that I had been carrying a secret that was killing me..."  silence followed, as Caspian thought back to that day.

He remembered throwing his wheelchair, and screaming...then he recalled her saying that she had been burdened with a secret...the rest was very hazy and jumbled.  She had, in fact, tried to tell him.  It was bad enough that he had thrown his wheelchair at her, out of anger and despair, but to find out that she was trying to share something that had been lying heavy on her heart for so long...

"Oh God, Mia...I didn't realize...You have been carrying this secret for all this time.  If I had allowed you to tell me that day...you would have been free from having to carry that with you."

"Well, better late than never...and now you know.  It wasn't your fault...it was her illness that finally broke her down.  She would have loved nothing more than to see you take your first steps, and she took that to the grave.  What would she think if she knew that you didn't even finish the surgeries?" When he didn't answer, she answered the question herself. "She would have been so disappointed."

"But what if I had…and I still couldn't walk? Would she still be disappointed in me?"

"No, I don't think that she would. I think that she would've been so proud of you for doing everything possible to make it happen and that you were brave, and you didn't give up."

"Well, it is too late now."

"It's never too late, Caspian. That's why I was on you about finishing the operations…because at least then, you would have done what you set out to do, and it would have been up to your body to do the rest. You wouldn't have any regrets."

"I honestly thought that you were pushing me to have the operation because you…"

"…because you thought that I had lied about not caring that you were in a chair. Why is it that you claimed to love me, and yet you never trusted that I would be honest with you about that, no matter what I did to prove myself? Now, I know why you stopped loving me…because you think that I…"

"Mia…I never stopped loving you. I pushed you away because I loved you too much to waste your life on a loser like me."

"You aren't a loser, Cass. Angie thinks that I am just putting myself through torture, holding on to what could have been, instead of what could be. She thinks that I should get on with my life, and find someone here is Chicago, but I told her that I couldn't see another man, knowing that he would never win my heart, because it wasn't mine to give to anyone else. It belongs to you."

"After everything that I have put you through…all the hurt I've caused you…all the tears you've cried because of me…" There was surprise in his voice, as clear as day, and it made her wonder.

"Yes, Cass…even after all that. Honestly, I wanted to move on with my life and forget all about everything between us…but the heart wants what the heart wants."

"Though I understand your need to move on, I hate hearing that you would want to forget everything between us. The bad stuff, yes, but the good stuff…you would want to forget the dance?" The hurt in his voice felt like a knife.

"Nothing I could do could make me forget that.  It was one of those nights that will go down in the history books" She giggled a little.  She heard the soft laugh of Caspian on the other end.

They continued to talk for hours, and finally, Amelia looked over at the clock, and couldn't believe that they had been on the phone for six hours. She had to get up for work at seven o'clock.

"Cass, as much as I hate to cut our conversation short, I have to work in a few hours…" There was silence, and then she heard him say some choice words.

"I am so sorry.  I didn't realize what time it was."

"Neither did I.  I guess that we needed this."

"Are we okay now?  I mean, can we consider ourselves friends again?"

"Seriously, Cass…we have never been just friends, am I right?"

"Now that I think about it…No, we have never really been 'just friends, but we could try…at least for now."

"Sounds like a plan…"  She yawned, and rubbed her eyes.  "I am gonna go to bed now."

"Alright…good night.  I hope that we can talk again soon."

"We will.  'Night."  And she hung up the phone.

He hung up the phone on his end, and leaned back against his headboard. That phone call had been the biggest emotional roller coaster he had been on in a long time. His heart was thumping hard in his chest, as he tried to absorb the conversation, and understand everything he had just learned.

The reality that his grandmother had suffered in silence for many many years, worrying more about bringing up three children that were not hers than about herself, made him wonder what else he didn't know about her. The burden of believing that he was the reason that she had gone downhill so quickly was gone, and yet the pain of her being gone was still there. However, knowing that he could have been on his feet, and possibly with the woman he loved, made him hurt just as badly. He picked up the picture from the night in the ballroom, and looked at it, studying every aspect of it, and his heart took him to that night; he could still smell her perfume, still feel the heat of her body against his. Things were going to be different from here on out, and he knew that he needed help getting to where he needed to be.

# *~Ten~*

A knock came to Caspian's door, and he opened his eyes. He had just gotten the best night's sleep that he could recall. He called out that the door was open, and his sister walked in.

"To what do I owe the honor of your presence?" He looked over at her, half expecting to get yelled at. He grabbed the picture he had repaired, and tucked it under his pillow.

"Did you call Mia last night?"

"Yes, I did. Why does it matter to you?"

"She is my best friend, and she deserves to be happy."

"I agree. She does deserve to be happy, but what does that have to do with whether or not I called her?" He propped himself on his elbows.

"It has a lot to do with you calling her. She needs to move on with her life, and she can never do that if you keep her hanging on. Just let her go…if you love her…Let her go."

"Never… I love her, yes, but I'm not going to let her go. She's my reason for being. I made mistakes, I'll admit, but she's forgiven me, and we're starting over."

"Yeah…starting over, huh? And, what exactly does that entail?" Her skepticism just made him laugh. "Why are you laughing? I don't find, you toying with Mia's heart, the least bit funny."

"I'm not toying with her heart, Angie. I love her. And if that means that I have to start at the bottom, and earn her trust again, then that is what I am going to do. I, my darling little sister, am a changed man. Now, do me a huge favor, and get my physical therapist on the phone. I have a ton of work to do."

"Are you messing with me, Cass?"

"Why would I be messing with you? I am dead serious."

"Seriously…who are you, and what did you do with my jerky, self-absorbed brother?" A smile crept across her freckled face, and she went into his desk, and pulled out his phonebook. She took his cell phone from the nightstand, dialed the number, and handed it to him. An hour later, a knock came to the front door. Evangeline escorted, Becky, the new physical therapist to her brother's room. Before she had a chance to leave, Caspian grabbed her arm.

"I know you have your doubts, and I don't blame you. I have been a complete bastard since Grandmother died. This is my chance to put things right. All I ask is that you don't tell Mia about what I am doing…you know, the physical therapist, and all that."

"Are you trying to hide the fact that your physical therapist is hot?"

"No, that's not what I meant. I am going to finish what I started, but I don't want her to know until the right time. It's very important that you don't mention it to her…can you do that for me, please?"

"Sure, if that is what you need me to do, I suppose that I could do that one thing for you…" She bent over, putting her finger in his face and giving him the stink-eye. " …but, dear brother, if I get one phone call…just one…and she's crying because you hurt her…I will make you wish that you never got the feeling back below your waist." She pointed at his lap, and then snapped her fingers in his face and left.

"She looks as though she would do it, so I'd watch it if I were you…" Becky winced, and then laughed.

*****

Mia walked out of the conference room, and sat down at her desk. Today, the meeting had gone very well, and she got many approving looks from Katrina. Everything was brighter, it seemed. She felt at home here. She couldn't wait to get home, and call Caspian. They had been talking for a few months now, and she was ready to try to convince him to join her in Chicago. With all their issues worked out, she felt there was a good chance he would say yes.

As she turned to straighten the picture on her desk, Danny from the mailroom rolled his cart by her desk.

"Hey Amelia…"

"Hi Danny. Do I have mail today?" She shot him a smile.

"No, sorry, you don't have any mail today. I just wanted to stop by your desk and tell you that I think you look especially beautiful today. You look good in blue." He had a lovesick puppy look on his tan face.

"Awe, thank you, Danny. That is really sweet of you to say." She tuned back to her desk, but he stood there, his foot propped on the bottom rack of his mail cart. She turned back to him, crossed her arms over her chest. "Is there something else, Danny?"

"Well, there's a festival at the Navy Pier... It goes on from Friday through Sunday...and I was wondering if you would like to...um...Would you like to go with me on Saturday?" He flashed his most flirtatious smile, but all she got was the gleam from the fluorescent lights hitting his braces.

"Oh...Danny...You are a sweet guy. I appreciate the invitation, but I can't..." she started, but Katrina cut her off and finished her sentence.

"...Can't wait until Saturday. She'll go with you on Friday, after work." Danny didn't even wait until Amelia could correct Katrina, and he was taking off with his mail cart. He yelled back at her before he got on the elevator.

"See you on Friday, Amelia!"

Amelia turned her head to her boss and gave her an evil look. All Katrina did was smile back.

"What was that? I didn't want to go the festival with him. Did you forget...I am not currently available."

"And why, exactly, are you not available? Are you dating someone?" She gave her a sideways look.

"Not exactly dating..." She turned back to the picture that she was straightening, and Katrina leaned over the top of her cubicle and grabbed it off her desk.

"Is he the reason why you are not currently available?"

"If you must know…" She grabbed the picture and put it in her desk drawer. "…Yes, he is."

"So, does he live in Chicago?"

"No, He's back in Boston."

"So, a guy, who lives almost a thousand miles away, is preventing you from going to a festival at the Navy Pier with a friend from work?"

"No, a guy, who lives almost a thousand miles away, is preventing me from going to a festival at the Navy Pier with a guy from work, who has been known to put his hands where he shouldn't. He has asked me out almost every day since I started working here. Casey, in Accounting, told me that he has asked out several girls from her floor, and he has copped a feel with every single one of them. And then, when they don't return his calls, he goes all 'stalker' on them. Two of them have restraining orders against him."

"Well, you see, if you had read the policies on inter-office dating, you would also have read that people from different positions are not permitted to date. For instance, general employees are not allowed to date anyone in a management or executive position."

"I read that, but what does that have to do with me or Danny? We are both general employees."

"Actually, you aren't. You see, I've spoken to our shareholders, and they feel that you deserve a more appropriate position here at Fashionista. You have bumped our profits, with your brilliant ideas, and insightful input, that you are making them rich. So, as of today, you are now the executive assistant to the Editor-in-Chief...me! Now, seeing as Danny just works in the mailroom, and you are now in a different position class as him, you are not permitted to date him, per the company policy." She grinned, waiting for it all to sink in.

"Wait a second...I'm your executive assistant?! Seriously? Oh my God, Katrina!!" She jumped out of her seat, and put her hands to her mouth, trying not to squeal.

"You've earned it, honey. Pack your personal belongings. I am going to, personally, escort you to your new office." She revealed a box from behind the wall of the cubicle.

"I get an office?" She took the box from her boss, and began to put her things in it. The last thing she grabbed was the small 5X7 photo frame from her drawer. She waved goodbye to all of her cubicle neighbors, who were cheering for her, and followed Katrina onto the elevator.

Walking into her new office, she got weak in the knees. There was a beautiful view from the tenth floor, so much different from the eight floor view. She had a door, which was new for her. Her desk was close to three times bigger than her old one, and she had shelves behind it. The computer on the desk was not fat and bulky, but thin and space efficient. She couldn't get over the fact that the whole computer consisted of was the monitor, keyboard, and mouse. The whole hard drive and motherboard was contained within the monitor.

Amelia was like a child in a toy store, and she sat down at her desk, and the chair was like a cloud, with lumbar support, and arm rests. She set her box on the floor and got up, walking over to what looked like a closet. She opened the door, to see how much space the closet had. It must have been a pretty big closet, because it contained a sink, toilet and even a small shower.

"I have my own bathroom! And it has a shower! I thought this was a closet."

"So, I can assume that you like it."

"This is all too much, Katrina."

"Oh, but if this is too much…then, what I have to show you next is going to blow your mind."

"There's more?" Amelia was overwhelmed. She could hardly get over what she had already received. She watched as Katrina walked over, stuck her head out the door, and then stepped aside as a young woman entered the office. She was about a foot shorter than her, and very well endowed. The girl smiled at Amelia, and put out her hand for her to shake it. "I'm Amelia…the new executive assistant."

"Oh, I know all about you, Ms. Landon. I'm Stacy, and I am *your* assistant…so, I suppose that makes me the executive assistant's assistant." She made a giggle that sounded like a bird chirping. "My job is to make sure that you are taken care of. I take your calls, get your coffee, pick up your dry cleaning, take memos for you, and whatever else you need me for."

Taking a deep breath, she tried to contain her emotions. Just when she thought that she couldn't take much more, there was a knock at the door. A handsome gentleman stuck his head into the office. He flashed Amelia a sweet, toothy smile. He stood back up and walked in, a notepad in his hand.

"I'm Joey, and I am here to get your lunch order. So, what would you like, Miss?"

"Lunch order?" She glanced to Katrina, then to Stacy, and then looked back at Joey. "I didn't know...I usually go to the deli cart outside the building for my lunch. What do you suggest?" He looked at her, almost like he was analyzing her, and then he smiled.

"I will get you a Pastrami and Swiss on rye, with sundried tomatoes and honey mustard...on the side. How does that sound?"

"That sounds like heaven. How did you do that?"

"I've seen you at the deli cart outside the building..." He laughed, and a dimple appeared on his right cheek.

"Hey, that's cheating. I thought that you were psychic for a minute there."

"Sorry to disappoint you, Ms. Landon. Ms. Larson, what can I get for you, since you are right here?"

"You know what...I think I will have what Amelia is having. That sounds very good." Katrina, smiled, and turned to her protégé, and put her hands on her shoulders. "Welcome to the team, Ms. Landon. I, for one, am very happy to have someone competent directly below me. And, yes, I truly believe that you deserve every bit of this promotion. You have proved yourself in such a short time. No one has shown their value as quickly as you have, and that is saying a lot."

"Thank you, Katrina. I will do my best to make sure that I continue to succeed."

"Don't do too much better…the only thing that they could promote you to would be my job." She winked at Amelia, and left the office, followed by Stacy and the "sandwich guy," who flashed another smile before leaving.

She was now alone, in her office, and she could hardly contain herself. She went over to her desk, lifted the box containing her belongings, and began to put everything where she felt it ought to go. When almost everything else was put in their designated spots, she took the framed portrait, and placed it on her desk top.

"Caspian, I have a great job, my own office, and soon, I'll have you here with me. Things couldn't be any better." She, lovingly, caressed the photo on her desk with her thumb. She stood back up, walked over to the window, and got lost in the pure joy she was feeling.

When she got back to her apartment, she pressed the button on the machine, and went in the kitchen to make something to eat. She had received her daily message from Caspian, telling her that he was thinking of her, and couldn't wait for their phone conversation. She smiled and put the kettle on. The phone rang almost immediately after she had finished eating the bowl of cream of broccoli soup.

"Hello, Beautiful." Caspian drawled out.

"And hello to you to…How was your day? You sound exhausted." She took a sip of her tea.

"I am tired, but I will be fine. It's been pretty busy around here."

"Yeah, so I've heard. Angie told me that her boyfriend asked her to marry him, before leaving for the service. I, honestly, don't see how she can deal with being someone in the military. We lost our fathers that way."

"I don't know either, but she is really happy, and the guy is really cool. You can tell he loves her, so I really can't say anything about it. Personally, I think that she is better when she is with him."

"Well, I will try to see if I can make it home for the wedding. Work has been really crazy. I may not be able to get back in time."

"It's been crazy…at a fashion magazine? All they do is talk about clothes, shoes and make-up…they are only busy when there is new stuff to talk about." He laughed.

"Do you even watch television anymore, Cass? There is *always* new stuff to talk about. Not to mention, we have articles on other things as well. It's actually quite exhausting."

"Well, if it is that bad, you should just come home. You could probably get a job at a magazine based out of Boston, with your experience at the magazine you are at. It's a lot calmer here."

"It would be the same at any fashion magazine I worked at, Cass. The Fashionista doesn't just write about the fashion in Chicago, but rather, all over. If you are so worried for my well-being, why don't you just move here?" That wasn't how she had planned to ask him, but it was on the table now. There was silence. "Cass, are you still there?"

"Yeah...I'm here. Did you just ask me to move to Chicago again?"

"Yes, I did. Cass, I miss you. And with my job, I can't leave now."

"And why not? What's so special about working in a cubicle day after day?"

"That's actually why I couldn't wait for you to call. I am not in a cubicle anymore. I have my own office now, and have an assistant...and a guy that gets me lunch. And I have my own bathroom…with a shower!" She couldn't contain her excitement.

"Wow. So…your job is really going well." Amelia could tell that he wasn't really excited, but rather disappointed.

"You aren't excited for me? I thought, for sure, that you would be happy that I am doing so well."

"Oh, I am, sweetheart. I'm very happy for you. I guess a part of me was hoping that things weren't going well, so you would come back to Boston. I am proud of you for doing so well." The tone in his voice seemed to perk up a little bit toward the end.

"I have a job as the Executive Assistant to the Editor-in-Chief, and a good size apartment…things are a lot better between us…Please come to Chicago. You can visit for a bit, and if you decide that you want to stay, we can just send for your things…"

"Mia…As much as I would love to…I just can't."

"Not even a visit, Cass?"

"Do you not realize…if I come there, even for a visit, I won't leave? I hate that you are there and I am here. Ever since we started talking again, all I have thought about is holding you again. If I came there, one of two things would happen; either I wouldn't leave, or you would lose your job because I would bring you back home, where you belong." His words made her warm.

"This is a once-in-a-lifetime opportunity for me. Believe me; if I had not been promoted...I would come back there. To be honest with you...I miss you, Angie, and everyone else. I miss the house...." She sighed.

"I know there's a but...what is it? Your job is a big deal. This is the first time that you have been on your own. The house will always be here. We will always be here." It went silent for a moment. "I'll make you a deal. I will come and visit you in Chicago. But, then you have to come back with me for Angie's wedding."

"I can't take all that time off."

"Who says you have to? I don't need a babysitter. I will be at the apartment, waiting until you get home, and then we can spend the evenings together. Angie is getting married on a Saturday. We can fly back here, after you get off work on Friday, and you can fly back on Monday. You would only miss one day of work." The excitement in his voice was very clear.

"Why would I fly back on Monday? The wedding is on Saturday, so I would just fly back here on Sunday."

"Nope…you'll fly back on Monday. I want you to myself on Sunday."

"Is that so? You know…If you came to live here, you could have me all to yourself every day." She wanted to slap herself, as she sounded desperate and pathetic.

"That's very true…but, let's just start with my plan…for now." His deep laugh sent tingles up and down her spine.

As he spoke to Amelia, he couldn't help himself. Slowly, he used his free hand and lifted his leg, and attempted to use his muscles to extend his leg out in front of him. All he managed to do was flex his ankle. He still had a long road ahead, and progress had been made, but not as quickly as he would have liked. He had gotten around her knowing about the last surgery, though it wasn't easy. Thankfully, she had been pretty busy with work, which left her distracted, and he knew how to hide pain and exhaustion in his voice when talking to her on the phone.

"Well, it's getting late, and I have to be at work early in the morning. Let me know when Angie is getting married, so I can request the following Monday off."

"That's my girl." There was a growl in his voice, and it sounded almost primal. "Alright, beautiful...you get a good night's rest and I will talk to you tomorrow night."

"Every night...just like clockwork. Talk to you tomorrow night." She laughed, and then placed the receiver on the base, and rolled over. Clicking the lamp, she placed her head on the pillow, and drifted off, thoughts of Cass floating through her mind.

*****

A couple weeks had gone by, and Amelia was enjoying her job more and more. Her assistant, Stacy, had a knack for learning quickly of her boss's like and dislikes. Every morning, Amelia would find a caramel mocha frozen cappuccino and a cinnamon raisin bagel on her desk. All of her messages were color-coded according to priority, and all her mail was stacked neatly on her desk.

She sat at her desk, staring out at the beautiful skyline, when her phone buzzed. She reached over and pressed the intercom button without looking.

"Yes, Stacy?"

"Good Afternoon, Ms. Landon. You have a call on line one, and Joey is here for your lunch order. Do you want the usual?"

"Yes, please…um…wait, no. Tell joey to come back in ten minutes. And, as I have asked you many times, Stacy, call me Amelia." She laughed. She pressed a button on the phone, and put it on speaker. "Amelia Landon, Executive Assistant, Fashionista…How can I help you?"

"Did you get the dress yet?" A cheerfully nervous voice asked over the phone. Amelia looked up, from her desk, over to where a long garment bag was hanging.

"Yes, I got it. Stacy picked it up from the cleaners this morning. It is really beautiful, Angie." She remarked, getting up from her chair and walking over to the dress. It was sunflower yellow, with a robin's egg blue sash. The crepe-like material was light and silky.

"Oh, thank goodness. I was worried that you would hate it…not that your opinion matters…I'm the bride."

"That you are, my dear. And I don't hate it one bit. It is the kind of dress I would wear again and again. How are you holding up?"

"I am so nervous, and really excited. Wait until you meet Kent. You are going to love him. He is really excited to meet you."

"I am equally excited to finally meet him as well. If he makes you happy, I am sure that I will love him." She zipped the garment bag back up, and walked back over to her desk, leaning against the edge.

"When is Caspian's plane supposed to arrive? He was really nervous, seeing as he really doesn't like planes, but he was flying to you, so he took some motion sickness pills and got on the plane."

"His plane arrives in about an hour. I was getting set to have a car go pick him up, but I think that I better go myself. I cannot believe that he is actually coming here for a week." Her heart skipped a beat at the thought that she would be seeing him again, after such a long time. The phone calls were great, but she wanted to see his face, smell his aftershave, and run her fingers through his long dark locks.

"He is beyond excited to see you, Mia. I don't remember the last time I saw him this revved up. Seeing you is all he has talked about for the last week. It kind of makes me sad, being that he was more excited about seeing you than his own sister's upcoming wedding."

"I am excited enough for both of us" She smiled, and squealed. Out of the corner of her eye, she saw the sandwich guy waving from her doorway. She signaled him to wait a moment. "I have to get back to work. I will call you later tonight, okay?"

"Oh, please. Cass will be there, so I won't hear from you until I see you back here in Boston. Have a good visit. I love you, Mia!"

"I love you, too, Angie. Talk to you later." Both of them hung up the phone, and Amelia walked over to the door. "Hey Joey…"

"Hello to you, too. You look awfully chipper today. Were you looking forward to seeing me?" He winked at her, and his dimple sunk deeper into his cheek as he smiled at her.

"I always look forward to seeing you. You bring me yummy food." She joked. "And I am chipper because I was just talking to my best friend. She's getting married next weekend."

"Oh…that's awesome. I assume you are going to the wedding."

"She would hunt me down and kill me if I missed it."

"So, where in Chicago is she getting married? I bet it's the Navy Pier…Do you have a date? If not, I would be happy to go with you. I love weddings." He started rambling, which she found kind of cute.

"Oh, Joey…I'm sorry, but the wedding isn't here in Chicago. It's back home in Boston. And I have a date already. Sorry, sweetie. I am going with the bride's brother."

"Aw…that sucks. I was hoping that you would ask me to be your date. I am starting to think that you don't like me. I have asked you out like ten times already, and you never say yes." He pouted his lower lip, and gave her pitiful puppy-dog eyes.

"I do like you, Jocy, but I have told you before. I am already in a committed relationship. Besides, we can't date…company policy." She felt bad, but her heart belonged to Cass, and she wasn't willing to risk that or her job to make Joey happy.

"You are in a committed relationship with a guy living in Boston, whom I assume is the bride's brother. You are in Chicago. One date won't hurt anyone. Come on, Gorgeous. And, we *can* date, because I don't work for the magazine…I work for the food craft services…company policy doesn't apply in this case." He winked and flashed a big smile. "I don't see a ring on your finger yet. When I see a ring on your finger, I will stop asking. In the meantime, I will work at breaking you down. You have to give in, eventually."

"You can keep trying all you want, Joey. I won't change my mind. I love the guy I am with."

"You're breaking my heart, Amelia." He clutched his chest, as if he was in pain. He smiled at her, and leaned against the door frame. "Well, since you have your mind made up already…what can I get you for lunch?"

"Yeah, um, nothing today... I have to leave to go pick up my *boyfriend* from the airport." She emphasized who she was picking up, and he acted like she had just shot him in the heart with an arrow.

"You're killing me, Mon Cheri…killing me."

"Oh, stop it, Joey. You are gorgeous. You could get any girl here…and I know one that would love to go out with a strapping Adonis such as yourself" She motioned to her assistant, who quickly looked down at her computer keyboard, hoping that he hadn't noticed her staring at him.

"Stacy…really…I don't know." He gave Amelia a look, as if shocked that Stacy would be interested in him.

"You must be blind, then. She can't stop staring at you, with those love-sick eyes. I bet…if you walked over and asked her to go out sometime, she would jump at it." She smiled, and noticed that Stacy was gawking again, her chin in her hand.

"Oh, I believe you…I mean, about her wanting me to ask her out, but the thing is, Amelia…" He reached out, took her hand in his, and kissed it. Her skin tingled at the touch of his lips. He looked at her through his dark lashes, giving her the most smoldering look he could muster. "…I only have eyes for you, and you alone." He bent to kiss her hand again, but she yanked her hand away.

"I'm sorry, Joey. I'm afraid, then, that you are as deaf as you are blind. I have told you several times before, and I will say it again…I am *not* available. I have a man, whom I love very much. I would appreciate it if you remembered that." Her temper began to rise at his advances, but she tried to keep her voice at an even tone. "Now, if you will excuse me, I have to go. And, if I am not mistaken, you have a job to do. People are waiting on their lunches." She shot him a half-smile.

"I'm sorry if I stepped over the line. It was very unprofessional, and very disrespectful." He moved aside, allowing her to pass by him, closing the door behind. "It won't happen again."

"Good, because I like you as a friend, and I'd hate for this to put a damper on our friendship." She walked to the elevator. As the door closed, she saw Joey walk over and say something to Stacy, and her reply was an obvious squeal of delight, which made her smile.

Amelia traveled down the elevators, and walked toward the parking garage. All that she could think about was seeing Caspian, and wrapping her arms around him again. All that had happened in the past seemed like a dream. Evangeline quite often had called her a glutton for punishment when it came to Cass, especially with the way things had been left before she left Boston. She tried really hard to get past how she felt about him back then, but as she got into her car, she was so glad that her heart had stood firm. She started the car, put it in reverse, and went to back out, when she noticed a rose tucked into her back wiper. She threw the car back in park, got out of her car, and went to the back hatch.

"That's an odd place to put a flower. I wonder who did this." She looked around, and after not seeing anyone, plucked the rose from the wiper, and threw it to the ground, before getting back in her car, and heading out. It was a long drive to the airport, and she was already running late. By the time she arrived at the airport valet section, she had totally forgotten about the rosette in her wiper.

# *~Eleven~*

Overhead, she could hear a woman, announcing boarding flights. The skylights above allowed her to see planes as they flew in and out from the landing strips. Her heart leapt into her throat as she heard the woman announce that the flight from Boston had landed. Amelia walked to the window, as the plane touched down, and rolled down the runway toward the terminal. The jet bridge extended out to where the plane was pulling up. She began to fidget and pace as it connected and locked into place, and shadows of the passengers were seen as they entered the tunnel. She walked slowly over to the gate, and waited, other people gathering with her to await their loved ones. Person after person came out from the tunnel, and her breathing became more labored. She watched as men and women were reunited, hugging and crying in happiness. Out of the corner of her eye, she caught a glimmer of light reflecting on chrome. She turned her head, and her eyes met with the smoky depths of Caspian's. Her heart felt as if it were pounding out of her chest. She took two steps forward, and stopped.

"Be still my heart...I have died, gone to Heaven, and they have sent the most beautiful angel to greet me." His deep voice had a force that seemed to pull her toward him.

He looked completely different than he had when she had seen him last. His skin was freshly shaved and smooth, and seemed to glow as if kissed by the sun itself. The bags and dark circles, which were once under his eyes still lingered but were less noticeable. His eyes were not red and bloodshot, but clear and smiling. His hair had grown out a bit more, but was pulled back in a neat ponytail at the nape of his neck, like a chocolate waterfall. His chest was broad, and the muscles were outlined in the material of his shirt. Even women who had companions of their own, couldn't help but gaze in his direction, but he never even saw anyone else, as he was focused on the vision of raw beauty in front of him.

"I'm no angel, I assure you." She smiled. Even if she wanted to, she couldn't pull her eyes from his.

"Oh, but you most certainly are…To me…." He reached up, taking her hand in his. A wave of electricity surged though him when their skin touched, as it had been a long time since they had had any physical contact. The urge to leap out of the chair and take her in his arms was unbearable. He pulled her to him, though it didn't take much. She fell onto his lap, and their faces were so close that it would have taken just a whisper for their lips to touch. Caspian's hand slid up her leg and pulled the edge of her dress down, but the feeling of his hand sent sensations through her whole body, that only he could give her.

"I feel like I am dreaming that you're here with me…" That was all she could get out of her mouth. She ran her hand up his chest, and her fingers found their way to his neck.

"We have been apart too long…far, far too long. I had almost forgotten what you smelled like…the sweet mix of Honeysuckle…" He buried his face in her silky crimson hair, and took in the scent of her, nuzzling her neck though the red curtain. "…fresh air, and sunflowers."

"I could never forget what you smell like…but I started to forget what it felt like to be in your arms. I wished, every time that I heard your voice, that you were here with me. Now, you are, and I couldn't be happier. I love you, Cass. And I have missed you more than anything."

Her lip trembled, and she couldn't hold in the tears of happiness she shed. She laid her hand on the side of his face, and he closed his eyes, leaning into her touch.

"I love you, too, my beautiful one…I will make up for any hurt I have ever caused you…for every tear you ever shed because of me. I was lost without you. I can't take back what has happened, but I can do my hardest to never cause you pain again. I have you in my arms, and I am never letting go again." He wrapped his arms around her, and buried his face in her chest. She could feel his breath and his heart racing against her skin.

They had an audience now, as the people around them in the terminal were watching them. It was almost as if they were witnessing a love scene from a romantic movie. The reunion between all of them and their companions paled in comparison to the one in front of them. A hush came over the group, and the sudden silence caught Amelia and Caspian's attention. She blushed, looking around at the strangers. Caspian sighed, and rolled his eyes.

"Alright, folks... The show is over now." He chuckled.

"That was the most beautiful and heartwarming thing I have ever seen…" One lady said to the woman standing next to her. She turned to her husband and slapped him, then pointed at Amelia and Caspian. "I want that to be us! Why can't that be us?"

Caspian whispered in Amelia's ear, urging her to get them out of the terminal before a riot ensued. She giggled and got off his lap, quickly moving behind him to push him out of the crowd.

They went to baggage claim, retrieved his suitcase, and made their way to the valet outside. When her silver sedan rolled up, the nice young man driving it assisted them in getting the suitcase. Cass hoisted himself into the car, and the valet took the wheelchair, folded it up, and put it in the trunk. Thoughts of freedom from the wheelchair and the inconvenience of it crossed Cass's mind, as he buckled his safety belt, and watched as Amelia tipped the valet, and then got into the driver's seat.

"Are you ready for this?" She glanced over at him and smiled, shifting the car into gear.

"I am ready for anything when I am with you." He put his sunglasses on, and leaned back in his seat, cracking the window slightly, letting the warm air blow on his face.

They pulled away from the curb and were on their way down the road in no time at all. Though the airport was not in Chicago itself, it was a nice drive, and it gave them a chance to talk on the trip back to her apartment. They passed many beautiful sights, many of which Cass

clicked pictures of with his phone. They caught I-90 and took it into

Chicago, and stopped at an old fashioned diner right off the interstate.

Driving the main streets through Chicago was quite exciting for Cass, as it

was very busy and very crowded, unlike what he was used to. They took

South Michigan Avenue, where they passed her place of employment,

Fashionista Inc. He had to crane his neck to see the whole building. Soon,

they were turning into a parking garage, with a large sign over it, "The

Boulevard Residential Parking Only."

"The Boulevard? That's a strange name for an apartment

complex."

"Don't let the name fool you. It is really surprising." She smiled,

giving him a sideways glance as she found a spot to park. She hopped out,

and yanked his chair out of the trunk. When he got into the chair, she

closed the door, pulled the handle up for his suitcase, and pointed him to

the doors into the actual building. She slid a key card in the slot and the

door buzzed, allowing them to open the door. He found out quickly what

she meant.

Everything in the lobby was so bright, welcoming, and very symmetrical. Chairs and couches were strategically placed. He spun his chair, looking up at the vaulted ceilings.

"Ms. Landon!" The girl at the desk was smiling and waving. Amelia waved back, and urged Cass toward the elevators.

When they got in, she pressed a button, and they felt a jolt as the iron box ascended. She turned his chair, and the back of the elevator opened up to reveal windows to the outside. Cass's breath caught in his throat as he saw the beauty before him. It was dusk, and the sun set the sky on fire as it made its descent into the horizon, and he saw the people turn to ants as they went higher and higher. Finally, after a moment, the elevator came to a halt.

"Come on. This is my floor." She tapped him on the shoulder, grabbed the handle of the suitcase, and reached into her purse for her keys. He followed her, still in awe of what he had already seen. He finally understood why she loved it so much in Chicago. He would never be able to take her from this, and convince her to come back home to Boston for good. Amelia unlocked her door, and opened it, allowing Caspian to enter it first. He rolled his wheelchair through the door, and stopped in the middle of the floor.

"This is absolutely amazing. This is where you have been living since you moved here?" He was entranced by the beauty and elegance of her home. Everything was color-coordinated, with hues of blues and greens, khaki and ivory. The space was open and inviting, and every aspect of it had Amelia's heart and personality. There were pictures on shelves and end tables.

"Yes, this is my home, and for now, yours too." She put his suitcase by the bedroom door, and walked over to him. "I am so glad that you came. How do you like it?"

"It's almost as beautiful as the woman living here." He took her hand, and pulled her onto his lap. "I understand why you are so happy here. This place is like the Emerald City and Wonderland all rolled up in one. It is amazing, and I haven't even seen all of it yet." He swept a strand of her hair away, and tucked it behind her ear.

"I am even happier now that you are here with me." She ran her fingers through his long, dark hair, and looked deep into his eyes. Over a year had passed since she had looked so deeply into those very eyes, and she could see that something in him had changed. They had aged far more than a year, and yet the light in them seemed brighter and full of life. "You're different...somehow." Her eyes narrowed, but her smile didn't fade. "A lot has happened in the last year…more than what you have told me."

"A lot *has* happened, but I don't want to talk about it right now. I just want to sit and hold you for a while, if that's alright." There was a hint of sadness in his eyes, and she nodded, understanding.

They rolled over to the couch, and she got up. He turned the chair, and maneuvered over to the couch, and pushed his chair away. She sat down next to him, and snuggled up under his arms. They sat there, warm and safe and back where they belonged. Silence fell in the apartment, and all that could be heard was their breathing; all they could feel was each other's heartbeats and the heat of each other's bodies.

*****

Stacy and Joey sat across the table from each other, their meal ordered. Stacy smiled wildly, and looked at him. It was surreal that he had asked her out for dinner and a show, and she was purely giddy. Her cheeks were flushed as her eyes met his. She nearly jumped out of her own skin when he slid his hands across the table and took her hands in his.

"Are you having a good time tonight?" He spoke.

"I most certainly am. Thank you. Are you? I mean, I know that I wasn't exactly your first choice for a date, but I am glad that I'm the one here with you now."

"I'm having a great time, Stacy. And I am sorry that you *weren't* my first choice. You are beautiful, and funny, and smart, but I have to be honest with you. You and I can't be more than just friends."

"Then why did you take me out tonight? This isn't the cheapest place to eat. You could have just taken me out to a fast food joint, and saved yourself the money." Her smile faded, and her eyes began to fill with hot tears.

"I brought you here, because you deserve it. Sure, I could have taken you to some Podunk diner or bought food from a cart on the Navy Pier, but I was trying to be nice, and take you to a nice place." He patted her hand.

"If you don't mind my asking…who was your first choice?" She pulled her hands away and put them in her lap.

"I am pretty sure you already know who it was…is." He looked at her, and something clicked in her head.

"Oh, Joey…You know that she is in a very serious relationship. She loves him."

"I know, but they aren't married. Heck, Stacy, he lives in Boston…over a thousand miles away. She deserves better than that."

"She deserves to be happy, and he makes her happy. I can tell how happy she is…every time that she talks about him. She's my boss, and my friend."

"Are you saying this because she is your boss and friend, or because you can't have what she has? Or is it just me…."

"Joey, I have loved you from afar for the last three years. I have watched you flirt with every girl in my office except me, but I didn't care. I didn't know what to say to you, but I tried to tell you how I felt in different ways. Then, today, you just walked up to me and asked me out. I thought that you finally got the message, actually saw me, and that you felt the same way." She folded her napkin and put it on the table. "I want what Amelia has, yes, and I thought that I'd finally have that with you. However, you brought me out, not to be with me, but to help you be with her…to give you an inside scoop on the one you can't have. I understand now...expensive dinner, a movie…you are trying to bribe me." The smirk was not from amusement, as his supposed plan was not the least bit amusing.

"It's not like that, Stacy. I like you. I really do, just not the way you want me to."

"Amelia is my friend, and I won't have a part in helping you bring her relationship to an end for your own selfish needs. I am not, and will not help you hurt her." She stood up, and grabbed her handbag. She pulled some money out and threw it on the table. "Enjoy your expensive dinner alone. Don't worry…I won't tell her about tonight, but you need to back off and grow up." She walked out of the restaurant.

"Dammit. If I can't get her help, I guess I will just have to get Amelia on my own. I am Joey Maynard. I get every girl I go after. She is no different, just a bit more challenging." He sat back in his chair, ignoring the disgusted looks from the people at tables nearby who had heard the conversation.

*****

"Are you sure that your boss is okay with this?"

"I already talked to her about it. She is very excited to meet you. And with you there, I can work and spend time with you. You can see what I do, and who I work with. You will absolutely adore my assistant, Stacy. She is an absolute angel." She pressed the button on the elevator and it moaned and creaked before moving upward. "Katrina is the only one that knows that you are coming in to work with me."

"Shouldn't I have dressed a bit differently, though? I look like a bum you pulled off the street." He surveyed his outfit; a dark grey form-fitting t-shirt, a pair of dark denim jeans, and black boots. He took his hand and smoothed out his hair.

"Stop your fussing, Cass. You are fine. Besides, it isn't 'Bring a Bum to Work Day' until Thursday…" She gave him a half smile, and he smiled back.

The elevator stopped on the floor and she pressed the button to keep the door shut for a moment longer. She looked at him, and felt an overwhelming sense of pride, as her coworkers were about to meet the man she loved.

"It may get a little crazy out there. Most of the people on this floor are women…single women, and they drool every time they see our sandwich guy…and it isn't cuz they are hungry, either. Just smile, wave, say hello…I will get you to my office as quickly as possible, before they strip you down like a male prostitute…" She laughed, and motioned for him to take a deep breath, and then she released the button, and stepped aside. The doors opened and whatever chatter was going on before came to a staggering halt. She got behind his chair and pushed him forward, as he was not moving. People stood up and watched, as they made their way to her office. The women seemed almost entranced by the sight of the handsome new face in their workspace. He smiled and nodded at everyone as they passed, trying to be polite, and to not show how nervous he was at being there.

The hush in the large room was broken by a familiar squeal. If he didn't know any better, he would have sworn that it had been his sister that came shuffling toward them.

"Good morning, Stacy. This is Caspian. Caspian, this is my assistant and very good friend, Stacy." She introduced them, and smiled at her friend, her eyes beaming with happiness.

"It is a pleasure to finally meet you, Caspian. Amelia talks about you all the time...well, not ALL the time." Stacy was so excited she could hardly stand still. "Good Morning, Ms. Landon."

"It's a pleasure to meet you as well." He extended his hand to shake hers, and she returned the gesture. When their introductions were done, Amelia wheeled him into her office, and Stacy closed the door behind them.

A sense of dread filled Stacy's stomach, as she stood against the closed door. She knew that Joey would be in the office in a matter of a few hours, getting lunch orders. Though she already knew about Caspian's wheelchair, she knew that Joey would use that to his advantage if he could, to try to manipulate the situation. She wanted to say something to Amelia, but was afraid to, just in case it came back to bite her. It took her a few minutes before she decided what she was going to do. Taking a deep breath, she walked over to her desk, and wrote an email to her boss, telling her everything that happened when she went to dinner with Joey, and that she had already spoken to Katrina about it, just in case he did try to start something. She knew she was doing the right thing, for Amelia's sake. If Amelia thought that she was in on it, then she would just have to deal with the consequences, but that was a chance she was willing to take. Hitting send on the screen, she sighed and sat back in her chair.

Meanwhile, Amelia and Caspian were in her office, looking out the window at the view. It was an amazing day outside, and the sun was shining like a jewel in the sky.

"I am so proud of you for all you have accomplished here. And to think, this all started out as an internship."

"I know…crazy, right? I am still trying to wrap my mind around it, myself. It's like I am living someone else's life." She sat down in the chair nearest to him, and leaned her head back against the window. "Katrina says that she has never had an intern excel as I have. My input actually helped sales ratings to go up. Speaking of Katrina…hold on." She walked over to her phone and dialed, then put it on speaker.

"Hello, this is Katrina, Editor-in-Chief, Fashionista. How can I help you?"

"Katrina, it's Amelia. Could you please come to my office, if you aren't too busy? There is someone here I would like you to meet."

"If it is who I think it is….I will be down in a moment." She sounded almost as excited as Stacy did.

It didn't take her as long as Amelia thought, as she heard a frantic knocking at the door. She smiled at Caspian, tweaked his nose, and went to answer the door. Katrina didn't even wait for her protégé to greet her, blasting through the doorway and sliding to a halt in her high heels just a few feet from his chair wheel.

"My goodness…Now I see what the fuss was all about. You are really as gorgeous as Mia said." She straightened up, correcting her stance to look more professional. "I am Katrina, Mia's boss. It is very nice to finally match a face to all the stories. Your pictures don't do you a bit of justice." She held out her hand, and he shook it.

"It is a pleasure to meet the woman who made all of this possible for my Amelia."

"Oh, Amelia made this all possible on her own, I assure you. I just gave her an outlet to grow, and that she has, far beyond even my expectations. We are very fortunate to have her here at our magazine. It was only fitting that we give her a job that matched her abilities. If she works any harder, I may be out of a job pretty soon." She chuckled, sitting down in a chair near him.

"Oh, she would never do that to you. But, I have to say, being a co-editor would be kind of cool…" He smiled, and she gave a nervous laugh.

"A funny guy too…Mia never told me you were so funny…" She glanced up at Amelia, and gave her a look, and she shrugged.

"What can I say…Cass thinks he's a comedian..."

"So, how was your trip here? No problems with your flight, I assume." Katrina focused back on Caspian, who was trying to refrain from being overly humorous and sarcastic.

"It went well.  I haven't ever been on a plane before, so it was a whole new experience for me.  I didn't really get the concept of the hot towels, and I would have liked to take advantage of the reclining seats…this seat doesn't give…at all."

"Oh, so you flew first class…must be nice.  I've never been in first class, so I couldn't tell you what the hot towels are for."

"Sorry, but it really isn't as great as everyone thinks.  They are too snooty and snobby for my taste."

"So, anyhow…You've been here for a couple days.  What do you think of our beautiful city, so far, Caspian?"

"I have to admit…I was not expecting it to be like this.  There is so much to do here, so much to see…It literally takes my breath away.  And Mia's apartment…wow!"

"Believe it or not, the Boulevard complex is the low end of apartments that were selected for our interns.  And, I will have you know, that Amelia is actually paying for her apartment now, as she is no longer an intern, but a full-time employee.  She could afford something much better, but she seems very modest."

"It isn't that I am modest, Katrina…" Amelia interrupted, "…it's that I chose not to pack all of my things up and move. I'm lazy. That and I absolutely love the view from my balcony."

"You are a lot of things, my dear, but lazy is not one of them." Katrina rebutted. She directed her next statement to Caspian. "You ought to be exceptionally proud of your girlfriend. She has taken this magazine to new heights. She has impressed everyone here, as well as our shareholders, and all of our readers…so much so that our sales are blowing the other magazines out of the water."

"Oh, I am very proud of her…couldn't be more proud. She has really made a life for herself here." There was a hint of sadness in his eyes that only Mia noticed.

"Now that you said that, is it safe to assume that you are not going to try to take her away from us?" She gave Caspian a stern look.

"Katrina, I am sure that you know that she is a very strong willed person…Even if I wanted to convince her to come home to Boston, she wouldn't do it. She's happy here, and successful. I would never try to get in the way of her career or her happiness." He took Amelia's hand in his, and kissed it. "We have managed to keep our relationship alive for over a year. I have no doubt that we can continue."

"Well, why don't you just move here? I am sure that her apartment is more than big enough. Even if it isn't…she can afford to get a larger one."

"I have obligations back in Boston that prevent me from moving here. Otherwise, I would move here in a heartbeat. Though we have kept things going, long distance, nothing compares to seeing her face every day."

"From what I hear, your sister will be married this coming weekend, and so your obligations should be concluded once she is…"

"Katrina, we have talked about it several times…and if he chooses to stay in Boston, I am not going to pressure him. The house he lives in has been in the family for generations. I would never expect him to give that up for me. Not to mention, the staff employed there would be out of jobs, and they are like family to us." She tried to convince Caspian that this form of questioning by her boss was not brought on by anything that she may have said. She didn't want him to think that she had recruited her boss to convince him where she had failed.

"Yes, my sister is getting married, true, but Mia is right…I don't want to give up our home, and leave our people without jobs or a home. I love Mia more than life itself, and I would love nothing more than to be here with her every day, but I cannot, in clear conscience, leave Boston."

"That is quite unfortunate, because Chicago has so much to offer. I understand, though, and really it comes down to what you and our Amelia decide to do. I just have noticed how much brighter, happier, more focused she has been since you arrived." Katrina prodded.

The subject was changed, and the three of them spoke about life in Boston, how they met, and soon an hour and a half had passed. Katrina was not, in Caspian's opinion, the typical boss. She was down to Earth, and very friendly. The thing he liked the best was that she spoke very highly of Amelia, which made her blush.

Katrina, laughing at something that Cass had said, casually looked at her watch, and abruptly stood up. "Well, I would love to sit and chat, but I have to get back to work. Enjoy your day here at the office. And Amelia, please let Joey know that Caspian's lunch is on me. He should be doing his rounds and taking orders anytime now."

"It was very nice to have finally met you, Katrina." Caspian extended his hand to shake her hand again, and she shook it then headed toward the door.

"The feeling is mutual." Katrina grabbed Amelia's arm and pulled her to the door with her. "He is absolutely delicious. Either you convince him to move here, or you may lose him to another girl in Boston…a man like him doesn't last long alone…some Boston Bimbo may swipe him right out from under you. If you weren't my friend, and employee, I would sink my teeth into him myself."

"Oh Katrina! That's horrible…" She laughed, and opened her door for her superior. As she began to close the door, she spotted Joey getting off the elevator. After the other day, when he started flirting with her and insisted that she go out with him, they had barely said two words to each other. She wanted to keep him as a friend, but if he insisted on pushing himself at her, she would have to cut him off at the knees, letting him know that she couldn't even be friends with him any longer.

She thought of this as she made her way over to Caspian, who watched her so intensely, she felt almost naked.

"Why are looking at me like that?"

"What was all that about? I thought we talked about…" He seemed almost angry.

"Baby, I had nothing to do with that. Katrina has her opinions and it best to just let her talk. I had no idea she was going to interrogate you like that, and try to pressure you. That is just the ways she is. You and I have discussed this countless times, and as much as I *would* love for you to live here with me, I respect your decision." She walked over and sat on his lap, taking his face in her hands. "I love you so much, but I would not want you to move here unless you wanted to. Moving here against your own free will would just ruin things between us, and I don't want that."

"Okay, I was just making sure...Sorry if I accused you of being sneaky..."

"Oh, honey, you don't know how sneaky I really can be..." She rubbed the tip of her nose on his, and attempted tickle him. They were laughing, and looking out the window, when the door flew open, causing Amelia to jump, almost tipping them both over.

"How's the most beautiful girl in the world doing today?" Joey sang as he walked in, but stopped dead in his tracks, the smile on his face, turning to a scowl.

"Have you ever heard of knocking?" Mia jumped up, and charged at him.

"I tried to tell him to come back, Amelia, but he didn't listen to me." Stacy pleaded, hoping that she wouldn't be blamed for Joey's blatant disregard for privacy and respect.

"I didn't realize you had company." He growled at her.

"My door was closed, Joey. Usually, that means that I am busy. When Stacy says for you to come back, there is a good reason. She's my assistant, and your disrespect for her is obvious disrespect for me as well."

"Good God, Amelia…chill out, would you? You have never had a problem with me stopping in to get your lunch order before…And you, clearly, weren't in a business meeting. It looked as though it had nothing to do with work…is that the boyfriend?"

"Not that it is any of your business, but yes, that is the…my boyfriend. He has a name, too. It's Caspian." Her temper faded slightly.

"May I meet him? I mean, you were going to introduce us, weren't you? I think he has a right to know about me…about us" His snide remark made her temper flare up again. She was unaware that the door has swung open behind her, and Caspian was hearing the whole conversation, a confused look on his face, having just remembered her saying that he had no idea how sneaky she really was. *Was she referring to this?* He thought to himself, as he watched. Joey had a clear view of Amelia's guest, and wanted to make the most of it.

"Why does he have a right to know about you…about us? There is no US, Joey!"

"He cannot honestly believe that you have been here all this time, and you haven't found someone to keep you company…"

"What on earth are you talking about? I work, then go home and talk to him on the phone, then go to bed, just to do it all over the next day. When would I have time for company?" She crossed her arms over her chest, her wiry red locks shaking with her body. "Are you on something?"

"You and I have flirted and talked every day since you came here…"

"Actually, you were the one doing all the flirting….what are you trying to accomplish with this senseless rambling?"

"Mia….Could you and your friend please come in here, before you both make more of a scene than you already have…NOW!" Cass was at the door, a demanding tone in his voice. Mia, startled, turned on her heels, and faced him, her face red from anger and embarrassment. She walked in her office, and Joey followed. Caspian slammed the door hard enough that it shook the glass in the door. "Could you please explain to me what this is all about?" Joey started talking fast, not allowing Amelia to defend herself before he could twist the proverbial knife even deeper.

"I'm Joe. I work for the food service. For the last few months, Mia and I have been speaking, and becoming friendlier. I just assumed that it was alright, as she said that her boyfriend was in Boston, and wouldn't find out about our relationship... But, now you are here, and I thought that you had a right to know." He could see that Amelia was getting progressively nervous and agitated.

"So, the two of you are in a type of relationship?"

"That's a laugh!" Mia blurted out, her arms still folded over her chest, her nails digging into her upper arms.

"Yes, Sir. In a manner of speaking, we are. However, company policy forbids us from dating, so we have kept it on the down-low."

"So which is it, Amelia? Are you seeing this...guy while you are here, and hiding it from me? Or is he just screwing with me? Right about now, I am not in the mood for being screwed with."

"You are actually listening to him?! I cannot believe this! Do you honestly mean to tell me that you are actually buying this crap?" She was seething with rage, both at Joey's lies, and at the questioning coming from the man she loves.

"It's okay....it's out now, Mia. You owe him to be honest. There is nothing to be ashamed of. He must understand how hard it is for you to be here, when he is back in Boston. You are lonely, and since he refuses to commit to your relationship, fully, you have me to fill the void."

"What do you mean, 'commit fully'? I am committed to our relationship with everything I have. Is this how you feel, Mia? By not moving here, and abandoning those who count on me, to be here as your house boy...I am not committed?" Cass was gripping the armrests on his chair. "This is the second time that this has come up today...I am starting to see a pattern here."

"Joey, why are you doing this? Why are you trying to ruin my relationship? You and I both know that these are lies. There is no relationship other than the fact that you get me lunch every day, same as everyone else here. I told you, from the very beginning, that I am not available. Why can't you accept that, and move on? Instead, you are trying to destroy the best thing in my life so that, what...so you can take his place? That will *never* happen. I love Caspian...with my whole heart, and every breath I breathe. Why would I betray him with someone like you?"

"Well, obviously, he believes a little of the 'lies', because he wants answers..." Joey's expression was cold and unyielding. "Besides, who else would take you dancing, and on those walks along the beach that you love so much...I am sure that he knows that an extremely sexy and desirable woman, such as yourself, has needs that he could never meet…especially from that chair." It felt as though Caspian's heart was about to explode, hearing the last statement about his disability having an effect on the relationship. All of his worst fears had come to light, as he heard this stranger speak of things that he always assumed were Amelia's deepest and most hidden feelings.

"I have heard quite enough!!" Katrina came storming into the office. "Thank the heavens that Stacy called me. I have been outside the office for the last few minutes, listening to this balderdash. Security has been called to escort you out of the building, Mr. Maynard. Someone else will be taking you place on this floor from now on."

"Security…Escorted…why?" Joey got a panicked look on his face. "This is none of Stacy's business. She had no right to call you…if anything, she should be getting escorted out too. She was in on it."

"That is exactly what she thought that you would say…" Katrina handed a piece of paper to Amelia. "Apparently, Stacy knew that he was going to try to drag her in on it, so she emailed me and filled out a statement with human resources early this morning, before the two of you arrived today. She said that she emailed you as well, but it is clear that you have not checked your computer yet today." She looked over at Amelia's desk, where her computer was still off.

"Stacy? Can you please come here?" Mia pleaded, tears burning her eyes. She looked over at Caspian, who was both confused and furious. He looked at Mia, seeing how hurt she was, and his heart broke as he finally figured out what had just happened. He wanted to go to her and hold her, but he was afraid to.

Stacy walked into the office, purposely bumping Joey as she walked over to her boss, and put her hand on her shoulder.

"I warned you, Joey. She is my friend, and I was not going to help you, nor was I willing to go down in flames as your accomplice." She turned to Caspian, and spoke to him, wanting to make certain he was listening. "Anything that he said about Amelia betraying you has been a lie. He has asked her out on several occasions, to which she was very clear that her answer was no. Amelia has been more than faithful to you, in every way possible. She loves you, and if you believed anything that he said, then you obviously don't love her nor do you trust her. He asked me out, under false pretenses. I thought that he wanted to get to know me, but it was all a ploy. He was trying to get me to...he was wanting me to aid him in his plan to put a wedge between you. I refused to help him, but when he got caught...and I knew he would...I knew he would try to take me down as well."

"I know that you would never do that to me, Stacy. Thank you for trying to help…but he did believe Joey, at least a part of him did." She looked at Katrina. "He doesn't believe that I am innocent of any of it. I would never hurt him, never ever." She walked over and sat down, putting her face in her hands. Her shoulders shook as she wept, and the band holding her crimson mane back broke, releasing the curly strands, which now were hanging like a curtain, hiding her from view.

"I am truly sorry if his shenanigans and scheming caused any discord in your relationship. Caspian, I assure you, Amelia had no part in why I asked you about your decision of whether to move here or not, if that is part of this. As I said, she has been a brighter, happier person since you came to town. Please don't blame her for that, or any of what this sick, sadistic idiot has said." She saw the state that Amelia was in, and knew that it would affect her work immensely. "You need to take her out of here. Go spend the rest of the day together, and work things out. I will cover her work."

Caspian felt horrible for all the accusations and hurt that she had just endured. He should have known better, but his fears got the best of him. A big part of him always thought that another guy would come along and sweep her off her feet, and he could do absolutely nothing to stop it from happening. He rolled over to her, and reached under her mound of curly hair until he found her hands. He leaned his head toward her ear, and whispered to her all the regrets and fears that he was feeling; his worst fear being that he would lose her forever. To him, it seemed inevitable, and he told her that he wouldn't blame her if she hated him for even considering her to be unfaithful and deceitful. His heart swelled as he felt her squeeze his fingers.

"I'm so sorry, honey. I promised that I wouldn't hurt or doubt you, and yet, I've broken that promise over the words of a stranger. I love you, and I'd die if I ever lost you." He swallowed hard. "Maybe, this was a sign…the push I needed to make a very important decision. Let's go, like your boss said. We have some talking to do." He knew that he needed to make things up to her; especially considering that he just shown her that he doubted her heart, even in the slightest way.

She got up off the chair, and went into the bathroom, intending to clean herself up. Stacy followed her in there, to assist in wrangling her hair back into a clip or hairband. Caspian sat and waited for Security to come and retrieve Joey. When they arrived, Caspian rolled over, and said something to Joey that made his eyes burn with hatred.

"You know, the sad thing is, if you had been honorable and worthy of her, I would have stepped aside, and allowed her to be with you, if that is what she truly wanted. I only care about her happiness. I needed to tell you that, because, now you have made certain that she will never want you, even if the two of us can't repair the damage you have caused. You tried to use lies and deception to break us up, and she doesn't tolerate that." He cracked a smile, looking behind him to see if Amelia was still out of sight. "And by the way, you only *assumed*, with me in this chair, that I would never be able to take her dancing or walking down the beach at sunset..." He locked the wheels on his chair, and put his feet on the floor, and lifted himself up. For a minute or two, before he heard the bathroom door begin to open, he was standing on his own. "Now you know..." He quickly sat back down before anyone else saw. "...you gotta love the miracles of modern medicine."

Before Joey had a chance to tell anyone what he had just witnessed, the security guards hauled him away, and Katrina, who was waiting outside the office, followed right behind.

Amelia had washed her face, and Stacy had used makeup to lessen the redness around her eyes. Stacy, also, tamed Amelia's mane, and fastened it back into a messy bun with a ton of bobby pins. It wasn't perfect, but it did the job. She retrieved Mia's purse, and keys, and handed them to Cass, angrily, and walked her out of the office, rubbing her back to calm her.

*You have really screwed up things this time, Cass.* He thought to himself, as he wheeled through the gaggle of chattering women, and entered the elevator with his crimson-haired girlfriend.

"You better fix this, mister, or you will have to answer to me. I cannot believe that you made her cry!! If your legs worked, I'd break them myself…jerk!" Stacy sniped as the door closed.

They made it to the car, and still, no words were spoken. He got in, and she took the chair, and heaved it into the trunk. As they exited the parking lot, he could tell that she was deep in thought as she drove.

# *~Twelve~*

After driving around for a while, Amelia and Caspian went to the park near her apartment building, and took a stroll. He saw a cluster of beautiful trees, and decided that that was where they could sit down and talk. She had barely said two words to him since they left her office. The guilt that weighed on his heart was only made heavier by the silence. *How could he have been so easily deceived by someone he knew nothing about?* It was, as if, he thought that the day had finally come that she would realize that she deserved a man who could do the things that he never could. It took great strength and determination for him to get to where he was now, and yet he had not shared it with her yet. He wanted to wait until the perfect moment to sweep her off her feet, and sharing his momentous news.

He locked the wheels on his chair, and pulled her toward him. Usually, she would automatically sit on his lap, but she just stood there. He squeezed her hand, lovingly, but she just pulled away, and crossed her arms over her chest, still looking down at the ground. He leaned against the back of his chair, and shoved his hands into his pockets.

"Please, talk to me, Mia. I want to fix this." He pleaded.

"There is nothing to fix, Caspian. I know how you feel, what you think of me. I am sorry that I am not the girl you thought I was." She was kicking at the grass with the toe of her shoe, and talking in a very solemn tone.

"What I think of you is that you have taken far too much pain and hurt from me, that you have come to expect *that* more than love and understanding. I don't know why I let that guy get into my head, Mia, and I am sorry that I made it seem as if I took what he said to be the truth. I am sorry that I didn't prove how much faith and trust I have in you."

"It doesn't matter, Caspian. I put myself in the situation by bringing you to my work. I thought that, if he saw you here with me, that he would finally get the picture, and back off. He stooped to a whole new level, and you fell right into his scheming, conniving trap. I should have known this was coming, but I didn't think he would stoop so low….and to try to drag Stacy down with him…." She began to pace.

"I should not have let him get inside my head, and manipulate me."

"Though, I agree with you, I think that this goes beyond what happened today. You have said to me, on countless occasions, that I deserved someone better than you. It wasn't *you* that was feeding on what he was saying, it was your fears. So many things have happened, and our relationship has taken so many twists and turns, it makes my head dizzy just thinking about it. I just worry that the next twist or turn could be the last."

"Not if I can help it...I will fight until the end for us, Mia. You have to know that."

"I do, and I think that that is the problem. Our relationship has never been easy. We have had to fight so hard for our relationship, and yet, one of us hurts the other, somehow. I don't like that you still have fears of me leaving you for another man. I have no desire to be with anyone else but you." She was chewing on her fingernails now, which meant that she was thinking hard of a solution.

"I don't like that you feel as though I am the best you can do. I also don't like that you always seem to make excuses for my blatant disregard for your feelings." He paused. "Seriously, though, we've been together since we were teenagers, Mia. Neither you, nor I have been with anyone else. How do you know that I am the one you are supposed to be with? If I thought that there was a possibility that someone else could love you better, deeper, or more fiercely than I do…"

"Okay…so, we both love each other deeply…we both have an overwhelming fear of losing the other… but neither of us even has ever had a minute desire to be with anyone else..." As she paced, Cass slipped his hands out of his pockets, both of which were curled into fists. She turned to him, her eyes locking onto his like two magnets.

"I think I know where this is leading..." With a very serious expression on his face, he reached for her hand, and she offered it to him without hesitation. He pulled her to him. She sat on his lap, and he used his thumb to sweep a strand of hair from her face. Tears were building in their eyes, and her bottom lip began to tremble.

"Are you…breaking up with me?" She choked on the words, as her biggest fear made itself known. "This wasn't the solution I was expecting…I don't want to…we have fought our way back from worse things than this…please…You have to know that this is not what I want. Is this the end?"

"Quite the opposite, my dear…I was hoping to do this a bit differently, with more flare and romance, but I think that…beneath these amazingly beautiful Cherry blossom trees, and in light of today's events…." The confusion on her face made his heart skip, and he looked down at her hand, and slipped something onto her palm.

"What is this? What's going on, Cass?" She lifted her closed hand, and slowly opened it, revealing a stunning ring, with a beautiful Sapphire, surrounded by diamonds.

"Amelia Catherine Landon…you deserve the very best…someone who will back you up without question. You deserve someone who will let you grow without borders, limitations, or hidden agendas. And, most importantly, someone to love you without end…and I don't think that it's possible for any man to *ever* love you more completely than I do. You would make me the happiest man alive if you would…" He removed the ring from her hand, and held it up, allowing the sunlight to catch the jewels, but she wasn't looking at the ring anymore. Her hands were shaking as they covered her mouth, trying not to interrupt him, but she couldn't hold it in any longer.

"Cass!! Are you serious?!" she blubbered.

"Marry me, Mia…" As he whispered the words to her, a breeze blew through the trees, and thousands of petals floated down from overhead, showering them like confetti. "As I said, this isn't how I had imagined this to go, but this seemed like as good a moment as any." He plucked flower petals from her hair, and then put his hand to the back of her neck, and pulled her in closer. "So, what's your answer?"

"Do you even have to ask? You know what I am going to say…" She sniffled, and smiled. Her right hand slid up his chest, over his shoulder, and her fingers entwined the dark ponytail at the back of his head.

"I need to hear you say it…out loud." There was an arousing growl in his voice. Their lips were so close, that she just had to sigh the word, and he tasted the sweet deliciousness of it.

"Yes…"

"I thought so." The corners of his lips curled up, and his dimples sunk deep, sending the smile into the depths of his smoky hazel eyes. With his free hand, he slipped the golden band onto her finger without looking away.

Both their hearts were racing, and neither of them loosened their grips, but reinforced them by locking on with their other hands. The perfect moment had finally come, and it was time to finally give in to their need for the most intimate connection. He took one last, shaky breathe, and pulled her to him, closing the gap.

The sky exploded above them, the ground trembled below them, and they were engulfed in flames. Her fingers curled in his hair, not willing to let go. He felt her chest heave against his, and he took in the sweet smell of her tender skin. He felt as though he had a lust for the blood that pulsated in her lips. He felt like a vampire, wanting to taste her. He had finally claimed what was rightfully his, and yet, he couldn't get enough of it. He slid his hand down her vibrating body, and braced her at the base of her spine, feeling her pulse against his palm, which was against her bare skin. He took in a deep breath through his nose, causing his nostrils to flare. A pleasurable growl rumbled in the back of his throat.

She didn't try to pull away, though she was gasping for air. Her fantasies of what it would be like were nothing compared to reality. Nothing she could have seen or read could have prepared her for the singular moment that their lips finally met. An instant spark ignited in her, and sent shockwaves of lightning to every cell in her body. She realized, in that instant, that 'Love' was simply just a word, and no amount of hearing it from another person would ever compare to feeling its meaning rush through her veins like hot lava.

They continued until their bodies could take no more, becoming weak from the strength they had exerted in efforts to clutch to one another.

With a combined effort to break the link, they simultaneously released, and fireworks exploded. They struggled to catch their breath, not allowing too much distance to come between them.

Amelia was startled to discover that her lips were on fire and throbbing from the blood that had filled them. They felt slightly fuller, and she could feel her pulse. Her cheeks were warmer as well. However, this was inconsequential, compared to what this encounter had done to her vision. Cass looked different, compared to before. As tired and weathered as he may have looked before, it was as if her kiss were the fountain of youth for him. His skin seemed smoother, his eyes were brighter, his smile wider, his dimples deeper; overall, he looked as though five years had disappeared.

Cass couldn't look away from her eyes. Just as she had seen a change in his appearance, he was captivated by the change in her eyes, which were dilated slightly. The gold flecks that just slightly appeared, were now brighter, and more vivid, glowing from under a curtain of long, thick lashes. There was a glow to her skin, almost dreamlike. He blinked a couple times, thinking his eyes had gone fuzzy, but nothing changed.

"It's not possible..." he panted.

"What..." She took in a gulp of oxygen.

"You are even more beautiful than before... It's surreal how much more stunning you are…" His hand brushed her cheek, and she became very warm.

"I am the same as I was before…" Her eyes took in every inch of his face, as if she were looking at him with new eyes. "You, on the other hand, look just as you did the first time I saw you. All that sadness, despair, regret, and hopelessness that lingered in your eyes…they are gone…I see only happiness, contentment, peace…and hope" She gently swept a strand of his russet hair from his temple, and tucked it in, neatly, with the rest.

"You are the most beautiful creature that God created, and now that I have stolen your first kiss, I honestly don't believe I will be able to restrain myself anymore."

"You can't steal something that belongs to you. I told you…that kiss was always yours for the taking." She ran her fingers along the edge of his lips. "Now, I get to kiss you whenever I want to…and there is absolutely nothing you can do to stop me." She didn't give him a chance to say anything, because she began to lay soft kisses, one after another, on his lips. He laughed, and attempted to kiss her back.

"Pace yourself, sweetheart…we have time." She grabbed her shoulders, and pushed her back. She growled at him, like he had just tried stealing a rawhide bone from a pit bull. "My Goodness…I've unleashed a monster…" She wriggled, laughing, until she decided to tickle him, which worked quite well. She released his grip on her, and she dove back at him at full force. Wrapping her arms around his neck, she kissed his lips with a desperation that surprised them both. Her kisses moved to his cheeks, along his jawline, and down onto his neck. He felt it useless to fight her, so he just enjoyed her openly public displays of affection. He even waved, happily, as people walked by, and stared. "I just proposed…Have a good day!!" Some people got the idea, and yelled their congratulations, while others gave them strange looks and picked up their pace to get away quicker.

When she had finished covering his face and neck with kisses, she leaned back, and smiled at him, like a child on Christmas morning.

"We are engaged…we are getting married…" She sighed, and then it hit her, as she looked at the ring. "Oh my God… We're Getting *MARRIED*!!!" She leapt up, and looked at him. "Who else knew you were going to propose?! Your sister…Henry…"

"No one, actually. I brought that ring from home. It was Grandmother's. She told me that if I ever found the right girl…I brought it, figuring that if I ever worked up the courage to ask, I would have it ready…" He tried to grab her, but she was dancing around, kicking up flower petals as she twirled around. "What do you say about us keeping this a secret until after Angie's wedding? She's the bride, and should be the center of attention on her big day, don't you think?"

"Of course…I would never want to rain on her parade or overshadow her on her special day. I have got to tell someone, though, or I am gonna bust!" They looked at one another and solved the problem, immediately.

"Stacy!" They said in unison, and she ran over to him, flinging her arms around him. She kissed him softly and tenderly on the lips, and then gave him a peck on the tip of his nose.

"I am never going to get tired of kissing you, you know that…Sweet man of mine. Let's head back to the office. This is too big of news to tell over the phone. This ring is your reprieve from getting your legs broken. Let me tell you, she may be small, but she is mighty…" She got up, and skipped as she rolled him to where the car was parked.

"You are absolutely adorable when you are like this…I will have to thank Joey when I see him…He was the reason that I finally got the courage to pop the question. I cannot risk losing you to anyone, even if the relationship is all in their head…"

"Good, you thank him, and then I will strangle him." When she said that, they both laughed.

Mia stuck her hands in her pockets, and strolled up to Stacy's desk, and leaned over.

"Hi."

"Goodness, Amelia…I thought you left. You were supposed to take the rest of the day off, on account of what happened."

"I know, but I wanted to drop in real quick and let you know I was okay." She stood up, and smiled.

"You could have told me that over the phone. What's really going on? Did you and the 'Wheeled Wonder' work things out?" She looked suspiciously over at Cass, who was lingering by the elevator.

"I don't know…you tell me!" She whipped her hand out, and stuck the ring right in front of her. At first, it startled Stacy, but then she saw the glitter and shine and slowly looked up at her boss. "Shut up….SHUT UP!!!! Seriously!?! Oh my goodness." She took her hand in hers and looked at the ring thoroughly. "Is that a real Sapphire...real diamonds?" Amelia nodded in response. "I guess that means that I can't snap him like a twig now...that's alright. It looks like he wouldn't snap very easy, anyhow." She raced over to Caspian, and hugged him, congratulated him and gave him a kiss on the cheek. Amelia was trapped by a crowd of women, wanting to see her ring.

"I guess you decided that you had courted her long enough, huh?" She nudged him with her elbow, watching Amelia being handed off to one group after another. "She looks different...something has changed in her. I mean, I know that she is newly engaged and all, but there is just something really different. She's glowing...Is she pregnant?" She looked down at him.

"Nope...not pregnant...not until *after* we are married." He smiled.

"I would hope not. She has a career. She can't afford to take the time off of work for maternity leave." Katrina piped in, having walked up behind them at the very end of their conversation. "Besides, it would be hard to get pregnant when you live a thousand plus miles away, and being that you are not moving here, and she is not leaving here...we really have nothing to worry about, now, do we?" She paused for a moment, and then looked down at Caspian. "Didn't I send you two out of here after that debacle earlier? What are you doing back here?"

"Cass proposed!" Amelia squealed as she approached, finally having broken free from the mob of women. She held out her hand to show her boss the ring. Katrina examined it, thoroughly.

"Hmm…perfect clarity, exquisite cut, twenty-four carat gold band…it looks old, and new at the same time…Family heirloom, I imagine…worth more than a year's salary, at least…" She looked up at Amelia, a smile on her face. "It's beautiful, honey. Congratulations to you both." She walked around Caspian and Stacy, and gave Amelia a hug.

"Thank you, Katrina."

"So, have you set a date yet?"

"No, not yet, but when we do, you are most definitely invited…both of you." She looked from Katrina to Stacy, and then back again.

"We'd better be…" She winked, and set off again, after she hugged Amelia again. "Now get out of here, and celebrate. Go!" She pointed to the elevators.

*****

After leaving the office, Amelia and Caspian went to dinner, and then spent time at the Navy Pier. They got back to the apartment right before sundown, and settled in for the night. Amelia made tea for them both and they adjourned to the bedroom.

They cuddled up on the bed, Amelia in a tank top, and cotton shorts, and Caspian in flannel sleeping pants. She had helped him up onto the bed, before climbing in herself, and nuzzling up next to him. Though the day had come to a close on a positive note, Amelia could tell that something was on Caspian's mind.

"A penny for your thoughts…"

"I was just thinking…about some things that were said earlier."

"Like what, for instance?" She looked up at him.

"Stacy asked if you were pregnant…she said you were glowing." He shot her a half smile.

"If I am, it's by immaculate conception. You're smooth, but even you aren't *that* smooth. I am pretty sure I am still a virgin. Sometimes, that girl makes me wonder…" She giggled, running her fingers through Caspian's hair. "I assume you told her that I wasn't pregnant, just really happy."

"Yeah, I told her that. But, it got me thinking…You do want children, right? I mean, eventually…after we are married, you wanna have babies?"

"Of course, Caspian. I want to have your babies…cute little mini-Cass's running around…"

"And little ginger-headed daddy's girls…" He spun a strand of her hair around his finger.

"Can you just imagine that house being filled with children again? Our kids, and Evangeline's…chasing Henry and the rest of them around the halls…"

"That would be wonderful." His smile faded, and he tuned his head to look at his fiancé. "I would love nothing more than to see you glowingly beautiful, and pregnant with a child that we created together, but I am worried. What if I can't give you that?"

"What do you mean? Why wouldn't you be able to?"

"I am concerned that, after my accident, it did more damage to me than just my spine. What if I can't…you know…"

"Don't be silly. Why wouldn't you be able to? It was your spine that was injured, not your…man zone." She awkwardly swirled her fingers in the direction of his groin area.

"I'm just worried that I won't be able to…that something is wrong down there."

"Well, we could go see a doctor about that. Then, we would know for certain…"

"My question is this, though…What if the doctors say that I'm sterile?"

"If you can't give me children, biologically, there is always adoption. There are plenty of children out there, who need good homes. Even if you *can* give me babies, we may still adopt. I was an only child, and always wanted a big family. Either way it goes, we will have children to love. Okay?"

"You're really okay with that?"

"Why wouldn't I be?" She propped herself up on her elbow. "Are you worried that I would resent you for not being able to get me pregnant? If that's what you think, you're sadly mistaken. There are plenty of men out there, who aren't able to father children, biologically. It's a sad fact, but that has nothing to do with your accident. It has to do with biology."

"I just feel like, if I can't give you that one thing, I'm not much of a man."

"Now, you know how I feel about you talking nonsense like that. You're the man I want to grow old with. The ability to give me children doesn't define you as a man. Neither does your ability to walk. I fell in love with your heart, and your mind, and your personality. You're kind-hearted and smart…gentle, funny, loving…the list goes on, and none of it has to do with your physical abilities or disabilities."

"You're amazing, you know that? No matter how down I get, you always know just what to say to make me feel better. How did I get so lucky?"

"Luck had nothing to do with it. Now, is there anything else that you are worried about? If not, I would like to enjoy our first night of being engaged." She laid her head down on his chest, and listened to his heart beat against her ear.

"Are you all packed for Boston? Angie told me to remind you not to forget your dress." He began to yawn, and he stretched his arms over his head, before wrapping them around Amelia once more.

"I'm all packed and ready to go. The dress is in the garment bag in the living room, and the plane tickets are pinned to it, so I am certain to grab it. I get off work at three o'clock, and will get home around three-thirty. The car will be here at four-thirty to pick us up, to take us to the airport. We should arrive in Boston around seven o'clock, and Henry will be there to pick us up. We are going straight to the church for the rehearsal, and then the rehearsal dinner is at the house." She pretty much had Friday all planned out. Rather proud of herself, she smiled and looked up at him, figuring that he would look overwhelmed.

He was fast asleep. She stared at him for a few minutes, and debated about waking him. He looked so comfortable, and she was in awe of how peaceful he looked. She figured that it would not hurt anything to just let him sleep, as that was all they were doing, and, technically they had done it before, years ago, when she had fallen asleep after reconciling from a fight. Both of them had their religious convictions about pre-marital no-no's, and though it seemed wrong to "sleep together" before they were married, that was a lot different than this. Both of them were dressed, and all they were doing was sleeping, and cuddling, nothing more. She reached over, shut off the lamp, and curled back next to him, and fell asleep to the lullaby of his breathing and heartbeat.

*****

The morning came, and her alarm buzzed, alerting her that she needed to get ready for work. The buzzing had no effect on Cass, except that he snored slightly and turned his head away. Not wanting to wake him, she slid out of bed, and quietly crept around in the dark to get ready. The timer on the coffee pot had been set, so she had a pot of coffee waiting for her when she exited the room. She left him a note on the fridge, and softly closed the door behind her.

The morning at work was quite uneventful. She answered inquiries, looked over her emails, returned calls, and dictated memos to Stacy, to send out to people about her absence and what was expected of them upon her return on Tuesday morning. It was around noon, when Joey used to stop in to get the lunch orders, when she became very anxious. She stepped out of her office, and was talking to Stacy when the elevator dinged and the doors opened. Both women tensed up, momentarily, as they saw an older, dark-skinned gentleman, wearing the same uniform as Joey, step through the opening. They looked at each other, and sighed. As bad as she felt that Joey was no longer working the floor, she was relieved that Katrina had followed through with what she had said about having him removed from lunch duty on their floor.

"Good afternoon, ladies. I'm Mike. I'm the new lunch guy. Which one of you is Ms. Landon?" He smiled, and Mia raised her hand. He handed her an envelope, and then asked for their lunch orders.

"What's this?" She took the envelope, flipping it over, looking for a name or something on it.

"I don't know, Ma'am. I was just asked to give it to you by one of the other workers." He said, politely, and she could tell that he was being sincere. She looked at Stacy, then back at Mike.

"It's not going to explode or anything, is it?" She asked, nervously.

"I didn't hear it ticking and it seems too thin to be a bomb. And, the security guys in the lobby put it through a machine, so I am pretty sure it is safe of any poisonous substance. Why?"

"Just curious…the last sandwich guy that worked here isn't too fond of me right now. I had him transferred off this floor…personal reasons."

"I don't know anything about that. I was just asked to give you the envelope. Now, what can I get you ladies for lunch?" He pulled out his order pad, and looked from Stacy to Amelia. They gave him their orders, and then both of them went into her office.

"Let me open it…" Stacy took the envelope from Amelia, and used the letter opener to make a slit in the paper along the side. She shook it over the garbage can, covering her nose and mouth, and signaling

Amelia to do the same. All that came out of the envelope was a piece of paper. Stacy took a tissue, and picked it up out of the garbage, unfolded it, and began to read it aloud.

Amelia,

I am writing this letter to you to apologize for my behavior. I had no right to do what I did, and to act as I had. Please extend my apologies to your boyfriend. Upon reflection, I realize that your personal life is neither my concern, nor my business. I stepped over the line, causing a hostile work environment for you and others at the Fashionista. I hope that, one day, you can find it in your heart to forgive me. I, honestly, didn't intend on causing you or your guest any ill will. I tend to come on rather strong when I want something, but I went too far. Again, I apologize, and I do hope that you have a good and happy life.

Joey Maynard

They looked at each other, and then both read the letter a couple more times. They could not believe that he had written such a formal letter of apology. Amelia came to the conclusion that, in order to keep his job, he was told to write an apology. It was very carefully worded, and sounded absolutely nothing like him.

"Honestly, I don't believe that he would apologize for what he did. He took great pleasure in causing turmoil in your relationship. He had one goal in mind, and that was for you to choose him over Caspian. You would think that being a nice guy would have been enough, but not for Joey…He would much rather throw a tantrum, kick up dust, and hope that it falls in his favor." Stacy crumpled the paper and dropped it into the waste paper basket.

"I would love to believe that he meant 'no ill will,' but actions speak much louder than words. He is a good looking guy, but his personality is ugly."

"It's a good thing that Caspian had more faith and trust in you than to believe his bull."

"That's the thing, Stacy…Had you and Katrina not vouched for me, I think that Cass's insecurities would have gotten the best of him, and I would have lost him." Amelia sat down at her desk. "He is so afraid that I am going to choose to be with someone else, that he would believe anyone if they said that I was sneaking around. He is so hung up on his disability, and it making him seem like less than a man…He's always been like this. It's been a constant battle inside him. I think the worse part of it is that he wasn't always in that chair. He lived the first eleven years of his life like any other little boy…running, playing, walking…but, that accident took away his independence, and he had to rely on others to do things for him that he feels that he should be able to do himself."

"Didn't you tell me that he was going through surgeries to change that?" Stacy leaned on the edge of the desk.

"Yes, and he was so close to doing so. Then, Gran passed away, and he gave up hope. Don't get me wrong, Stacy, I love him completely as he is. I fell in love with him, despite the chair, but sometimes... No matter what I say to him to reassure him that his disability has no influence on my feelings for him, he tries to come up with excuses of why I would be better off with someone else. Isn't that weird? He doesn't want to lose me, yet he is constantly trying to convince me to leave him."

"Maybe he is just having trouble with the fact that you haven't left…that you have stuck by him, no matter how good his reasoning has been for you to leave. Has he lost a lot of people in his life? Have people left him?"

"His mom died, during his sister's birth, same as mine. Both of our fathers died in the military. Gran passed away. That's all I can think of. But, they didn't leave by choice…they all passed away. He's trying to *push* me away."

"Eventually, he will realize that his efforts to push you away have only made you cling tighter to him." Amelia gave Stacy a strange look, and smiled. "Why are you looking at me like that?"

"Stacy, among your many talents, I never realized that you were a therapist, too."

"I'm not a therapist...I'm an assistant."

"Well, then maybe you should reconsider your occupation...You would make one heck of a therapist. Do I have to pay you more money now? Do you charge by the hour?" She laughed, recalling their whole conversation. Stacy thought about it too, and started laughing as well. She looked at her watch, and stood up straight.

"Well, time's up. I'll bill you!" She walked over, hugged Amelia, and stepped back toward the door. "You need to talk to him about what we talked about. Tell him how you feel, not just what you think he needs to hear. You'll feel better when you do, and he'll thank you for it." She opened the door, winked, and closed the door behind her.

*****

Cass rolled over as the sun came in through the window. He had slept the best he had slept in a long time. He buried his face in the pillows, and took in a deep breath. Even without her there, physically, her intoxicating scent lingered as if she were right there next to him. He sat up in bed, and hung his legs over the edge. Just like every other day that she had left to go to work, leaving him alone, he took the chance to strengthen his legs and back by using them. Fully determined to be able to dance with her on their wedding day, he needed to build endurance. His muscles were not used to being used on a regular basis, so they cramped up in defiance. He slid off the edge of the bed, and slowly put weight on his feet.

The doctor said that he needed to teach himself to walk again, and at home, he could do so freely. He had mastered the stairs and used crutches for balance. He didn't have to worry about being caught, because everyone back home knew. Caspian has laid out the whole plan to them to surprise Mia, and they all agreed to go along with it. Henry pushed him hardest to be fully mobile.

He spent his days in the apartment walking, using his chair for support. And knowing when Mia was due home helped him keep up the charade. He hated lying to her about it, but he knew that it would pay off in the long run. He, however, did not lie about his concern of not being able to give her children. That had always been a concern of his. And now that they were officially engaged, he needed to know for sure.

After doing his routine morning sit-ups and push-ups, he made his way to the bathroom, and got in the shower. He knew that Amelia wanted him to live there with her, as she had gotten a handicapped accessible apartment, which included a shower with handles and a shower bench. She had loved him so much, that she was living in an apartment that would make life easier for him. He turned the faucet on, and stood there, allowing the water to engulf him. He must have stood there for fifteen minutes at least, unassisted, which was an accomplishment for him. He finished washing up, grabbed a towel and wrapped it around his waist, then went to the sink to shave. When he was done, he walked back into the room to get dressed. He brushed through his hair with his fingers as he headed over to her side of the bed, and picked up the phone receiver. When he had made his phone call, he hung up the phone, and smiled. The door buzzer went off, and he nearly fell on the floor out of surprise. He hopped into his chair, and sped to the door, looking in the monitor. His blood began to boil, as a familiar face was on the screen. He pressed the button, to speak through the intercom.

"What do you want?" He growled.

"I came to apologize for yesterday."

"Okay…so apologize."

"Can I come up?"

"Amelia isn't here. She's at work. Knowing that, do you still feel the need to apologize?"

"Yes, now can you please buzz me in?"

"No. Just say what you need to say, and be on your way."

"Dude, you know the lengths I can go to get what I want…do you really think it wise to piss me off right now?" There was contempt in his eyes. "Or did you forget that you have been lying to Amelia? What would stop me from going to the magazine and telling her that you can walk after all, and that you have been playing on her sympathies all along?"

"Well, for one, the security guards that escorted you out can prevent you from talking to her…"

"Not once she leaves the building…I will wait outside the building until she goes to her car, and tell her then."

"She wouldn't believe you anyway. She's known me for years. And after your theatrics yesterday, I wouldn't be surprised if she sprayed you with pepper spray before you could even get two words out."

"And yet, there is a hint of doubt in your voice. All you have to do is let me in, so we can talk. Or are you too scared to hear what I have to say?"

"Ha! I am not afraid of you or anything you have to say. I just don't want you coming into our home." His temper was beginning to get the best of him.

"It isn't your home, Caspian! It's hers!! And I have been there, sat on her couch, drank from her coffee mug…you know the one, with the little daisies on the handle. I have laid on her big queen sized bed, with the pillow top and the large goose down comforter." There was an evil look in Joey's eyes, and it sent a spark of fear to his heart. He had been in Mia's apartment. This situation was far worse than he had imagined. He was not just a jilted sandwich guy…he was a stalker. Amelia was in danger. Had he snuck into the apartment when she was sleeping?

"Stay away from her, do you hear me? If you go anywhere near her, so help me God, you will be sorry!"

"I will, but you have to let me come up there, so we can talk. If you don't, I will go straight to the paper and wait by her car. She should be leaving work soon. You guys are going to the airport to attend your sister's wedding, right? Evangeline? She would be ever so sad if her best friend didn't attend her wedding. She is the Maid-of-Honor, after all."

"Who are you?!"

"It's just Joey, the sandwich guy...harmless Joey, who is truly sorry for his bad behavior." He said, innocently. But as quickly as he has softened his face, his appearance became dark, and sinister. "Now, buzz...me...in."

As if he had no control over his actions, he pressed the button, and Joey was through the door with a flash. Caspian raced to the phone, and picked up the receiver. The phone was dead. He went to the bedroom, and grabbed his cell phone. "No Service" came up on the screen. He raced to the living room, and sat, like a sitting duck. Though he was able to walk and move on his own, he was not strong enough, physically, to overpower Joey if he decided to attack him, physically.

Preparing himself for pounding at the door, he braced himself, and locked the wheels on his chair. What he wasn't prepared for, was to hear a key in the door, and the door to slowly creak open. Joey stood in the doorway, his hands in his pockets, and a purely evil look in his eyes.

Caspian's heart pounded hard against his ribcage. Though he wasn't afraid of Joey, he was afraid of what his motives were, what he was capable of.

Joey stepped over the threshold, closed and locked the door behind him, not taking his eyes off of Caspian. When he had locked the last lock with a loud click, he walked over and bent down so they were eye-to-eye.

"Let's have a talk, Walking Man. Why don't you drop the act, and get rid of the chair? C'mon, get up and have a seat over here, like a real man." He stepped back and allowed Cass to move out of the wheelchair, before kicking it across the room. Caspian backed toward the couch and fell backward onto its cushions. Joey sat on a chair in close proximity to where he had landed, and looked at him, scanning his face.

"You are up here now. What on earth would you want to talk about?"

"Amelia, of course…she is a common interest between us. She is the only thing that we have in common."

"What is there to talk about? She and I are together. You tried to break us up, but we are stronger than ever. If anything, I should thank you." Cass gave a sly smile, knowing that he had the upper hand.

"Thank me…for what? Trying to take what is mine from someone who doesn't deserve her? If it hadn't been for those two meddling wenches…I would have accomplished it. You actually believed that she was cheating on you, and that is rather sad. Amelia is the purest, sweetest, gentlest woman to walk the earth. She would never be unfaithful. She doesn't have the capacity to be dishonest. The fact that you thought, even for a second, that she had gone behind your back just proves that you are unworthy of her."

"You know what, Joey...you are right! I let you get in my head, and made me doubt her, and that makes me a horrible person, unworthy of her."

"Don't patronize me!"

"I'm not. I am agreeing with you. I don't deserve her. She is too good of a person, too pure, too perfect...but, just as I don't deserve her, neither do you. You came into her office, fully intending on hurting her."

"I would never want to hurt her. I love her."

"If you loved her, then you would not try and break her heart by taking away her happiness."

"I DO LOVE HER!" He screamed, pulling a pistol from his pocket, and putting it to Cass's temple. "I needed to free her from you. You have a hold on her, even from a thousand miles away. She left Boston to start a new life, and you keep her from being free. She's like a bird, but you keep her caged up. She wanted you to move here to be with her, and you refuse. If you loved her, you would have given up everything to be with her.  You would have forsaken everyone and everything standing in your way.  Instead, you keep her caged up, forcing her to live a half-life."

"Alright, Joey, calm down.  You don't want to shoot me.  I understand what you are saying.  I am listening to you.  Put the gun away, and let's talk like real men.  That's what you wanted, right?  To come here and talk, man-to-man…but we can't do that with you pointing a gun at me."  He looked him straight in the eye, and put his hands up in front of him, trying to calm him.

"No, you are mocking me.  You are sitting there, acting like you understand and agree, but you are just trying to get in my head, so I let my guard down.  Sorry, buddy, but that isn't going to happen.  I came here with one purpose…"

"And what purpose was that?"

"…for you to let her go.  Go back to Boston, and let her live her life, here in Chicago…with me.  I will take care of her.  I love her.  I can protect her, and cherish her.  I can give her everything she could ever want.  I am good looking, young, strong, and virile…I can give her the children she wants, the life she wants.  She is from Chicago, originally.  Your grandmother stole her away, and now she has returned to her true home.  Why can't you just let her go and find yourself someone back in

Massachusetts?" He seemed to be pleading with Caspian, grasping at straws, trying to break him down.

"I can't do that, Joey. You know that. Just as you love her too much to let her go, I love her ten times more, and I refuse to live my life without her."

"I can remedy that for you. If I shoot you, right here, right now…you won't have to live your life without her, because you will cease to live."

"If that is what you feel you need to do, do it. But, before you do, think about the consequences. If you kill me, you will go to prison for first-degree murder. All the evidence will point to you. You made yourself look guilty when you acted as you did at the magazine. The Apartments have surveillance cameras all over the place, and they have you on camera coming here. There won't need to be a trial, because there will be no other suspects. Neither Amelia, nor I have any enemies. If you kill me, they will lock you away, and you will never see Amelia again."

"I covered my bases. I sent Amelia a very nice letter, apologizing to her, and wishing the two of you a long and happy life. Why would someone do that, and then kill the person that they were apologizing to, hmm?"

"That letter is inconsequential. Plenty of people think that saying they are sorry is a 'get-out-of-jail-free card,' but that is not the way that they law will see it. They will look at all the evidence, and it will point to you, and then we both lose her…forever. You want her to be happy, but you will be taking away the only happiness that she has ever known. The difference between the two of us is that we both love her, but she doesn't love *you* back."

"She'll learn to love me. She'll realize that I did this for us, and she will love me for it, because I set her free."

"All you will end up doing is taking her from one cage, and putting her into another. She will live in fear of you for the rest of her life. Do you really want that…for her to be afraid of you?"

"No…no. I want her to love me. I deserve to be with her, not you. You lie to her. You don't need that damn chair, you probably never have. She is only with you because she feels sorry for you. I would never lie to her like that."

"I don't need the chair now, but I lived my life in that chair. I had an accident when I was a kid, and I couldn't walk. That was my cage, and she freed me from it. She encouraged me to see doctors and surgeons, who specialize in spinal cord injuries. That is why I can stand, and walk. She gave me the courage to do it. She loved me enough to make me want to be the man she deserved, the man whom could dance with her, and to walk down the beach with her…"

"Okay, so if that is the case, why not just ditch the chair and show her what miracles her love has done? Instead, you continue to lie to her. You deceive her into believing that you are still bound to that chair. If she knows that you went through surgery to repair your spine, then she knows that you are lying to her."

"There were five surgeries that I had to go through. I only went through four of them before she came to Chicago. She doesn't know that I had the fifth surgery."

"Do you think that she is stupid? If you went through the first four, she would know that you went through the last one as well." He looked at him, as if he was brainless.

"Something happened and I chose to not finish the procedures. Amelia moved here, we reconciled and I decided that I would do it for her. I planned on surprising her this weekend, at the wedding."

"You reconciled? As in, you got back together, after she had moved to Chicago? Why the hell didn't you just let her go? She was free, and you put her back in the cage." Joey's hand began to shake, as she pressed the muzzle of the gun harder into Cass's head.

"She's not a bird, or a dog, Joey. She's a human being. I have never forced her to stay with me. Quite honestly, I'm surprised that she hasn't found someone else she wanted to be with. I would have let her go, if I knew that that is what she wanted. I told you that before the security guards hauled you off yesterday. If she wanted to be with you, truly wanted you, I would have said goodbye, and would be back in Boston right now. But, by doing what you did, spouting lies about her, and trying to hurt her, you only pushed her away."

"I wasn't lying! She smiles at me every day. She is always happy to see me, and cheers up whenever I am around. We talk, and flirt, and joke. She hugs me, and touches my arm or hand….She wants to be with me. She is just too good of a person to break your heart."

"She smiles, and hugs, and touches you because she is a good person, a friendly person. She is a physical contact type of person. She hugs, and touches, and smiles at everyone because she likes to make other people feel important. If that is all it took to make people believe that she was in love with them, she would be in love with every single person she has ever met, and carried on a conversation with…the doorman, the guy at the grocery store, and the valet driver at the airport. If that was all it took to show that she was in love with someone, she's also in love with Stacy, Katrina, my sister…Do you understand what I am saying, Joey?"

"It's different with me!! She's different with me!" He hissed through his teeth, tears running down his cheeks. "She will be mine…with or without your cooperation." He took a deep breath, and wiped the tears from his face with his shirt sleeve. Suddenly, he was smiling again. "You were right, what you said earlier. I don't want to kill you. You are a good guy, and you gave Amelia the love she deserved, but you don't deserve her love in return. You had your time with her, but that is over now. I'll promise you that I could never hurt her. I would never bring harm to her, in any way, but you have to leave. Go back to Boston. If you leave now, then everything will be fine. She may be sad at first, but I will be here to dry her tears and heal her heart. So, what is your decision? Are you going to leave, and release her heart for her to love me, or are you going to fight me, and make me do something that I don't want to do? It's your choice, but you need to make it quickly." Joey, pulled the gun away long enough to cock the gun, then he placed it back to his temple, and began to put pressure on the trigger.

# *~Thirteen~*

"Amelia, I just called your apartment, like you asked…it is still coming up busy." Stacy said, concern in her voice.

"I don't understand it. I have been trying to call him for the last hour. I even tried his cell phone, and that goes straight to voicemail. Something's not right. We talk everyday around lunchtime." She got out of her chair, slamming her finger down on the speaker button, disconnecting the call.

"You don't think that Joey…"

"No, it couldn't be…he doesn't know where I live. And even if he knew what apartment building I lived in, he wouldn't know which apartment it was, right? I mean, you either need a key card, or you need to be buzzed in by a resident."

"I wouldn't put it past him to find a way around that…" Stacy whined.

"I don't think he is that smart, to be honest." Katrina sighed, trying to convince herself. "How good is security in your building, Mia? Do they have cameras on every floor, by the elevators and such?"

"Yes, and there is no way to dodge them. They are motion activated. As soon as the elevator door opens, the camera gets the whole elevator opening." She crossed her arms over her chest.

"I'm calling the Police. Stacy, get ahold of The Boulevard. Ask them to check their cameras for anyone fitting Joey's description."

"If he knows where I live, what else does he know? How long has he been following me? Is he a violent person?" Mia began to shake, uncontrollably. Her fear was not only for herself, but for Caspian. In that chair, he could easily be overpowered. If Joey was a violent person, what would he do to Caspian? The apartment was fourteen floors up, and the railing on the balcony wasn't that tall. Her hands shot to her face, as she imagined what could happen.

When both of the other women got off the phone, they rushed over to Mia, who looked as though she was about to pass out. She had gotten incredibly pale, and was shaking more than before.

"Sit, Mia. You need to breathe. The police have been contacted, and Stacy got ahold of the apartments. What did they say?"

"You don't want to know…it is not good news."

"Oh my God, no…."

"Don't worry, sweetie. The cops are going there as we speak." Katrina tried to calm Mia, but she just got more upset.

"No! We don't know how Joey will react to the police. He could hurt Caspian. Oh God…he's defenseless. I have to go home. Joey wants me…If I go, maybe he will let Cass go."

"Or, maybe he is expecting you to come to Caspian's rescue, and so he is waiting, so he can hurt him in front of you. We don't know what he is capable of, Mia. Cass loves you. He would never want you to put yourself in danger's way for him. The farther you are from that psycho, the better." Katrina grabbed Amelia's arm.

"I cannot stand here, idly, and allow Cass to get hurt. I refuse to lose the only man I have ever loved. I would rather throw myself at Joey's mercies, rather than let him harm one hair on Cass's head. Joey wants me. If I go to him, maybe he will stop whatever he is doing."

"We could be wrong about this whole thing. He could just be there talking to him. Caspian might not be in any danger at all. Caspian seems as though he could talk Joey down, but if you go there, it could start

something and someone could get hurt." Stacy grabbed her other arm.

"Please…I am begging you. Just let me go there. I won't go in,

but I need to be there. Please…" She was sobbing as she begged them.

"Fine, I will go with you. But, we are not going into the building

until the police have Mr. Maynard in custody. Is that understood?"

Katrina grabbed Mia's face, and made her look her in the eye.

"Fine. I understand. Can we please go now?" Mia turned and

grabbed her purse, and car keys. Katrina grabbed the keys from her and led

the way. Stacy gave Mia a strong hug.

"He'll be fine. Just you wait…he'll be just fine and in no danger at

all."

"Oh, Stacy, I really hope you are right." She hugged her back, and

then raced out the door, and got into the elevator, where Katrina was

already waiting.

*****

Officer Cooper and his partner, Officer Blake were the first ones

on the scene. The building's security staff had been alerted that the Police

were on their way, so they were waiting at the door to let them in.

"Ms. Landon's apartment is 1412. Take those elevators to the fourteenth floor, straight down, sixth door on the right." The security guard pointed to the elevator. Soon, two more units were there. One set went up to the floor, positioning themselves by the elevators. The other duo, stayed on the ground floor, and prevented people from using them until the situation was under control.

Officer Cooper signaled his partner to stand out of sight, and he knocked on the door.

Cass closed his eyes shut, thinking that the banging was from the gun. It took him a moment to realize that there was someone at the door. Joey looked at him, checked his hands, making sure that he didn't have some kind of communication device he hadn't disabled. When he couldn't find anything to suggest that Caspian had called or signaled for help, he put his finger to his mouth, and whispered that he would kill whoever was at the door if he didn't keep quiet. He went to the door, and looked through the spyhole, then back at Caspian.

"Who is it?" He yelled through the door.

"Officer Cooper, Chicago Police Department...I am responding to a disturbance that was reported through 911. Please open the door."

"I'm afraid that you have the wrong apartment, sir."

"The caller said it was apartment 1412, sir...which is this apartment. Open the door."

"The caller must have been mistaken. Nothing wrong here, Officer. I am home alone."

"Open the door, sir. We have to verify that there is nothing going on."

"I'm afraid that I cannot do that, Officer. You see, I'm naked."

"I don't care. Let me do my job. Open the door, now, or I will have no choice but to come in, forcibly. If you say that there is no disturbance, than let me in, so that I can verify that. By not cooperating, you are interfering in a police investigation. Now, I say this one last time...Open the door, and let me and my associate enter, or we will come in by force."

"Do you have a warrant, officer? You cannot search my apartment unless you have a warrant to do so."

"I have something better than a warrant. I have the verbal consent of the building superintendent and the owner of this specific apartment to enter. I suggest you stand back and cover yourself up, because we are coming in." The Officer pulled his gun from his holster and pointed it at the lock.  In a moment of pure desperation, Joey yelled something he would soon regret.

"If you come in, I will put a bullet in the temple of my friend here. Now, I doubt you want a dead hostage on your hands, so I would suggest you back away from the door and put your guns away."

"He has a weapon, and a hostage."  Officer Cooper whispered to his partner.  "Radio the other officers, we need more backup."  With that, Officer Blake stepped about twenty feet further away, and called it in.

Out on the ground, Mia and Katrina stood behind the yellow tape, near one of the police cars.  Over the radio, she heard the words that she feared.

"Suspect is armed and dangerous, and has a hostage.  Requesting immediate backup.  I repeat, suspect is armed and dangerous, and has a hostage, requesting immediate backup."

"Oh no…Katrina…They have to do something."  She cried.  She turned, and tried to get the attention of the officer ten feet away.  "Sir! Officer!"

"Did you not hear that, lady?  We have a hostage situation.  Quiet down…"

"Please officer!! I need to talk to you!" She pleaded, putting her hands down on the hood of the police car.

"Hey! Like I told you, be quiet! Sheesh. And get your damn hands off my car!" He charged at her, putting his hand on his holster, and Mia jumped back out of fear.

"Listen up, Officer! This lady is the owner of the apartment where your hostage situation is taking place. Her fiancé is the hostage, and your attitude is not helping her at all. I am the editor-in-chief of the Fashionista, and I have my connections with every paper in this town. I would hate to report this to them, and have them print a story in tomorrow's paper about police brutality toward innocent victims!"

"My God, Miss… I am terribly sorry. I didn't know. As you can tell, the situation is pretty tense." He lifted the tape, allowing Amelia to join him, and sit in his car.

"My fiancé is in a wheelchair…his name is Caspian Wallingford. The guy holding him hostage is Joey Maynard. He's been harassing my fiancé and I and I believe he has been stalking me. Please help my fiancé…please. Let me talk to Joey. I won't be in any danger…I don't even have to enter the building"

He got on is radio, and reported back. "10-4. we have radioed for backup. Listen, we have the hostage's fiancé down here. The suspect's name is Joey Maynard. What is the status of the hostage?"

Officer Blake walked over to his partner, and whispered in his ear. Officer Cooper nodded, and then lifted his gun.

"Listen, Joey…We know that you don't want to hurt anyone. But, in order for us to help you, you need to do something for us…we need to talk to the gentleman that you are holding hostage."

"Why do you need to talk to him? He's just fine and dandy. And how do you know my name?"

"We have a very worried fiancé outside. We just want to calm her. Please, let us talk to him."

"Fiancé?" He looked at Caspian, anger in his eyes. "And when were you going to tell me that you were marrying her? I ought to shoot you right now!" He stepped toward Caspian, gun drawn.

"No, Joey…you don't want to do that." The officer yelled. A voice came over the radio, and he spoke again. "Joey, Someone wants to talk to you…go to the intercom." That caught his attention, and he looked toward the video screen.

"Who would want to talk to me?" He stepped closer, his gun still pointed at Caspian. He motioned for him to come over. Caspian slowly moved toward his wheelchair, and sat down, wheeling himself over a few feet from the door. A voice that sounded like angels came over the speaker.

"Joey…Joey, are you there?"

"Amelia…oh my god, it's you."

"Joey, listen to me very carefully." He nodded. "I don't want either of you to get hurt. Things have gotten way out of hand. You don't want to hurt anyone, do you?" He rubbed his head, and began to cry.

"No, baby…I just want us to be together. I want it to be you and I. I almost convinced your *fiancé* to go home, and let you free…but then the police came…"

"I know, Joey. It'll be okay though. All you have to do is just let the nice police officers in, and let them get Caspian. I will have them drive him straight to the airport, and make sure he gets on a plane."

"What about you? As soon as I let them in, I will lose you. They will take me to jail, and I will lose you forever. You will go with him to Boston. I can't let that happen."

"I won't go with him. I swear on my brother's grave, I will stay right here in Chicago and wait for you to get out."

"I don't believe you!"

"Joey, I swore on my brother's grave. That has to mean something, right?"

"Yeah, I suppose it does..." he wiped the tears away, and smiled. "It means a lot actually. But you need to tell your fake fiancé here." He pulled Caspian's chair over to the monitor, and positioned it so that he could see her face, and she could see his.

"Cass? Are you okay?" Mia tried to remain cold and distant, though she was screaming inside.

"I'm fine."

"I need you to go back to Boston. Go home, and find another girl. It's been fun, but Joey needs me." Her right eye began to twitch slightly.

"But, Mia, I love you. We were going to get married, and have little babies. You told me that I was the only one you wanted to be with. You promised to never leave me." He began to cry, and it was so convincing that it affected Mia's ability to hold back tears.

"I know, Cass...But I lied to you. I didn't realize until I received Joey's letter of apology, that he was truly the one who I wanted to be with." She felt her heart breaking. She was lying to the only man she loved, telling him that she had lied about loving him. The worst part was that he was so insecure, that he actually believed her, or at least it looked as though he did. That felt like a knife through her heart.

"If that is what you truly want…I have to confess something to you. After you moved to Chicago, and we had begun to talk again, I decided to finish what I had started. I had the last surgery. I have been lying to you. I can walk now, but seeing as you have chosen another man, I have no reason to keep it a secret any longer." He was hoping that she would have caught on that he was just saying things to make it seem as though they were over, to appease Joey. However the look of surprise in her eyes made him realize that she really believed that he thought they were over, and was just trying to hurt her. The sad thing was that he had just told her that he could walk again, he had told her the truth, and yet he felt no better. To her, it was just a mean lie to tell her, to break her heart worse than it was already breaking. But, she straightened up, and her face went stone cold.

"I want you out of my apartment, and out of my life, Caspian…Joey, please, just open the door, and get this over with. The sooner you deal with the police…the sooner we can be together." It was her last words, that made him lose grip on the gun, and it hit the floor, discharging a couple times. The stray bullets ricocheted around the room, and one hit the monitor, causing Amelia to lose all contact.

"Caspian!!!" Amelia screamed. Luckily, there had been officers surrounding her, because she fainted. They gently lowered her to the ground, and one of the officers began to fan her.

When the officers in the hallway heard the gun go off, they charged the door, and blasted through, tackling the only man on his feet. Joey allowed them to handcuff him, while the other officers checked Caspian to make certain he had not been injured.

They all traveled down the elevators; Caspian and Officer Cooper in one, and Officer Blake took Joey in the other.

They were at the ground floor in no time, and as Caspian wheeled off the elevator, he saw Amelia on the ground outside. Not thinking twice, he leapt up and ran for the door.

"Mia!! Oh My God! What happened?" He knelt next to her and lifted her into his arms.

"She heard the gunshot, the screen went blank…She called your name…you're Caspian, right?" The officer said, still fanning her.

"Yeah, I'm Caspian…"

"Well, she called your name…then she fainted. I thought you were in a wheelchair."

"I am, well, I was….were none of you listening?"

"So, it's true? What you said about your surgery…" Katrina was shocked.

"Yes, it is. I hated to not tell her, but I wanted to surprise her…I wish I had just been honest with her…you must think horribly of me."

"Actually, it is kinda romantic. I didn't see anything…" She looked at the officers around her. "Did any of you see anything?" Looking scared to argue with the woman in front of them, they shook their heads. "See, no one saw anything, but you better get back in that chair before she wakes up. The other elevator is getting ready to open.

Officer Cooper walked up behind Caspian and handed him his chair, which he had wheeled from where he had abandoned it. He sat down in it, and waited by her side until her eyes began to flutter open. The first face she saw was Caspian's. So relieved that he was okay, she leapt up and wrapped her arms around him, and began to cry uncontrollably.

Officer Blake was escorting Joey out of the building, and he saw the spectacle in front of him.

"Amelia! Amelia, what are you doing?" He cried out, struggling to free himself from the officer's grip. "You swore on your brother's grave...You said you were finished with him and wanted to be with me...you swore!!"

"You're a moron!! She doesn't have a brother...she's an only child!!" Cass screamed at him, clutching to Mia's shaking body. "Officers, you need to get him out of here. We are pressing charges for harassment, assault, and stalking. I also believe that he has bugged her apartment. I will pay any expense to your department if they can make sure that this guy never sees the outside of a prison cell again."

"You lied to me, Mia!!! I would have given you the world...but you chose that manipulative lying jerk over me...I wish I had shot you when I had the chance..." Something that Joey said flipped a switch in Mia. She stopped crying, leapt off of Caspian and walked over to Joey.

"How DARE you!?! You broke into my home, you harassed and threatened my fiancé, and you made me say those horrible things in order to get you to let him free. I was never going to leave him for you. You are nothing to me! I would rather kill myself than to ever be manipulated into being with you...you nasty, disgusting, ugly, infuriating, petty creep!" And just as she finished her statement, she hauled back and slapped him across the face. The sting in her palm was one of the most painful she had ever felt, but she felt gratified. Joey winced, and screamed out in pain. Almost immediately, a bright red handprint appeared across his cheek. The police officer winked at Mia, and then pushed Joey into the back of his car, slamming the door in his face.

She turned on her heels, and ran to Caspian again. She held his face between her hands and kissed him, soft and sweet.

"Can you ever forgive me for doing that to you? I didn't mean anything I said, I swear it."

"Do you swear it on your brother's grave?" He gave her a sly smile. She looked at him, dazed. "I know you were just lying…saying what you thought that he wanted to hear. There is no need to apologize. I just played along…"

"How did you know? You were crying…"

"You have a tell, sweetheart. I always know when you lie…your eye twitches."

"I hate to interrupt, but I am going to need you to come down to the station to make a statement." Officer Cooper said, trying to be as discreet as possible. Cass looked at his watch.

"We have a plane to catch very soon. Can we just give you my statements now? My sister is getting married in the morning in Boston."

"I suppose you have been through enough for one day. Let me make arrangements to get your statement. Be right back." With that, he walked over to the other officers that were there.

"Go with one of the officers and get our things, while I am giving my official statement. Most likely, they will want to talk to you and Katrina as well."

"Okay, I'll be back down as quickly as possible." She kissed him again, and then grabbed Katrina, and an officer, and the three of them went to retrieve the stuff for their trip.

*****

After all three of them told the officers, verbally and in writing, about the last forty-eight hours, they stood and watched the line of vehicles drive away, a screaming and cussing Joey in tow. Mia wrapped her arms around her boss, and thanked her for everything.

"After all you have been through, Mia, take a week off. Visit with your family, and unwind. You have earned it."

"I couldn't possibly…"

"Fashionista can survive without you for a week, Mia. Be with your fiancé, and go be with your family back home." She hugged Amelia again, just as the limo came to pick them up and take them to the airport.

The chauffer put their things in the trunk, and Amelia climbed into the car first. Katrina bent over, and gave Caspian a hug, and whispered something in his ear. He laughed, nodded, and got into the car next to Amelia. Katrina shut the door, and waved at the two of them. The chauffer loaded the chair into the trunk, slammed it shut, and then ran to the driver's seat. And as they drove away from the Apartments, and the waving woman, Mia slipped her hand under Cass's, and entwined her fingers in his.

They boarded the plane just in time, and the engines of the giant aircraft roared as they rumbled down the tarmac. Amelia leaned back in her reclining seat, and looked at Caspian. She insisted that he sit in one of the reclining plane seats, to which he had no argument.

She couldn't believe all that had happened in the last week. Before this week had started, if someone had asked her if she would give up her job to move back to Boston, she would have told them no. Now, if someone had asked her that same question, she would have answered with a very simple answer, "If it meant that I could wake up next to this man every morning, I would live anywhere."

The whole flight, her hand didn't leave his. She fell asleep, leaning against his shoulder. When the plane touched down, it jolted her awake. She looked up at him, and he was watching her, a look of unyielding love in his eyes.

"Hello beautiful...we're home." He ran a finger down her cheek, and she smiled.

"Yes...we are." She sat up and unbuckled her belt when the light went off, then reach over and unbuckled his.

As they walked through the tunnel toward the terminal, she could hear a crowd of familiar screaming voices. The screams and whistles continued to get louder until the group came into view. Amelia didn't realize how much she had missed this group of people until she saw them in front of her.

Caspian looked up and saw her eyes filled with tears, and he motioned for her to go ahead. She didn't hesitate, and ran to the crowd. She wrapped her arms around Evangeline first, and he couldn't tell which bush of hair was whose. She embraced each of the ladies almost as enthusiastically. However, the group parted, and she ran into the big bear arms of the large black man standing in the back. He picked her up off the ground like he was picking up a balloon. There were tears running down Henry's face, and his hearty laugh rumbled through the terminal like thunder.

"Eh Babette!" He held her for a moment or two, and then set her back down, gently on the floor. She didn't release her arms from around his neck until she was ready. Of all the staff that she missed, she missed Henry the most. When she finally let go of his neck, she kissed him on the cheek, and wiped the tears from his face, and he used his handkerchief to wipe the tears from hers.

Angie walked over to her brother, hugged him and then walked around the back of his wheelchair, and began to push him forward. She leaned over and began to whisper in his ear.

"Just so you know…everything is set. The seamstress from Chicago sent us all of her measurements." She tried to be as discreet as possible.

"Good. I know that it was supposed to be your big day, but…"

"She's my best friend…I would gladly share the spotlight." She stood back up and pushed her brother forward without another word.

They all arrived at the church, where Angie's fiancé was waiting patiently on the front steps. Mia practically climbed on top of Caspian's lap to get a good look at him before they got out of the car.

Kent Morris was a very handsome young man, by any standards. He had a chiseled look to him, reminding Mia of a Greek statue. He had very broad shoulders, and his posture was without flaw. He wore his fatigues, and saluted everyone as they clamored out of the cars. Angie grabbed Mia's hand and rushed her over to meet the man she would be marrying in less than twenty four hours.

"Baby, this is my best friend, Amelia. Amelia, this is Kent Morris." She shoved Mia at him and stepped back. Amelia, unsure as to how to greet him, put her hand out for him to shake. He smiled, and put his arms around her, and hugged her.

"It is great to finally meet you. Angie talks about you all the time." He sighed, seeming less formal.

"You, too. I'm sorry that we hadn't met sooner than now." She smiled, more at ease.

"Okay, enough of that! Amelia, come with me. I want you to see the bride's dressing suite...." Angie grabbed her hand and, again, dragged her along behind her. When they were out of sight, Kent gave Caspian the thumbs up, and he got out of his chair, and ascended the stairs to stand beside his future brother-in-law. Henry carried the chair up the stairs and placed it inside the doors.

"Man, you were not kidding when you told me she was gorgeous. Are you ready to do this?"

"Are you? You do know that we are both going to have our hands full with those two." Caspian laughed, nudging Kent with his elbow.

"I thought that Angie was a spitfire, but she seems to be the lesser of the two." He chuckled back.

"Now, I just wanted to say that it means a lot to me…agreeing to the wedding's revisions."

"It makes Angie happy, and if she's happy, I'm happy." He looked into the church, and heard his fiancé, so he signaled for Henry, who walked over, and hauled Caspian up into his arms, and acted as though he was just reaching the top step.

"Hey, honey. I want to get married in this church. Can we talk to the minister after the rehearsal?" Mia smiled at him, sweetly.

"I am sure that something can be arranged." He smiled back. Behind Amelia, Evangeline gave him a cheesy grin and two thumbs up.

"So, shall we all go in and get this rehearsal going. I want to get back home...I'm famished." Caspian sighed, and everyone started to enter the church. Henry set him down in his chair.

"I am so glad that I only have to do this a couple more times. You are getting heavy!" Henry wiped his brow, and walked in with everyone else.

"Say that a little louder, Henry...I don't think they heard you in CHINA!" He laughed. He wheeled forward, and joined everyone else at the front of the church.

Approaching the pastor, he made a point to introduce Amelia to him. As the clergyman went through what was expected of them, Caspian made sure that Amelia was paying attention to every detail.

She looked back at him quite a few times, and smiled, and he knew that she was planning their wedding as they went over Evangeline's. They practiced walking down the exceptionally long aisle several times, and also made certain that the timing was right, as well as where they were supposed to stand.

The rehearsal went as any normal rehearsal would go. The minister discussed timing, where everyone was to stand, and the structure of the service. After they had gone over it a few times, it was time to head back to the house.  They all loaded in the cars, and once again, Henry made a big deal about Caspian's weight becoming a problem and how he wished that Cass could just get up and walk himself up and down the stairs, but Amelia just laughed because she thought that Henry was trying to be funny. Caspian finally realized, in that moment, that Henry was not real good at keeping secrets, and he was even worse at dropping hints to Amelia.

# *~Fourteen~*

Everyone made their way to the house, where the kitchen staff had a spread laid out for them.  There was a lot of laughter and everyone wanted to hear about what happened that day in Chicago.  Angie almost burst into tears, hearing how Amelia had come to her brother's rescue. At around eleven o'clock, Angie got up from her seat.  Kent got up with her, as he felt that any gentleman should do when a lady gets up from the table.

"Well, I don't know about you all, but I need to get some beauty sleep.  I'm getting married tomorrow." Angie sighed.

"Well, if you needed beauty sleep for your wedding, you should have gone to bed five hours ago…" Cass jibed, and ducked as a silk napkin came flying toward his head.  When it missed, Mia smacked him on the shoulder.

"That was not nice, Cass. Your sister is going to be the most beautiful woman there tomorrow."

"Well, *one* of the most beautiful women, anyway…" He crooned, giving her a toothy smile.

"Oh Brother…Come on, sweetie. I'll go up with you. We need to have girl time."

The two redheads kissed their fiancés and went running up the grand staircase, arm in arm. Cass had a flashback of them doing that back when they were both at the Academy, and his heart filled with pride.

When they were out of view, and earshot, everyone began to plan tomorrow's festivities.

\*\*\*\*\*

The sun came shining through Amelia's window. She opened her eyes, and rolled over, and she felt as though she had traveled back in time. She was back in her old bedroom, and nothing had changed. She lay there, thinking of the first time she had been in that very room. Cass had rolled in, introducing himself to a very scared and sad fourteen year old version of herself. She couldn't help but smile. Out of the corner of her eye, she saw something in her hair. When she removed it, she realized what it was; they were flower petals from a cherry blossom tree just like the ones that

Cass had proposed to her under. She giggled, and looked across the room, where her full length mirror stood. Her eyes opened wide, as she stared at her reflection. She was covered in flower petals. They were strewn through her hair, on her pillow, on the comforter, and on the floor, surrounding the bed.

There was a knock at the door, and then it opened. Claudette came in, a tray in hand.

"Good morning, Miss. It is so good to have you home again. And from what I see, I am not the only one that feels that way. I've brought you breakfast."

"Oh, Claudette…you didn't have to do that. I was planning on having breakfast with Caspian in the dining room."

"Oh, Miss, Master Caspian cannot attend breakfast with you this morning. He is busy helping Master Kent with his vows. He had me bring you breakfast in bed." She set the tray down on her bedside table. On the silver platter, there was a cinnamon raisin bagel, and a frozen caramel mocha cappuccino, and a flower from the tree in the garden; a cutting from the cherry blossom tree. Amelia picked it up, and put it in her hair.

She ate her breakfast in the window seat, staring out at the beautiful setup of the garden. They had gone all out with decorations for the reception.  There were thousands of lights hung from the trees and the trellis.  Flowers and lights covered the huge gazebo, and the live band had already begun to set up their speakers, and what appeared to be fog machines.  They had turned the center of the garden into a huge dance floor.  It was absolutely perfect, and she needed to mention how much she liked it to Cass.  As much as she would hate to copy her best friend's wedding, it was exactly as she would want her wedding and reception to be.  Obviously, Angie and she had very similar tastes.

She got up, shook as many petals from her hair as she could, placed the flower from her hair onto her pillow, and grabbed her robe.  She ran and took a nice bath in the dog-footed tub.  After a while of soaking, she finished up, and dried herself off.  She crept into Angie's room, and climbed into bed with her.

"Dum dum de dum…dum dum de dum…"  She tapped the wedding march on her nose, and Angie smiled.

"You're up early."  She yawned.  "What time is it?"

"It's around nine."  She pulled the covers back.  "You are getting married in six hours. We have a lot to do.  So, get up."

"Yes…We're getting married today." She shot up, and tried to cover up what she had just said. "I cannot believe that Kent and I are getting married. I am so happy to have you here."

"I am your best friend. Where on Earth would I be? A Bride needs her Maid-of-Honor on her wedding day…to keep her focused and calm. And I know that you will do the same for me, when I get married."

"I will be right here beside you as well…right there…I'll be right there beside you." She got up. "I am going to go take a shower. I'll be back, so don't go anywhere."

"Sure thing, Boss!" She laughed at Angie, as she shuffled out of the room. It had to be frazzled nerves, because Angie was acting stranger than normal.

After they were both showered and dressed, they scurried downstairs, where a car was waiting for them, to take them to get their hair done. Evangeline had chosen to not have a gaggle of bridesmaids, but rather to just have Amelia stand up for her as her honor attendant. It made things so much simpler. At least that was the explanation that she had given to Amelia when she had asked about it. Jean Claude, the hairdresser that had done their hair years ago for the Spring Formal, did their hair. He chose to do Amelia first, as he felt that she needed a cut as well. After he had trimmed about six inches of red frizz off of her head, he worked hard

to tame the curls into some semblance of an elegant up-do, with a cascade

of curls going down her back like a waterfall.  He topped it off with fake,

clip-on flowers that resembled a common theme of the day; Cherry

blossoms.  It only made her laugh to herself.

"What's the deal with all the Cherry blossoms?  I saw a bunch of

petals scattered all over your room this morning."

"Cass proposed under some cherry blossom trees.  I think he is

trying to make me feel special, and loved…especially after all that stuff

happened yesterday."

"That is so sweet.  He really loves you, you know.  I am so glad

that you are getting married…eventually.  I'm glad that you guys didn't

listen to me, way back when.  I was young, stupid and hot headed, and I

didn't want to share him.  Now, I couldn't imagine sharing him with

anyone else." Angie whispered, sitting down in the chair to have her hair

done.

"Why are you whispering?"  She whispered back.

"I am trying to save my voice for my vows."  She giggled.  "Silly,

huh?"

"Not at all silly…you do what you need to do. It's your day. Who am I to question the bride?" She giggled, admiring her hair in the mirror. Even after all that hair had been cut off, her hair was still rather long, and still came down to the middle of her back. It was pulled together in what looked like a large ponytail surrounded by blossoms. The cascading curls down her back had small petals and blossoms throughout. She looked like a garden fairy, or wood nymph, and she absolutely loved it. For her wedding, she wanted her hair to be done just as such, but with white flowers.

Angie's hair was done in a similar fashion, but as her hair was not as long and thick as Amelia's, it looked more like a ball of curls on the back of her head. Her veil consisted of a short layered toule-like material with silk at the bottom, and jewels glimmering here and there, which attached to her head with a comb, hidden under the curls. White flowers, babies breathe, and pearls were placed on the sides, making it appear as though she had a crown of flowers surrounding her ringlets of hair.

After their hair was done, they had their nails touched up, and painted to match their hair; Angie had a French Manicure, and Mia's was a French manicure done with hues of pink darkening into red at the very tip, instead of pure white like Angie's. They left the salon, and were driven by white limo to the church, where their dresses were waiting for them in the room that Angie had shown her before the rehearsal.

"I have a question for you, Angie…"

"What is it?"

"If my dress is yellow and blue, why are my nails and the flowers in my hair like cherry blossoms? Won't that clash?"

"If it does, it will just ensure that I will be the most beautiful woman at the wedding."

"So, you wanted me to look ridiculous to make you look even more beautiful…I see now." She shook her head, and chuckled to herself.

Claudette and Eloise were waiting for them there. They walked them from the limo to the room, and both of them looked very different in regular dresses, as opposed to the normal black and white uniforms they normally were seen wearing.

Mia walked over to her garment bag, and noticed something weird on it that resembled a burn hole.

"Oh…no no no NO!" She quickly opened the bag to reveal a huge hole that went straight through the bag, through the front of the dress, and out the back. "Son of a Cracker Jack!"

"What?!?" Angie turned quickly, and ran over to Mia.

"HE SHOT MY DRESS!!!" She took it out, and proceeded to measure the size of the burn hole by sticking her finger through it. "Joey, that maniacal rat, shot my dress! Eloise can you do something to fix it? It's less than an hour until the wedding. and I don't care how ugly the BRIDE wants me to look, I cannot go out there in front of everyone with a bullet hole going through the center of my dress…Angie! Why are you laughing? This is so not funny!"

"I am not laughing, I am just smiling."

"Well, why are you smiling, then?" She was getting quite annoyed.

"I was just thinking about how hilariously perfect this is…"

"So, you want wedding pictures with your Maid-of-Honor with a bullet hole going through her torso? You have lost your mind, Evangeline!" As mad as she was trying to be at Angie, she couldn't help but start laughing with her.

"Luckily, for you, there is another garment bag in this closet…and it has your name on it, Miss Amelia." Eloise said, pulling out a huge opaque bag, and hanging it on the hook next to where Angie's dress was hanging moments before.

"What in the world…Where did this bag come from?  It wasn't here yesterday, when Angie showed me her dress."

"I don't know, Miss Amelia.  It must be a backup.  We really have no time to quibble about where it came from…you cannot walk down that aisle in denim capris and a button-down flannel shirt.  Take it out and get dressed…" Claudette urged, as she buttoned up the back of Evangeline's dress.

"It can't be another dress like mine…it's far too big of a bag.  There has to be a mistake…"

"Put on the damn dress, and shut up!"  Evangeline growled.  Mia jumped at the tone her best friend was using.

"Okay...Okay…Whatever you say, Bridezilla!"  She walked over the bag and slowly unzipped it, moving the bag aside to reveal the last thing she expected to find inside.

On the hanger, hung one of the most magnificent dressed she had ever seen in her life.  Angie and the other two ladies watched Amelia's face change from frustration and confusion to pure wonder and awe.  Layer upon layer of crinoline made up the skirt and train, and along the bottom, were pink and red flower petals held in place by a border of satin.  The bodice was satin, with clear, pink and red jewels, and a halter strap that faded from deep crimson to shiny white. There was a box at the bottom of the bag, which contained a pair of matching stilettos, and a smaller satin jewelry box. Mia picked it up, and opened it. There was a piece of paper in it, and beneath that was a beautiful sapphire pendant, and matching teardrop earrings. She opened the folded piece of paper. It was a note from Gran.

My Darling Amelia,

I fear that I will not be here on Earth to see your wedding day, as my time here is coming to a close. The first time I took you out shopping, you stopped in front of a dress shop and admired this dress. You told me that you would wear that dress on your wedding day. So, to ensure that your dream came true, I purchased the dress for your wedding day. I left instructions with Eloise, Claudette and Evangeline to make certain that it was ready, and fit you perfectly. Though I cannot be with you on that beautiful day, I will be there with you, in spirit, as you marry my grandson in the dress you, yourself, chose. I love you, my darling Girl. Welcome to the family. You are finally a Wallingford.

Love Always, Gran

The tears welled up in her eyes, and she looked over at Angie, who was blotting her tear-filled eyes.

"Angie…is this for real? I mean, this…entire .the proposal, the hair, the nails…It was all…" She choked on her words.

"Grandmother took Caspian to see the dress, and Caspian planned the rest. When he said that I would be one of the most beautiful women today, he meant it. You and I talked about having a double wedding…don't you remember?" Amelia nodded, and smiled.

"I remember…And I was sad because you were getting married without me…" She looked up at the dress. Holding the note to her chest, she closed her eyes, and took a moment. "Okay, so, I am going to need help getting into this thing. Eloise…would you please…" She blotted away her tears, and began to get undressed.

After twenty minutes of wrestling with the layers of crinoline, and trying not to catch the strap or the jewelry in her hair, she was dressed, and standing in the mirror with her best friend, and soon to be sister-in-law. They looked at one another, and then at the ladies standing behind them. Eloise snapped a couple pictures of them, and then opened the double doors revealing two very fine looking gentlemen; Robert and Henry, both dressed in tuxedoes with the exception of the flowers in their lapels.

Robert, with his white carnation, held out his arm to Evangeline, handed her the bouquet with white roses, and proceeded out into the hall. Henry bowed to Amelia, and held out his hand. He had a red and white carnation in his lapel to match her dress, as well as the bouquet of red, pink and white roses.

"If I had only known…I promised to invite Stacy and Katrina to my wedding…I am sure that they will understand." She walked forward, and waited behind Evangeline. The music began to start, and everyone stood up. Evangeline and Robert headed down the aisle. They waited until they were halfway down the aisle, and then Henry gave her hand a squeeze.

"You are absolutely beautiful, Mon Petite. I am proud to be the one to walk you down the aisle. You have always been like a daughter to me, and so I feel honored to be giving you away."

"I wouldn't have it any other way, Henry." She took a deep breath, and began to walk with Henry down the aisle.

The church had been decorated to match both of their weddings. There were alternating red and white flowers at the end of each pew, a white runner along the floor, with red petals scattered on top. The Alter had a large flowered arch, with red and white flowers covering it. There were red and white candles lit all around the sanctuary, and Mia could not think of a more beautiful sight.

A hush came over the church as they saw Amelia. As she approached the altar, she saw two familiar faces, smiling at her. Caspian had really pulled the rug out from under her, and surprised her once again. She smiled, blew them a kiss, and proceeded up the stairs, where Caspian was waiting, dressed in a white tuxedo, light pink shirt, and a tie that went from white at the top then gradually turned red, before being tucked behind a red vest. When he saw her, in all her radiance, he could not help but shed a tear.

The minister gestured for everyone to have a seat, and the shuffle soon died down.

"We are gathered here today, to witness the unions of two very special couples; Kent Morris and Evangeline Wallingford…" He gestured to the right of him, and then gestured to the left. "…Caspian Wallingford and Amelia Landon. Who gives these brides to be married?"

"We do, in honor of their parents, God rest their souls. Amen." Robert and Henry spoke in unison. They handed them off to their prospective partners, and then went to stand next to the grooms.

"Each couple has chosen to speak their own vows, and so we will start with Kent and Evangeline." He handed the microphone to Kent, and stepped back.

"Angie, I am but a simple man. I am not wealthy. But, what I lack in wealth, I can offer you in love, loyalty, and my vow of devotion in making sure that you will never want for anything. I give you my life, my heart, my body, and my soul. If you will have me, I would love nothing more than to be your servant forever more."

"Kent, I am not perfect, no matter how much I try to say that I am. I can be stubborn, and moody, and a downright pain in the butt. With that being said, you still choose to love me and spend the rest of your life with me. To you, today and every day after, I promise to love you, honor you, stand by your side and support you. I promise to *try* not to be stubborn, moody or a pain in the butt, but if I am, know that I love you with everything I have in me."

"Now, Caspian and Amelia…" The minister took the microphone from Angie, and handed it to Amelia. When she tried to hand it to Caspian, he told her to keep it. She looked out among their friends and family, and then back at Cass.

"Um, I honestly was not prepared for this. So, pardon me if I seem kind of scatterbrained." She cleared her throat, and looked straight at Caspian. "Cass, My father once told me that I would know that I had found the man I was going to marry by the way he treats the people around him, but mostly by the way he treated me. When I first met you, I was scared, and alone. I didn't know you or Gran, or anyone around me. But, you, seeing that I was afraid..." She reached out, and he put his hand in hers. "...Seeing that I was alone, you took my hand and you offered to be my friend. You didn't know me. I was a stranger in your home, and yet you treated me like I was an invited guest, and that I had nothing to fear. You laid your heart out in the open, and allowed me to be a part of it. And in turn, I took you into mine. From that day on, you have loved me, without restriction. You were my first love, my first kiss, and the first and only keeper of my heart. Thank you for being the man that my father wanted me to marry." A single tear streamed down her cheek as she handed the microphone to him. He held onto her hand, as he began to speak.

"Amelia, my beautiful Angel...You came into my life at a time when I felt so alone. Because of my disability and not so encouraging words from my bratty younger sister..." He smiled over at Angie. "...I believed that I would spend the rest of my life alone, and unloved except for my family. When you came to live with us, you were like the angel of Hope, sent from the heavens to prove that I wouldn't have to be alone. When you looked at me, you saw down to my very soul. You never looked at me with pity, or detestation. You looked at me with understanding, and love. You gave me hope to walk again, when I thought it wasn't possible. You held my hand, and assured me that no matter what happened tomorrow, you would be there. Your love has given me the strength to go on, to be a better man, and to love without feeling like I am less of a man because of this chair. I will spend the rest of my life, filling your heart with the fiercely abundant love you have given me, filling your eyes with laughter, and filling your soul with my undying gratitude. You make me feel like anything is possible with you by my side." He kissed her hand.

"Now, for the blessing and exchanging of the rings..." He held out his bible, where Robert and Henry placed the two sets of rings on its pages. Everyone bowed their heads as he began to speak. "Heavenly Father, we ask that you bless these rings, symbols of never-ending love and commitment. We pray that you fill this bands with your grace, mercy, and understanding; that when placed on their fingers, will seep into their very souls the virtues and teachings of your word. Give this rings the power of Patience, unity, honesty, and faithfulness, all of which you ask of your children, Lord. In your son's name we pray, Amen"

"Amen" The whole room spoke in unison. He offered the rings to the couples. And as a group, they placed the rings on each other's fingers.

"By the power invested in me, by the state of Massachusetts and the Almighty God above, I now pronounce you husband and wife, and husband and wife...You may now kiss your brides."

Angie, despite wearing heels, still had to stand on her tip-toes to kiss Kent. He picked her up, and her feet dangled at least twelve inches off the floor. Amelia slid herself onto Cass's lap and kissed him ever so softly on the lips. Just as she began to pull away, he slid his hand around to the back of her neck, and pulled her in for a deeper kiss. She instantly got warm, and her breathing became labored. But, before they made a scene in front of everyone, he released her.

"I love you, Amelia."

"I love you, Caspian."

Amelia and Evangeline stepped off to the side, and hugged one another. Kent, Robert and Henry all worked together to lift and carry Caspian down the few steps that were in front of him. They set him down on the floor, and Amelia stepped behind him and pushed him down the aisle behind her new sister and Brother-in-law. All the guests stood up and clapped as they exited the church. Some of the male guests came and helped get Caspian down the stairs outside and carry him to the bottom. Henry assisted in lifting him up into the Horse-drawn carriage that was waiting for them all, to take them back to the house by way of through the park.

Amelia looked at Caspian, and her heart seemed to overflow with love for him.

"I cannot believe that we are married…You planned this whole thing, didn't you?"

"From the very beginning…with a little help, yes." He laughed, kissing her hand, which he held tightly in his own.

"You were all in on it? Henry and Robert too?"

Caspian, Kent and Evangeline all nodded.

"As much as my head is spinning…I don't think this day could get more perfect." She was glowing from the inside out.

"That's your problem, Mia….you jump the gun. This day still has more to come!" Angie giggled.

\*\*\*\*\*

As they entered the garden, they were announced, and they went to sit at the beautiful table near the Gazebo. Their friends and loved ones were distributed at the ten other smaller tables surrounding them and the man-made dance floor. One by one, people got up to make speeches as the microphone got passed. Katrina was the final person to receive the microphone.

"Hello, everyone. I am Katrina, editor-in-Chief of Fashionista, and I am Amelia's boss, and her friend. She was originally brought to my attention by some work she had done in her sophmore year of college. We welcomed her into our elite internship program, and I did not know it yet, but she would soon become a huge asset to our paper and to our lives. We welcomed her into the fold, and she became an essential member of our staff. I have watched her grow, and I have watched her blossom as a journalist, colleague and friend. And, I also learned that though her career was very important to her, the man sitting next to her was just as, if not more important. I know that coming back to Chicago, back to work, will be a struggle, as she has a life here, in Boston. So, in cooperation with the Editor-in-Chief of Fab-Fashion, Mr. Craig Lowry, we will be sharing an Executive Assistant. Six months of the year will be spent here in Boston, at

Fab-Fashion, and six months of the year will be spent in Chicago, at Fashionista."

Amelia was so overwhelmed, that she leapt from the table and ran to hug her friend. She knew what a sacrifice this was for her and for the paper, but she would make it work.

Dinner was served soon afterward, as the band played some soft music in the background. After everyone had had time to digest their food, the lead singer got on the microphone, and announced that the first couple on the floor for their first official dance as husband and wife would be Kent and Evangeline Morris. They took to the floor, and soft music began to play, and they swayed to the music, while the crowd chattered about them, and how cute they were together.

"I'll be right back, sweetie. I have to go talk to Henry about helping out with getting me up on my feet for our first dance. I will not sit down for this… it's too important…"

"Baby, it's *not* important. I can just sit on your lap." She pleaded with him. "We are up next…" Her words faded as he rolled off to find Henry.

The song came to an end, and Angie kissed her new husband, and they returned to the table.

"And now, could the new Mr. and Mrs. Caspian Wallingford please come to the dance floor for their first dance as husband and wife…"

Mia walked around the table and looked for Caspian to join her but he was nowhere to be seen. She spotted Henry at the table a few feet away.

"Where's Caspian?"

"I haven't any idea, why?"

"He went to find you. He wants you to lift him up so that he can stand of our first dance." She looked around, through the crowd.

"Caspian and Amelia, please make your way to the dance floor for your first dance…" The singer repeated, and discreetly turned on the fog machines.

"I have been sitting here since before Angie's dance started." He looked around, and then got up. "I'll dance with you until he gets here. He probably had to use the bathroom." He whispered in her ear, and then led her to the dance floor. They began to dance to the music, surrounded by a cloud of smoke, and then she felt her eyes begin to tear up. Right before she began to cry, she heard his voice, from behind her.

"Excuse me, but I believe this is my dance…" Henry nodded, and before moving aside, he spun Amelia around a couple of times. When she came to a stop, it wasn't Henry, but Caspian standing in front of her; one hand was at her waist, the other clutching her hand, and he began to dance her around the floor, swirling fog around them like it was a dream. She felt lightheaded, and felt as though it was all a figment of her imagination. After a few moments, people were up on their feet, and they were making comments, and pointing. As they spun and glided across the floor, he held her close.

"I told you that our first dance was too important for me to sit it out." He whispered in her ear, and kissed her forehead.

"Caspian...you're not in...you can..."

"As I said to you, anything is possible when I am with you. You are my miracle." He picked her up, and spun her around, and then set her back down on her feet. And as though they had been dancing together for years, they dominated the whole area, the fog fading away, revealing their feet moving in unison. When the music started to fade, they just stood in the middle of the floor, and swayed together. His arms engulfed her and he pressed her against his body, his palms against her back.

She didn't care how long he had sat in that chair, fully able to walk...this was the perfect moment. And so, despite her feet getting tired and hurting, they spent the remainder of the night, dancing. When she couldn't dance any longer, her lifted up into his arms, and danced her around, cradling her against him.

He carried her into the house at the very end of the night, up the whole staircase, and set her down on the edge of his bed, removing her shoes with the softest of touches, massaging her feet. She leaned back and enjoyed the pain that was followed by relief. He took her jewelry, and set it on his table, and then assisted her with her dress. He hung it up on a heavy wooden hanger, leaving her standing in her lacy white undergarments. When he turned to remove his tuxedo, she climbed up onto his bed, and covered with a blanket. He turned around, standing there in nothing but his socks and boxers. He walked over to the bed, stubbing his toe, and crying out in pain.

"Are you okay?" She jumped up, and he flung himself onto the bed.

"Believe it or not, I love the pain."

"Do you want me to rub your tired, achy feet?" She gave him a sympathetic look.

"I welcome the tired achy feet. Let me enjoy the feeling for a little bit." He laid back on the pile of pillows and pulled her to him. "I want to hold my wife right now."

She nuzzled up next to him, and ran her hand up and down his chest. If there was a moment in her life, when she was her happiest, this moment topped it. So much had happened that led up to this moment, and she was thankful for every moment, whether it was good or bad. Every single thing that took them on this rollercoaster was there to test their resolve, their commitment to withstand anything and everything. They came out of it all, wiser, stronger and definitely more determined. She closed her eyes, and she listened to his heartbeat. His breathing slowed and his chest rose and fell steadily, his muscles relaxing. She looked up at him, and he had fallen asleep, a smile on his face. She slid from the bed, walked over, and quietly closed the door, then returned to lay with her husband, and enjoy her first night as Mrs. Amelia Wallingford.

*~Seven Years Later~*

# *~Epilogue~*

The sun was shining, as the staff rushed about getting the house ready for Mrs. Wallingford's return. She had been gone for four days, and the excitement of her return was mixed with the chaos of laughter, squealing, and crying. The nursery was stocked to the gills with diapers, wipes, ointments, powders, lotions, and other essentials.

It had been a long and exciting few years, and Caspian never needed to visit the doctor to make sure that he could have children. Almost exactly nine months after the weddings, the cries of new life rang through the hallowed halls of the old Wallingford Estate. And it hadn't stopped since. Between Amelia, and Evangeline, who had come to live with them while Kent was overseas, they had a herd of gingers and one brunette, Annabelle, who was adopted. No one wanted to adopt her from the children's home, on account of her having Downs Syndrome, but she was a very special little girl, and was in need of a loving accepting home. Anyone would have thought that she was their natural child, because she had Amelia's flare for writing, and Caspian's sense of humor.

Amelia had forgone going back to work completely, as every time she was recovered enough from childbirth, just to find out that either she or Evangeline was pregnant again.

"Do you see the car yet?"

"Nope, but they will be home soon. Henry said so." Taylor said, pulling his sister closer, to straighten her hair. "Where's Maddie?" Taylor took off, and dragged the walker back to the foyer. "Watch her, please, Annabelle. I need to get her pacifier." The young boy raced into the kitchen, and grabbed a pacifier out of the sterilizer. His flaming red hair stuck to the sweat on his face, and he worked hard to keep his younger sisters together and looking proper for the return of their parents.

They heard the car pull up in front of the house, and Annabelle began to hop about, her curls bouncing and bobbing.

"Doooodeeee" Maddie gurgled. "Moooomeee" She began to speed away, and Taylor chased after her. Henry stopped the speedster in her tracks, and picked her up in his massive hands.

"Not so fast, Madison…" He cradled the small, ginger headed toddler in his arms, and began to make faces at her. She laughed and cooed, and he joined her brother and sister.

The front door opened, and Cass came in first, carrying a blue carrier on one hand, and a pink one in the other. Amelia followed slowly behind her husband, with another blue carrier. She looked thoroughly exhausted, and set the carrier down, collapsing on a chair.

"Settle down, Annabelle. Your new brothers and sister are right there, and I don't think they would like it if you fell on them."

"Yes, Mommy. I be very careful…" She got down on all fours, and snuck a peek under each of the blankets. "Shhh, babies are sleeping" She put her finger to her lips, and made a shushing noise at everyone who made a sound.

Amelia suddenly felt very uncomfortable, and reached under behind to find a squishy ball, a small tractor and the pieced to a block building set. She pulled them out, and then tried to get comfortable again.

"Let's try one more time he says…Let's even it out. One last time, and then we're done. Four is enough….now, we have six! If you want anymore, Cass, you can carry them for nine months and then try to push them out! I am done. Three at once…that is my breaking point."

"Did I tell you today how much I love you?" She walked over and kissed her, and gave her an apologetic look. "I love you oodles and oodles. Pugs and poodles"

"Poodles!" Annabelle laughed, and ran over to hug her daddy.

"Hey Tater tot, can you go get Aunt Angie, and tell her that mommy and babies are home from the hospital…Please…" He motioned for his eldest child to go. He then proceeded over to Henry, and took Madison from him.

"Doooodeeee!" She squished his face between her chubby hands, giving him a wet, open-mouthed kiss. He shifted her to his hip, and picked his second oldest up, and gave her some kisses and hugs. He carried both of the girls over and setting them down by their mother.

"More babies!! Yay!" Bellowed a voice from above. Two more boys came stampeding down the stairs, followed by their mother, who was waddling as fast as an eight month pregnant woman could possibly waddle. Taylor helped his aunt down the stairs. When he reached the bottom, he walked over and hugged his mother.

"After that one, I suggest you tell the doctor to yank everything out with it…" She laughed, weakly.

"Hey, it isn't my fault that you guys are popping them out like candy dispensers." She looked at the three newborns in carriers. "Have you named them yet?"

"Pink baby, blue one and blue two…" Cass joked, but then cleared his throat when he got dirty looks from his wife and sister. "No, Morgan is the little miss pink, and Richie and Oliver, after our dads. Also, not that you care, but I have an appointment with the doctor to get snipped next week." He looked to Henry, for sympathy. "I'm being neutered, Henry…"

"Rightfully so…Any more kids in this house, and we're gonna need a permit!" He walked over and picked up two of the infants, and started up the stairs. He led the pack as the others followed behind him like he was the pied piper.

"Brady…Corbin, come on. Mommy needs to go put her feet up." She assisted Amelia in lifting little Morgan, and they waddled up the stairs together, the two girls slung over Caspian's shoulders, pulling up the rear.

"Will Kent be able to get home in time for the delivery of baby number three, Angie?" Cass asked his sister, bouncing the girls with each step.

"Caspian, I'm gonna say this, and you can take it to the bank and cash it... if he isn't in that delivery room, you aren't going to be the only neutered male in this house." She heard the hiss from her brother, and the two women gave each other a fist bump, and continued their trek up the stairs. "Goodness Gracious...I look forward to nap time. Hey, Caspian...if you were planning on bringing the babies upstairs anyway, why did you have me come all the way down to see them, just to go right back up? What was that supposed to accomplish?"

"Nothing, I just like to watch you waddle...it's like I live in in a house with a couple of Penguins...."

"You are so lucky that you have my little angels in your arms...I'd push you down the stairs." Amelia growled. "I think I liked you better when you were in the wheelchair. You are getting way too cocky."

"Well, I liked you better when you weren't..." She shot him a dirty look, and he didn't finish what he was about to say. "...never mind."

"Yeah, I thought so." She snickered, and Angie made the sound of a whip cracking.

"Hey now..." He protested his sister's reference.

"I love you, honey!" Mia looked over shoulder, and shot him a sweet smile.

"Yeah, I thought so…"

They finally reached the top of the stairs, and he kissed his wife, and took the infant from her, so now he had all his daughters.

"Don't drop one. You break one of them, she isn't gonna be able to make a new one. Snip Snip!" Angie teased.

"Shut up, Snot face." He called over his shoulder.

"No way, bubble butt…"

"Grouch!"

"Jerk!" She called back, sticking her tongue out at him as he turned the corner.

"Will the two of you stop it, or I am gonna make you both go into time out!" Mia yawned, barely getting the words out.

Caspian went down the hall, and placed his two older daughters in their room for their afternoon nap. He plopped Maddie into her toddler bed, and tucked her in, kissed her on the forehead, chin and nose. He laid Annabelle in her bed, beneath he pretty princes blanket, and handed her a stuffed animal to sleep with. He read them a story, and then took the littlest addition to the nursery. He took her out of her carrier, and placed her in the crib that was empty. He turned on the monitor, and then closed the door until it was open no more than a crack.

He checked on the boys as he went back toward his room. They were all on their beds, either reading or playing a handheld learning game.

"If you could try, please keep it down. The smaller ones are down for their naps."

"Yup, no problem dad…" Taylor sighed.

"We'll be quiet, Uncle Cass." The other two said in unison.

He crept into the bedroom, and Amelia was lying with an icepack on her head, and her feet elevated.

"Hello, beautiful. Do you want me to rub your feet?"

"Would you please?"

He sat at the end of the bed, and picked her feet up, one at a time, trying to make the swelling go down. After he was done rubbing her feet, he crawled up and leaned against the backboard, and she sprawled out, over his lap, and began to rub her back.

"In case I haven't said it lately, I love you very much. I am so proud of you. And our children are absolutely beautiful, and perfect….just like their mommy."

"I am far from perfect, but thank you" She managed to sit up and crane her neck to give her husband a kiss. Though having a baby was taxing on her body, she would not trade a single one of them for anything.

She wouldn't trade her life for anything. She couldn't get enough of it, and if her body would allow, she would have six more. But, right now, she just wanted to enjoy afternoon nap time with her loving and adoring husband. She leaned against him, and reached for the old worn out book on the nightstand. In the front cover, was written a small passage from her father;

**No matter where your life leads you, or how long it takes you to get to where you want to be, just remember that it is not the destination, but the journey that truly matters.**

**I love you, my darling Amelia.**

**Dad**